"In *Fair Game*, Evan McNamara
orado mountain landscape and th
hot suspense. Sharp plotting, a c
avalanche of thrills will leave rea

"   ol-
                                                          re.
                                                          nd

DATE

DATE DUE			
2/21	1201		
	1627		
	1626		

HIGHSMITH #45114

r
f
n

t
h
h
s
s
te

o,
p-
ts
g
of
irl

g
an
rs,

r®
Award-winning author of *Ice Run*

FAIR GAME

Evan McNamara

J
JOVE BOOKS, NEW YORK

THE BERKLEY PUBLISHING GROUP
Published by the Penguin Group
Penguin Group (USA) Inc.
375 Hudson Street, New York, New York 10014, USA
Penguin Group (Canada), 90 Eglinton Avenue East, Suite 700, Toronto, Ontario M4P 2Y3, Canada
(a division of Pearson Penguin Canada Inc.)
Penguin Books Ltd., 80 Strand, London WC2R 0RL, England
Penguin Group Ireland, 25 St. Stephen's Green, Dublin 2, Ireland (a division of Penguin Books Ltd.)
Penguin Group (Australia), 250 Camberwell Road, Camberwell, Victoria 3124, Australia
(a division of Pearson Australia Group Pty. Ltd.)
Penguin Books India Pvt. Ltd., 11 Community Centre, Panchsheel Park, New Delhi—110 017, India
Penguin Group (NZ), Cnr. Airborne and Rosedale Roads, Albany, Auckland 1310, New Zealand
(a division of Pearson New Zealand Ltd.)
Penguin Books (South Africa) (Pty.) Ltd., 24 Sturdee Avenue, Rosebank, Johannesburg 2196, South
Africa

Penguin Books Ltd., Registered Offices: 80 Strand, London WC2R 0RL, England

This is a work of fiction. Names, characters, places, and incidents either are the product of the author's imagination or are used fictitiously, and any resemblance to actual persons, living or dead, business establishments, events, or locales is entirely coincidental. The publisher does not have any control over and does not assume any responsibility for author or third-party websites or their content.

FAIR GAME

A Jove Book / published by arrangement with the author.

PRINTING HISTORY
Jove mass market edition / February 2006

Copyright © 2006 by Evan McNamara.
Cover design by Pyrographx.
Text design by Stacy Irwin.

ISBN: 0-515-14067-8

JOVE®
Jove Books are published by The Berkley Publishing Group,
a division of Penguin Group (USA) Inc.,
375 Hudson Street, New York, New York 10014.
JOVE is a registered trademark of Penguin Group (USA) Inc.
The "J" design is a trademark belonging to Penguin Group (USA) Inc.
The Edgar® name is a registered service mark of the Mystery Writers of America, Inc.

PRINTED IN THE UNITED STATES OF AMERICA

10 9 8 7 6 5 4 3 2 1

To my family.
If not for their support, patience, and creativity,
they would still be getting unpublished manuscripts for
Christmas.

And thank you to Samantha Mandor and Scott Miller,
who brought the Mineral County mystery series to life.

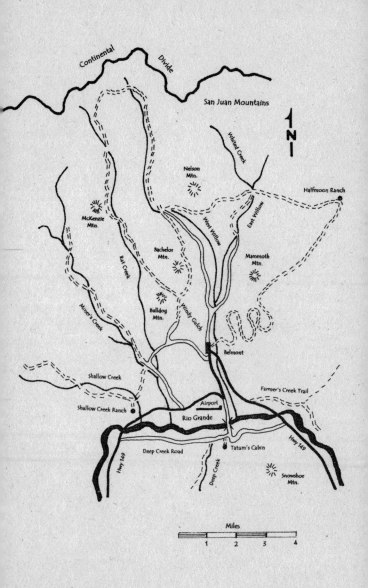

One

E VER SINCE WE SHOT HALF OF THE MINERAL County sheriff's department, my deputy and I have been a little shorthanded.

It was Indian summer in Belmont, which meant it was still cold as frozen hell, only without all the snow. Pancho climbed out of the low country, and we emerged on Wason Plateau. Multiple creeks traced these foothills of the La Garita Range. Engelmann and blue spruce lined the draws and towered over us. I turned up the collar of my sheepskin coat to the coldest part of the day and the incessant wind that introduced it. Pancho's breath came out in milky clouds, and frost covered the hairs around his muzzle.

I let my horse forage for tender shoots of alpine grass while I glassed the ridge. Once the terrain broke from the wooded canyons below, it sloped gently upward, all the way to the continental divide. I felt stupid, moving about in the early light on a brown horse with hunters about. I had wrapped a band of blaze orange around the crown of my cowboy hat, as if that would help.

Sergeant Richter had always said only fools hunted for sport. Actually, he said: *Any fool who hunts some dumb animal from long range with a rifle ought to find out what it feels like to be in the crosshairs himself.*

Sergeant Richter would kick my ass if he knew I was shirking. I didn't see it that way, but I was running the ragged line between on-duty and off-duty. I ignored the disapproval of my old team leader and clicked Pancho up the trail.

A gunshot popped from the ridge, then was swallowed by the valley. The back of my neck burned, as if the scar tissue remembered the last time I stood at the wrong end of a scope. The ridge stood empty and quiet in the morning frost. A line of juniper and short spruce lay on the opposite side of a circular field. If I hunted this ridge, that's where I'd put my stand.

I thought about my big brown horse, standing in the open, looking a lot like an elk. I waved my arms and hoped the rising sun would catch the blaze orange on my hat. Silence from the ridge. Trees obscured the hunter within. I nudged Pancho, and we trotted up the slope, right for the source of the gunfire. I decided to confront my early-morning shooter.

The spruce grove on the ridge made a nice spot for an elk stand. The hunter could see down both sides of the ridge and ambush elk or mule deer as they emerged from the low ground, just as he had ambushed me. I stopped at the edge of the trees and dismounted.

"Hey!" I shouted into the thick evergreen. "This is Sheriff Tatum. You just shot at me. Come on out of there."

No response. I felt like I was talking to nothing but rocks and trees. I left Pancho happily foraging and stepped into the grove.

Thick pine boughs closed around me. I left the wind outside. The meager orange light turned gray, and silence pressed my ears. Pale dun pine straw muffled my approach.

Thomas Harding Pitcher lay face down in a bed of pine needles at the base of an ancient Engelmann spruce. I knew it was Councilman Pitcher from his red wool hunter's coat and the antique binoculars on a leather cord around his neck. Against the big trunk of the spruce rested his rifle, a brushed-stainless Remington with a black fiber stock. It had a big Nikon Titanium scope mounted on the top rail— a rich man's gun. Pitcher was a very rich man, probably the wealthiest man in Mineral County.

Not anymore.

I gently pushed his cap away to check his pulse, but pulled back when I saw the blackened hole in his head and the pool of blood soaking into the pine straw.

Turns out I was doing my job after all. Now I was standing in the middle of a crime scene.

Leaving my feet where they were, I pulled the radio off my belt. I took a few deep breaths, pressed the key, and spoke into the handset.

"Jenny, this is Sheriff Tatum. You in, yet?"

"Yes, Sir. What can I do for you, Sir?" Jenny Lange had been with the department about a year. We had to hire a new dispatcher when I shot the last one.

"Stop calling me 'Sir,'" I said. "We got a problem up here on Wason Plateau. Looks like it might be a hunting accident."

"Somebody get shot?"

"Roger."

Silence from the other end.

"Can you get ahold of Jerry?" I asked. More silence. "Jenny, you still there?"

"I'll see if I can get ahold of Jerry, Sir," she finally came back. "What do you want me to tell him?"

"Just have him meet me where Farmer's Creek Trail comes up on the ridge."

I stood still and tried to get my mind straight. I hadn't spent much time at the last murder scene in Mineral County—I'd been too busy keeping my head down.

Was this a murder at all? It looked more like a suicide or hunting accident—bullet hole in the head, no sign of struggle. Hunting accident seemed the more likely theory, and Councilman Thomas Pitcher wasn't the type for suicide. Drive others to suicide, maybe.

The sound of an engine broke my puzzled reverie. I stepped lightly around the body and out of the silent copse. Councilman Pitcher and I were about to have some company.

I looked to the western ridge and saw a short man driving an olive drab ATV along the line of trees. ATVs were forbidden on the Halfmoon Ranch. Dr. Ed risked Orville's wrath hunting on one. He quickly maneuvered down the slope while standing on the pegs. His old Weatherby 7mm Mag lay crossways on a rack attached to the handlebars.

Dr. Ed parked his vehicle and walked over to me. Frost coated his gray cowboy mustache, but that's where the cowboy resemblance ended. Dr. Ed was barely five and a half feet tall and thick everywhere. He looked more like a giant dwarf in a Stetson.

"Cold enough for you, Sheriff?"

"Orville's gonna kill you if he catches you driving that thing up here," I said.

"Sheriff Tatum, I have been a member of the Gun Club since you were in diapers, so I am entitled. Besides, Orville is hunting in the northwest quadrant today. Isn't this your week on duty?"

"Yes, Dr. Ed, I am on duty," I said. "I just happened to be up here patrolling this portion of the county."

Dr. Ed eyeballed me while he filled his pipe with Captain Black from an elk-skin pouch. When blue smoke replaced white vapor, he spoke. "What's happened? You look like you just found a dead possum in your bed."

"Councilman Pitcher's in there." I nodded to the stand of pine. "He's dead."

"Stroke?"

"I don't think so," I said. "Not with the hole in his head."

"Hunting accident?" Ed scanned the ridge to the west. "Is Jerry nearby?"

Now why would he ask that? "I don't know, Dr. Ed. I just got here."

"Jesus, not another sniper."

"Doesn't look that way. Why don't you and I go take a look?" Dr. Ed is the county coroner as well as the town doctor.

I led Dr. Ed into the clearing. Pitcher was still there, still dead.

"You check his pulse?" asked Dr. Ed. "Sometimes these old boys just look dead."

"He's dead," I told him. "You just can't see the bullet wound from this side."

Dr. Ed stretched the stems of his glasses over his ears and walked around the body. He squatted painfully and examined the big hole in the man's skull. I got down with him.

"Powder burns," we said at the same time. Exploding

powder from the barrel of the weapon had burned Pitcher's hair and skin.

"Not a hunting accident," said Dr. Ed.

"Self-inflicted?" I asked.

"Hard to say," said Dr. Ed. He looked at the rifle leaning up against the tree. "I can't imagine he shot himself with that. Did you find another weapon?"

"I haven't looked yet."

"Well, let's look."

We did our best not to trample any evidence. Booted feet had flattened much of the tender alpine turf and pine needles around the tree. Pitcher had used this stand for a few days. I found two cartridges on opposite sides of the Engelmann spruce. One was a rifle shell, the same caliber as Pitcher's weapon—Winchester .270. It lay next to the expensive hunting rifle. A small caliber, I thought, for hunting elk. The other shell was a wide, stubby handgun casing, lying to the left of the tree.

"Here's a forty-five." I held up the cold piece of brass, then I set it back down, exactly as I found it. *Dumbass.*

"That's what you carry, isn't it?" asked Dr. Ed.

"That's correct." Actually, both Jerry and I carried .45s. We upgraded from 9mm Berettas last year, trading capacity for stopping power. I wondered if Jerry had his with him.

"I don't see the weapon anywhere," said Dr. Ed. We looked at each other, then turned to the body.

"Underneath?" I asked.

"Let's turn him over."

Thomas Pitcher was a big man, six feet tall and close to 250 pounds. It took both of us to roll him onto his back. As we rolled him, the acrid odor of urine filled my dry nostrils. A dark patch stained the front of Pitcher's green wool pants from his crotch to his knees.

"Jesus Christ." I grimaced from the smell.

"Easy there, big fella," said Dr. Ed. "Dead people tend to lose control of these things."

Pitcher's right arm and a .45 automatic lay tucked under his heavy frame. The Colt was a nickel-plated Series 70 Mark IV—another rich man's gun.

I left the handgun and looked at the dead man. The ugly exit wound had exploded out of his right cheekbone, but I refused to let it distract me. I needed to find the subtle markers, to show Dr. Ed that I could analyze a crime scene, too.

Pitcher's face was gray and drawn, his eyes half-lidded. The tips of his fingers and nose were a frosty blue, and his lips were purple. Cracks and stretch marks radiated from the corners of his mouth, raw and red to the back of his jaw.

"His coat," I said.

"What about it?"

"It's buttoned all wrong," I said. Pitcher had misbuttoned his red wool coat. Carelessness from the only man in Belmont who wore a three-piece suit every day.

"I never expected Thomas Pitcher to kill himself." I stood. "The man was in such control of his world."

Dr. Ed stood, too, but did not respond to my inane statement. At the time, I didn't know it was inane, but I was about to find out.

"Let's take a step back, Sheriff," said Dr. Ed, "and talk a bit of field forensics."

"Okay."

"Take a look at Pitcher's rifle, Bill," said Dr. Ed. He called me Bill. Class had begun.

"Okay."

"Where is the bolt action?"

"It's on the right side," I said. "So he's right-handed."

"Very good. Now look at the councilman's wound."

"It's on the left side."

"And?" asked Dr. Ed. "Get closer if you need to."

I squatted back down and examined the position of the gunshot wound. The bullet penetrated behind the ear, right above the little knob in the skull.

"It's back kind of far," I said.

"Exactly," said Dr. Ed. "Just above the left mastoid process. A difficult spot for a right-handed man to shoot himself, don't you think? Now examine the marks extending from the sides of his mouth."

Bits of skin and whiskers had been torn away from Pitcher's face. Traces of adhesive remained embedded in the skin. Both the damaged skin and two-days' growth of beard struck an inconsistent chord. The folds of rough skin on his neck indicated decades of overshaving. Pitcher shaved every day, even while hunting.

"It looks like someone had duct tape over his mouth," I said.

"Very good," said Dr. Ed. "Now pull the cuffs of his coat back from his wrists."

I had to hold Pitcher's hands to do this. They were icecold lumps of dead wood.

"There are ligature marks on his wrists, and his hands are freezing cold."

"But he's been dead less than an hour," said Dr. Ed. "How can this be? His urine is still warm and stinking, not frozen to the ground, yet his extremities show evidence of prolonged exposure to the cold."

"He's not wearing gloves," I said.

"In this weather?" asked Dr. Ed.

I stood and walked over to the big spruce. Rope burns marred the bark on the uphill side.

"Someone tied him up, then shot him in the back of the head," I said.

"I will take that a step further, Sheriff," said Dr. Ed. "Someone had him tied up for a long while, in the cold, without his coat, hat, or gloves. This person kept Councilman Pitcher alive, then shot him in the back of the head with that gun, put his clothes back on, and left him here. Notice there is no blood on the coat or hat. I imagine we will find blood spatter on his undershirt. Dead men cannot put their coats back on."

I kicked myself for missing it, but he was right. The hat and coat were clean. Someone had done a poor job of staging a suicide.

"Dad!" A shout came from beyond the trees.

Two

THERE'S NOTHING LIKE A DEAD BODY TO BRING people out of the woodwork. You'd think that'd be harder on a four-thousand-acre hunting ranch, but they all found the dead guy.

"Dad, did you shoot?" asked Jerry. "Did you get him?"

I tried to intercept my deputy before he saw his dead father. I didn't make it.

Jerry used to be a fat kid in a young man's body. Now, he's an older, skinny kid in a young man's body, but he's my deputy, and he saved my life once, so I'll keep him.

Jerry stared at his father for a long time before seeing me. Jerry was as tall as his father and had on a matching red wool coat, but instead of the hunting cap, he wore his deputy sheriff cowboy hat. His rifle was slung over his shoulder, barrel down. He finally looked down at me, and in his pale blue eyes, I saw the fat kid again. Faint patches of black stubble peppered his pale face.

"Sheriff Tatum. What are you doing here?" he asked. "It's my week to hunt."

Jerry is only a few years younger than me, but he makes me feel like his uncle. An old one.

"I know, Jerry," I said. "I was up here patrolling."

His eyes shifted back to his father. "Is that my dad?" he asked.

"Yes."

"Is he dead?"

"Yes, Jerry. I'm sorry."

Jerry blinked a few slow blinks. "Well, *I* didn't shoot him."

I didn't want my only deputy going into shock on me, so I turned him around and led him out of the trees.

"Why don't we move away, and we'll talk about it," I said. "You got your radio with you?"

"Yeah, but I don't have it turned on when I'm hunting," said Jerry. His eyes glazed and focused on nothing.

The wind had picked up with the coming of the sun, and it splashed my face as we came out of the spruce grove. The dawn had turned from orange red to bright yellow— faint frost had burned away where the light touched the ground. My eyes watered in the light and wind. I turned to Jerry. Tears streamed down his face.

"You want to tell me what's going on?" I asked quietly.

"I don't know, Sheriff Tatum." Jerry turned back to the spruce grove. "I haven't seen my dad since we came up here. I figured he was hunting on this ridge, so I stayed a couple valleys away, in case he needed help with an elk."

"You haven't seen him?" I asked. "Is that normal?"

"Dad always hunts alone," said Jerry. "I never even see him go out or come in. He walks everywhere, so he leaves early and comes in late."

"Jerry, we're over four miles from the lodge," I said. "Are you telling me your Dad walked down here this morning in the dark?"

He shrugged. "Probably."

I waited for more, but Jerry was done talking. He sat down on an outcrop of gray rock and stared off into the valley.

Dr. Ed emerged from the scene and stood next to me. We both watched Jerry's sad perch for a moment, then he pulled me away.

"How's your deputy taking it?" asked Dr. Ed.

"Well, look at him."

"Can we leave him alone like this?"

"You okay, Jerry?" I called over.

Jerry slowly turned his head. "Yes, Sheriff Tatum. I'm okay."

"Okay. You just sit tight, Deputy." I wasn't very good at consoling. Ed and I returned to our dead councilman, but it wasn't long before the gathering continued.

"Who the fuck drove this goddamn ATV onto my ranch?" Orville James's voice called through the trees. The little man pushed into the clearing. He wore his winter uniform, which was the same as his summer uniform—jeans, boots, and Stetson—except with a sheepskin coat over the top. His face was a white potato with red ears sticking out. He gripped his Weatherby hunting rifle in one hand, thoughtfully pointing the barrel away from Dr. Ed and me.

"Doc, I figured it was you," said Orville. "Bet you thought I was hunting the northwest quadrant today. How many times I told you about that goddamn vehicle?" He finally noticed the body. "Say, is that Tommy Pitcher?"

"Yes, Orville," I said. "This is a crime scene. Would you please back away? I will be with you shortly."

Orville grunted and left the clearing.

"I need to talk to him," I said. "Maybe he saw someone."

"Go ahead," said Dr. Ed. "I have work to do here."

Four horses now milled about on the ridge.

Orville stood next to his horse, hands on hips, rifle now slung over his shoulder. Jerry continued to stare off into the valley.

The fourth horse was Emmet Springer's young paint. Emmet squatted next to Jerry, talking quietly. Emmet was a local artist, one of many in Belmont. The ridge was getting crowded.

Orville pulled out a pack of Marlboro Reds. He offered me one. I took two, along with a light from his Zippo and another squint from the old man. I didn't usually smoke on the ranch, and neither did Orville.

"Aren't you on duty, Sheriff?" said Orville.

Does everyone in town know our rotation? "Looks that way, doesn't it?"

"Then what are you doing up here?"

"Investigating a—"

Murder? Suicide? Patricide?

"You were scoutin', weren't ya?" said Orville.

"Investigating Councilman Pitcher's death," I said, finally.

"How'd he die?" asked Orville, "Someone shoot him?"

"Why would you think that, Orville?"

He snorted. "I can name at least five people in this county who would be happy to kill Tommy Pitcher. And if you gave me a few minutes, I could probably name about five more. I'd a killed that son of a bitch myself years ago, but he pays his dues on time and doesn't violate ranch rules."

I extracted my notebook from an inside pocket and took off a glove. *See? I was on duty.* I wondered how long it would take for my right hand to go numb.

"Did you hear any shooting this morning?" I asked.

"Yup, but that's not why I came down here," said Orville. "I heard that goddamn ATV of the Doc's, and knew I could ambush him."

"Which way did you come down?"

"From the north, down the pack trail. I was on my way over to Silver Park when I heard the engine."

"That's a long way," I said.

"I'm old, not deaf, Sheriff," said Orville. "Anyway, you were out here this morning. It's as quiet as a church before sunup."

He was right. Sound carries a long way in the mountains, especially in the cold air.

"Did you see anyone on your way down?" I asked.

"I met up with Emmet near the west branch of Bellows Creek," said Orville. "We came down together."

"What was he doing up here?" Emmet was not a member, nor did he hunt.

"Glassing the valley," said Orville. "I let him come on the ranch with his camera." Emmet made bronze wildlife sculptures.

"Kind of dangerous during the season, don't you think?" I asked.

"You were up here," said Orville. *Good point.*

"Why did he come with you?"

"You'll have to ask him yourself."

"You do any shooting today?" I asked.

"I don't harvest my own product, Sheriff. I leave that to my clients."

I'd forgotten. Orville only carried a rifle for show.

"Did you see anyone else up here?" I asked.

"Nope. No one."

My radio squawked, "Sheriff Tatum, this is Jenny."

"Go ahead, Jenny," I said into the handset.

"I can't seem to raise your deputy," she said. "He must have his radio turned off."

"Stand down, Jenny," I said. "He's up here with me."

"Roger, out." I turned back to the old man. "Orville, when was the last time you saw Councilman Pitcher?"

"Before just now? Let's see." He rubbed his wrinkled face. "Must have been a couple days ago, at least, maybe three. He grabbed an early breakfast from Wendy and walked out in the dark. He leaves earlier than anyone else, 'cause he walks everywhere. Old-school hunter."

"Did you know where he was hunting?" I asked.

"No one knows where Tommy Pitcher hunts," said Orville. "Not even me. He does his own scouting a couple weeks before the season, then goes off on his own. He's real secretive, but he brings back the bulls."

"What time did he leave?" I asked.

"Damn near two thirty," said Orville. "It must take him at least two hours to get down here in the dark. He hunts until he can't see, then walks back to the ranch for supper. Eats, then goes to bed. Don't talk to no one."

"Does anyone else get up that early?"

"Just Wendy and me, and I'm still puttin' on my socks and he's already out the back door."

"What about Jerry?" I asked. "Do you know his routine?"

The old man stared at Jerry for a moment. "That boy spends most of his time hunting for his father."

"Really?"

"You know what I mean, Sheriff. The boy just wants to hunt *with* his father."

Jerry was twenty-five years old, but he was doomed to being a boy for the rest of his life. Until now, maybe.

"How many other hunters do you have on the ranch today?" I asked.

" 'Bout ten," said Orville. "Five from town, one party of four from Denver, then a single. The Denver party drinks more than they hunt. They do not require a guide."

"And the single?"

"Fella from Chicago, does something with pork bellies. He's hired Darren to guide him every day, all day."

"Kind of slow for this time of year," I said.

Orville grimaced. "Goddamn drought is killing me, but we've had lean years before. It'll come back."

"Where have they all been hunting?" I asked. Ten hunters would disappear in Orville's four-thousand-acre ranch like raindrops in the desert.

"All over," said Orville, "but not down here. Mostly up higher, closer to the ranch. Prob'ly why Tommy walked this far, just to get away from everyone." He looked into the grove. "But someone must have found him."

"What makes you say that?"

"I ain't deaf, and I ain't stupid, either, Sheriff," said Orville. "Big as Tommy was, he wasn't out of shape. Most folks don't know how much he walked around these mountains, so that rules out heart attack. And suicide? Tommy loved himself too much to blow his brains out, so that leaves only one other option." He hissed out a stream of gray smoke. "Someone blew 'em out for him."

"Any idea who?" I asked.

"I told you already. I could name ten people in as many minutes who would leave Tommy Pitcher dead and bleeding up here on the mountain. What do you need me to do here, Sheriff?"

"Can you get one of your trucks down here?" I asked. Orville nodded. "Call one of them down, then just hold up while I talk to everyone."

He tucked another cigarette into the corner of his mouth and made the call.

Emmet had heard my radio squelch and left Jerry on his rock. Now, Emmet was a real-live, six-foot-three cowboy look-alike. He had a droopy mustache that covered his upper lip and gray-green eyes set deep in his wrinkled face.

"Howdy, Sheriff Tatum." His voice always sounded ready to break into a verse of cowboy poetry. He pulled off his dark brown Resistol and combed bare fingers through his dirty blond hair. His hair ended in a middle-aged ponytail. That's where the cowboy ended, too, and the artist began.

"How's Jerry doing?" I asked.

"Not too good," said Emmet. "I seen that look before. You aren't gonna put him on duty, are you?"

"No," I said, "but that might be the best thing for him." I took a drag from my cigarette. Emmet looked at it hungrily. "You'll have to ask Orville. I left my pack in the Bronco."

"I'm tryin' to quit, anyway," said Emmet. "Now, you have some questions for me?"

"Turns out I do." I opened my notebook. "Where were you this morning?"

"Henry and I came up Farmer's Creek Trail this morning before dawn, same way you came." Henry was Emmet's paint. I noted Emmet's saddle had no rifle scabbard. "We worked our way right around this spur and up the west branch of Bellows Creek. We were headed up toward the divide when we heard the shot."

"What were you doing up here so early?" I asked.

"Same as you, scoutin' for elk and deer." Emmet grinned. "They come up out of the low ground in the morning to feed and get warm."

"Did you see anyone else this morning?"

Emmet stared up at the LaGarita Mountains before answering. "Nope, just Orville."

"Did you hear the shooting?" I asked.

He refocused on me. "Sure. But I didn't think anything of it. It is hunting season, you know."

"Why did you come down here?"

"Orville was pretty steamed when he heard the ATV engine," said Emmet. "I didn't want him to shoot anybody, so I figured I could do the peacemakin'."

"Was today the first time you came up here?" I asked.

"Nope. Come this way every morning, at least when the bulls are in rut. Makes 'em crazy, so they just ignore me."

"Were you here yesterday?"

"Sure," said Emmet, "and the day before that, too. Been following a herd around. They like this valley, so I do."

"And you never saw Councilman Pitcher or anyone else?"

"Now, I never said that, Sheriff. I said I didn't see anyone else *this morning.*"

I waited. I was learning that people would talk if you just got out of the way.

"I saw Jerry milling about on top of the ridge the last few days," said Emmet.

"How could you tell it was Jerry?" I asked.

Emmet patted the high-power Bausch & Lomb binoculars around his neck.

"Right," I said. "What was he doing?"

"Well, hunting, I s'pose. Didn't pay much attention."

"Did he see you?" I asked.

"Well, he didn't shoot at me."

"But you didn't see him this morning?"

"Nope, not until I got here. I told you that already," said Emmet. He watched the end of my cigarette glow and smoke.

"You sure you don't want one, Emmet?" I asked. "I bummed two off Orville."

"No, really, Sheriff. I'm good."

"So, let me get this straight," I said. "You've been up here every morning for the last, how many days?"

"'Bout a week."

"And the only person you saw was Jerry Pitcher."

"That's correct."

"But not today."

"Nope." His eyes started flicking over my shoulder.

"Show me about where you saw him." I turned toward the ridge behind me.

"Right up there." Emmet pointed his hand over my shoulder so I could spot down his long arm.

"Which way was he going?" I asked.

"Hell, I don't remember," said Emmet. "Once I glassed him the first day, I just checked. The dawn was on him, so he was pretty easy to mark, with that coat and all."

"So you didn't positively identify him every day?"

"No, Sheriff."

"So, it could have been anyone."

"Yeah, I guess," said Emmet. "Anyone wearing a red hunting coat."

"Can you think of anything else that may have been out of the ordinary up here the last couple of days?" I asked. *What a lame question.*

"No, Sheriff, can't say that I can."

"All right, Emmet, thanks. If something else pops into your head, be sure to let me know."

"You got it. You need me to stick around? I'd like to get down off the mountain. Gettin' a little busy up here."

I couldn't think of any reason to keep Emmet around, besides that he was a suspect. Of course, everyone around me was a suspect, merely by their proximity to the body. There was just too much country up here to assume it was coincidence.

Emmet patted Jerry on the shoulder and got on his horse. Jerry shivered, his rifle barrel lodged in the dirt next to him. Orville stood apart, his sharp eyes watching for game and giving Dr. Ed's ATV a look that would melt the tires. Dr. Ed remained hidden in the trees with the body. Including me, that made five people within easy walking distance to a murder scene on a four-thousand-acre ranch in the middle of the San Juan Mountains.

Mike Stanford made it six.

We heard him coming down the ridge on one of Orville's horses. Even Jerry turned his head. Mike held out the reins like they were handlebars and bounced his way onto the spur. His horse stopped and snorted.

"Okay," said Mike, talking to his horse, "Okay, here we are. We made it." He eased out of the saddle and thudded to the ground, stumbling a little.

Mike Stanford was built like a tank, a short tank, a couple inches shorter than me. He wore a canvas hunter's coat that was a little too long. I couldn't help but think of him as the Michelin Man's younger brother.

"Just when we thought it was crowded enough up here, a lawyer shows up," said Orville.

"I'm not a lawyer, Orville," said Mike. "I am an accountant."

"Accountant, lawyer, what's the difference?" said Orville. "You know what Ben Franklin said, 'First thing we do is kill all the lawyers.'"

"That was Shakespeare, and I am a C-P-A. Get it straight, old man."

"Who taught you to ride a horse, your mom?" asked Orville.

"I think you did," said Mike. "Nice job, by the way." He noted the assembly of men. "Hey, Sheriff. What's going on? Someone shoot something?"

Emmet said nothing, just tipped his hat, turned his horse, and went south down Farmer's Creek Trail.

I waved Mike over, out of earshot from the others. He looked up at me and raised his eyebrows.

"Something's happened, Mike," I said. "Councilman Pitcher is dead. He's right in those trees. I found him this morning."

The light went out in Mike's eyes. "May I see him?"

"Not likely. This is a crime scene."

"A crime scene? Was he murdered?"

"Yes, Mike. That's what it looks like," I said. "You were up on the ranch this morning?"

"That's correct."

"Where?"

"You need a grid?" asked Mike.

"That would be nice." I called his bluff and pulled out my topographical of north Mineral County.

Mike's smile widened as he glanced at the map. "Three four eight, nine four two," he rattled off his position. Mike did this kind of thing all the time. I struggled to find the location on the map. Mike took off his left glove and pointed to the spot. For the first time, I noticed a thin wedding band on his ring finger.

"That's a few miles away," I said. "What brought you over here?"

"I knew Mr. Pitcher was hunting in this area," said Mike. "I heard the shooting and figured he might need some help. He doesn't have a horse, you know."

"Did you see anyone up here this morning?" I asked.

"Dr. Ed came up the pack trail from town, couple hours before daylight. I believe he stayed in the southern sector of the ranch, to keep away from Orville."

"Anyone else?"

"No. Just Dr. Ed."

"I didn't know you hunted, Mike," I said. I had been a member of the Halfmoon Ranch Gun Club for a year. Orville required an apprenticeship of sorts before allowing anyone on the rolls. The town CPA didn't seem the type to get past the old sniper.

"Sure do. I just don't get out very often," said Mike. "They accepted my membership while you were running for sheriff last fall. This is my first season. To be frank, I think Mr. Pitcher had a little influence on that." He turned to the trees where Pitcher lay.

"You any good?" I asked.

"I've had some luck, I guess."

"Are you a good shot?"

Mike looked back at me, his smile frozen on his cold face. "I'm okay. I can shoot well enough for Orville."

"You do any shooting this morning?" I asked.

"I . . . I took one long shot at a mule deer. Missed by a

mile," said Mike. "I'm a little embarrassed. Don't tell Orville."

"May I inspect your rifle?" I asked.

Mike's expression didn't change. He withdrew his rifle from the scabbard. He safed and cleared the weapon, then held the rifle at port arms, like he was standing in formation. I took it from him.

Four brass shells lay seated in the magazine well below the bolt. Round, black dots of powder residue speckled the brushed stainless steel of the chamber.

"Are you staying at the ranch?" I handed him the rifle.

"Orville won't let me keep one of his horses in my yard."

I knew that. "When did you come up?" I asked.

"A few days ago."

"Did you see Pitcher while you were up here?"

"Which one?"

"The dead one."

Mike's smile disappeared. "I saw him occasionally."

"But you knew where he was hunting."

"That's correct."

"What about Jerry?"

"What about him?" asked Mike.

"Did you see him, either at the lodge or in the field?"

"I might have. A man on a horse looks like any other at long range."

"How about this morning?"

"I told you," said Mike, "I only saw Dr. Ed coming up the trail from town."

"Right, well, I got nothing else for you right now, Mike," I said. "I need you to clear out of here."

"How are you getting Mr. Pitcher off the mountain?" he asked.

"Orville's got a truck coming."

"May I accompany the body to town?" asked Mike.

It was a strange request. "Sure, I guess. He's going straight to the morgue, though. Dr. Ed needs to do an autopsy."

"I will be honored to help Dr. Ed with Mr. Pitcher's transport." He looked over his shoulder at Jerry. "What about your deputy?"

"Jerry's staying with me," I said. Actually, I didn't know what I was going to do with Jerry, but I wasn't going to let him out of my sight just yet.

Just then, a big white Ford F350 came rumbling down the ridge. Orville waved it over. The truck sped to the downhill side of the spruce grove and braked hard, kicking up a little cloud of alpine turf. Wendy Schnuck's blonde curly bob bounced out of the driver's side while the truck still rocked with the abrupt halt. Wendy was the concierge at the Halfmoon Ranch.

"Hundred ten pounds of sweet hot fire," Mike said from behind me.

"Mornin' boys," she said to the group. "I got hot coffee in the truck if you need it." Wendy seemed to have everything her guests needed, especially the hunters.

"That won't be necessary, darlin'," said Orville. "C'mere." He put an arm around her and pulled her aside.

"No fuckin' way!" Jerry came alive behind me. "She ain't touchin' my father!"

We all stared at him like he'd risen up out of the ground. Jerry jumped up from where he'd been rooted and charged over to the truck, face red and eyes white. Wendy scooted around the big Ford.

I put my hand in Jerry's chest. "Easy there, deputy. She's just here to help. Why don't you go sit back down?"

I gently pushed him across the knoll and returned him to his mourning spot. We loaded the dead councilman in the back of the truck, and they took him away.

I stayed and watched Jerry. He glared at the procession until they disappeared over the ridge.

Three

I SAT DOWN NEXT TO MY DEPUTY AND TURNED MY face to the new sun. Solitary warmth when everything else was cold.

Jerry and I stared at the valley for a long time. From our vantage point, we could see the Rio Grande from where it twisted free of the sandy canyons by Becky Noonan's place, its slow meander through the green flats of the Wason's Ranch, its narrow plunge into Wagon Wheel Gap.

"I can see your cabin from here," said Jerry.

I spotted my little A-frame at the base of Snowshoe Mountain. I nodded. I waited.

"You know, I been shining my dad's shoes twice a week since I was four years old," said Jerry. "Twice a week for twenty years."

"Really?" I asked.

His tears had left salty streaks in the windburned skin. "I think my first memory of my father was him inspecting his shoes after I shined them."

"You still do it?" I asked.

"Oh, yeah. I don't even think about it anymore," said Jerry. "I actually get a week off when he's hunting, but I have to oil and seal his hunting boots for the season." Jerry laughed without humor. "Can you imagine, a grown man shining his father's shoes?"

"Sons have done worse things for their fathers."

"Yeah, I guess," said Jerry. "My wife doesn't even know I do it. I sneak into the basement before work. That's where I hide my shoeshine box. He lays them at the top of the stairs for me—black wing tips on Sunday, brown oxfords on Wednesday."

"You use Kiwi or paste?" I asked.

Jerry laughed again. This time, however, it was a real laugh. He tipped his head back and laughed at the dark blue sky.

"I use Kiwi," he said, smiling. Then the smile vanished. "I'll have to get his black shoes ready one last time."

I let him sit on that while I lit the other cigarette I'd bummed from Orville. I always smoked too much when someone was murdered.

"I gotta ask you some questions," I said, blowing out.

"I know, Sheriff."

"Where were you this morning when you heard the shots?" I asked.

"Up on the ridge, about half a mile to the northwest." Jerry pointed a thumb over his shoulder. "The elk like to come up out of the low ground in the morning. I wanted to find out where."

"Did you know that your father was down here?"

"Nope. Dad never tells . . . never told anyone where he hunted."

"Orville said you spent most of your time looking for him."

Jerry scoffed. "Orville is full of shit. Dad didn't want to be found, and I wasn't going to walk up on him. The season is the only time he gets out of the office, the only time I see him without a suit on. I'm not going to be the one to spoil his hunt."

"So, its just a coincidence that both of you were hunting in this sector?" I asked.

"Same coincidence that you, Emmet, Dr. Ed, Orville, and Mr. Stanford were all in this sector." At least he was paying attention.

"Anyway," said Jerry, "those drunks from Denver are hunting up north, near the lodge. No way I'm getting in range of them."

"Did you see anyone else this morning?" I asked.

"No. No one."

"What brought you down the mountain? You showed up pretty quick."

Jerry paused. I think, for the first time, he realized I considered him a suspect.

"I figured he was down here, somewhere, but I guess I was closer to Dad than I thought. I heard the shot and knew it was him. He only takes one shot. I came down to help him."

"Help him do what?" I asked.

"Recover his elk, of course," said Jerry. "Dad walks everywhere when he's hunting. There's no way he was going to get an animal out of here without help."

"When was the last time you saw your father?" I asked.

"You mean, before just now?" Jerry thought for a moment. "We drove up to the lodge together, earlier this week. Once we're up here, he does his own thing. Leaves early, comes in late, goes to bed."

"He didn't talk to you?"

"I told you, he does his own thing up here. He doesn't tell anyone where he's hunting, least of all me."

"Jerry, we changed over five days ago," I said. "You haven't seen your father in five days?"

"I guess."

"That didn't concern you?" I asked.

"Not really. Dad's been hunting up here since 1965—that's forty years, Sheriff. Longer than I've been around. Dad could take care of himself."

"Do you share a room at the lodge? Did you hear him come in, at least?"

"Dad gets his own room and pays for mine, too. He likes his privacy."

"Did anyone else at the Halfmoon see him leave or come in?" I asked.

"Orville and Wendy are the only ones up early enough."

"What's the deal with you and Wendy?" I asked. "I didn't know you hated her so much."

Jerry said something evil under his breath. "I don't hate her. I just hate what she does. She has no respect for anyone, not even herself."

I let that go for another time. "What about when your father came in from hunting? Someone had to spot him."

"He comes in after dark and goes straight to his room to look at his maps and plan the next day's hunt. You think my father was a social person? He wasn't."

I decided to change the subject. "Does your father own any handguns?"

"He carried a nickel-plated .45 with him all the time. Has a permit for it."

"Even in town?"

"Even in town," said Jerry.

"Did he have any enemies?" I had just broken my long-held promise to myself never to ask any question that I'd heard on a cop show.

"Dad had lots of enemies," said Jerry. "When he moved here in 1965, he worked for the mines—engineering, then management. He was in charge of payroll. Said you never knew when some crazy miner would get a wild hair up his ass and come after you, so Dad learned to carry his .45 with him all the time. Never gave up the habit."

"You think he needed it now?" I asked.

"Beats me. We got some pretty whacked-out artists in Belmont," said Jerry. I couldn't tell if he was joking. "You know Emmet's a little off."

"Why do you say that?" I asked.

"Anybody who comes up here without any orange on during the hunting season is asking for it," said Jerry. "You know he almost killed someone a few years ago?"

"I was here a few years ago, Jerry. I don't recall anything like that."

"It was a couple years before you showed up," said Jerry. "He damn near choked some guy to death in the San Juan Tavern."

"Who was it?" I asked.

"Some guy from out of town," said Jerry. "Went to the hospital in Del Norte and never came back."

"Was Emmet charged with anything?"

"Nope. Sheriff Dale let him off. Johnny Spotten and three others at the Tavern said the other guy started it."

Sheriff Dale Boggett was my predecessor. Jerry shot him a year ago, saving my life.

"Hey, wait a sec," I said. "Emmet doesn't drink. I've never seen him in the Tavern."

"That's because he's been in AA since then," said Jerry. "That was part of Sheriff Dale's deal with him."

I didn't know how we'd gotten so far off track. I wasn't satisfied with what I'd heard from Jerry or anyone else up here, but I couldn't think of any other questions.

"You want to go to work?" I stood.

"Sure," said Jerry, "I'll have to go down and talk to Mom. I hope Dr. Ed keeps his mouth shut, so I can get to her first."

"Do you want to go down now?"

"No, it's okay," said Jerry. He stood up with me and took a deep breath. "You know, Julie and I were going to move out, buy one of the new places Dana Pratt built west of town. Things were getting pretty crowded with the new baby. I guess that won't happen, now. Someone has to take care of Mom."

I wasn't going to let Jerry back into the spruce grove, so I had him circle the perimeter. I went back in to recover the shells, the rifle, and the handgun.

Placing the items on a horse blanket and leaving my gloves on, I inspected the .45. I dropped the magazine, cleared the chamber, and shucked out the rounds onto the blanket. There were eight rounds total—one short of a full magazine. The chamber smelled of fresh gunpowder and had small flakes of it at the back of the barrel. I did the same with the Remington 700. Like the Colt, it was one round short of a full load, and it, too, showed signs of recent firing. The shell cases I found at the base of the tree matched the loaded shells in both weapons.

I made one more turn around the little clearing but found nothing more, only the bloodstain in the brown pine needles. I was reminded how limited my crime scene resources were, being a mountain county sheriff. On top of that, I was still pretty new at my job. I had spent more time in the Army killing terrorists than I had wearing a badge. It would take a long time before my investigative technique outmatched my skill with a rifle.

"Sheriff Tatum, I think I found something," Jerry called from the uphill side of the grove.

Jerry had found horse tracks, a lot of them, but not our own. I was no tracker, but they looked like they were made by a single animal making repeated visits. I could see his trampled path up the ridge. The shooter had left his horse here while keeping Pitcher tied up in the cold.

"You wanna follow them?" asked Jerry.

"Yup," I said. "Let's get our horses."

I didn't have to be a tracker to follow this trail. I didn't even have to get off my horse. Only short brown grass and pincushion cacti covered the northwest slope of the spur, and the shod hooves of the killer's mount had torn up the delicate alpine turf. The killer had come this way repeatedly, staying below the top of the ridge, running parallel to Farmer's Creek Trail. He'd traversed the ridge until coming to the west branch of Bellows Creek, where the terrain fell away, too steep to negotiate in the dark. I suspected he'd moved in the dark, mostly because of his reliance on the same path to his place of torture.

I don't know when I began to think of Pitcher's experience as torture. One night in the icy dryness of the mountains would kill anyone, but Pitcher had been missing for at least two. The killer had kept him alive, freezing, hovering between shock and hypothermia. I couldn't shake the image of Pitcher's blue skin and purple lips from my head.

The narrow draw that held the west branch of Bellows Creek ran generally north and west, toward the top of Wason Plateau. To our right, the draw deepened into a canyon where it sought the main watershed of Bellows Creek. The killer had turned northwest, following the creek, and so did we.

A vein of trees—blue spruce and mountain juniper— traced the watercourse up the plateau, nourished by the scarce moisture. Cold air nestled in the low ground and found its way over my collar and down my neck.

The v-shaped draw flattened as we gained altitude. At a turn, we came upon the intersection of the draw and Farmer's Creek Trail. Jerry and I dismounted where the killer's track merged with the other.

"We'll lose him here," said Jerry.

I said nothing. I didn't think the shooter had taken the main trail. Both Orville and Emmet had come down this way, and they would have seen him.

Unless one of them did it.

One of the men who converged on the scene this morning was the killer. That many people in such proximity to a murder in the middle of the San Juan Mountains was simply more than coincidence. They all had perfectly acceptable explanations for their presence in the southeast quadrant of the ranch, but I couldn't shake the fact that one of them probably did it.

While Jerry milled about on the main trail, I searched the edge, looking for a step-off. I found it on the near side of the stream. The vein of trees continued up the slope with the shallow draw, providing the killer a hidden avenue of approach and escape. Instead of taking the trail, he stayed in the low ground and followed the line of the stream farther up the slope.

I pulled out my topographical and found the draw among the grid lines. It climbed the plateau for another four kilometers before crossing another man-made path, this time at the junction of two trails—the main pack trail from town, and another track that traversed the plateau from east to west. The killer could emerge from his hidden path miles from the murder scene, then choose one of two busy pack trails and cover his escape completely.

"He went this way," I said, folding up my map. "Let's go."

We got on our horses and stared at each other. Jerry waited for me to take the lead. I thought that wasn't such a good idea.

"Hey, bud," I said, "why don't you ride up here with me?"

"Draw gets pretty narrow up there," said Jerry. "I don't think we can ride two abreast."

"Then why don't you go first?" I said. "Be good training for you." I was a bad liar. Sergeant Richter had kicked my ass every time he caught me lying.

Jerry stared at me for a moment. I think, in that short span of time, I watched my deputy finally grow up. He dropped his bumbling innocence like he had shed his baby fat. His blue eyes hardened.

"You think I did it, maybe," he said.

I couldn't lie to my own deputy. "Maybe."

"I wouldn't shoot my own father," said Jerry.

"Maybe," I repeated.

"Will you stop sayin' 'maybe'? I told you I didn't do it. That should be enough for you."

"I trusted our last deputy, and look where that got me." I rubbed the scar on the back of my neck.

"Marty Three Stones was crazy," said Jerry. "She killed

because she liked to, and Sheriff Dale let her do it." He turned away. "This is different."

"Different?"

"I mean I'm different," said Jerry. I waited.

"I don't like killing, Sheriff Tatum," said Jerry. "Ever since I shot Sheriff Dale, I can't even load my rifle, let alone shoot it, not even at an elk."

I nudged Pancho over to Jerry's mount and withdrew his rifle from the scabbard. I tried to clear it, but hesitated— the bolt action was on the wrong side.

"I didn't know you were left-handed, Jerry," I said.

"You never asked."

"You carry your .45 on your right hip."

Jerry shrugged. "I don't take it out, much."

I lay the left-handed rifle in my lap and studied my deputy. "You and I have been to the range many times, Jerry. You always fired your service weapon with your right hand. I would have noticed. I trained you to shoot the .45, remember?"

Jerry looked away from me. I waited for his answer.

"You trained me to shoot the Colt, but my dad taught me to shoot a handgun." He stared long across the Wason Plateau.

"I thought you told me your dad never did stuff like that with you. Marty had to."

In a strange twist of fate, Marty Three Stones, the ex-deputy and ex-Belmont Sniper, had helped Jerry hone his rifle skills and earn a membership into the Halfmoon Gun Club. Jerry's proficiency with his .270 had saved my life.

"Dad made sure I knew how to shoot a handgun—he was paranoid, remember? He wanted me to be able to kill an intruder, coming in the house, in case I woke up first. He started taking me out to shoot his 9mm when I was only eight. He actually used the word 'kill' when he was teaching me. Had me shoot man-shaped targets, taught me to keep both eyes open and aim for the heart."

"What does that have to do with being left-handed?"

Jerry's mouth rippled with bad memory. "Dad tried to work it out of me. Made me write and throw and bat right-handed. I never could get it. Never played on any team in school because he wouldn't let me do it with my left." He paused. "But I could shoot right-handed. It just clicked for me."

"But your rifle—"

Jerry glared at me, interrupting. "My rifle is mine. I bought it, I taught myself to shoot it . . . with Marty's help. I'm still left-eye dominant, so I couldn't use the scope if I tried to shoot the other way. Dad didn't care. He hunted alone."

I didn't know my own deputy, this angry man-child living under his father's boot heel, or polished wing tip. I shot back the bolt of Jerry's .270—both the chamber and the magazine were empty. I sniffed the metal—it smelled of Hoppes and gun oil. The inside of the barrel was a mirror.

"Then why do you hunt?" I replaced his rifle in its scabbard. "Why do you and I rotate shifts?"

Jerry shrugged. "My dad expects me to come up here with him, so I do."

"But you don't hunt together," I said. "Everybody seems to know that your father hunted on his own."

"You don't understand," said Jerry. "Your father still alive?"

"No," I said.

"You hunted with him, though, when he was alive?"

"Sure," I said, "all the time, until I joined the Army, but I usually loaded my gun."

Jerry was sullen. "Are you going to let me help you on this case? Help you find my father's killer?"

I stared at him, hard. He held up under my gaze, but I still didn't trust him. I couldn't. That implicit trust in my team had died when Deputy Three Stones put me in her crosshairs. Jerry would have to earn it back. Until then, he wouldn't walk behind me.

I sighed. "Look, Jerry. You're a suspect, just like everyone else who seemed to crawl out of the rocks right after your father was killed. Until I make an arrest, you will remain a suspect, but I still expect you to do your duty."

Jerry stared back at me, unblinking, for a few beats. I waited for his response.

"Maybe you killed him," he said quietly.

"Say again?" I asked.

"Maybe you killed him," he repeated. "How do I know that you're not a suspect? You were up here, just like the rest of us, in the middle of nowhere. What do you have to patrol up here in the mountains? Was that just a coincidence, Sheriff, or was it something else? Maybe I should inspect *your* weapon."

Sergeant Richter had taught me early on how to deal with belligerence.

"Shut the fuck up, Deputy," I said, "and move out up the trail."

Four

BELMONT'S INDIAN SUMMER HAD JUST ENDED. Slate gray clouds crept across the big San Juan sky and denied the scant heat of the autumn sun. The wind picked up out of the northwest, and the trees swayed in the draw. In the wind, I smelled the first snow of the year. San Luis Peak already shimmered in white. I decided that the old slagheap looked much better with snow.

I had ignored Sergeant Richter's demand to wear my warm field boots—I didn't like the way they felt in the stirrups. I wore cowboy boots, and my feet felt like lead, but I sure looked cool. I flexed my fingers constantly inside my gloves to keep them from freezing into claws wrapped around the reins.

Watch out for that alpine climate, Specialist Tatum. You never know when it'll turn on you.

Had Councilman Pitcher, tied up and shirtless in this cold, fought to stay alive, his body seizing with violent shivers? Or did he let the wakeless sleep overtake him, only to be kept from death by his tormenter until the killer chose his time to die?

I had seen men surrender to the cold. Soldiers wet and naked in the Florida phase of U.S. Army Ranger School, wandered about in the swamps, hypothermia warping their minds. One guy in my squad just took off his clothes one night and walked into the darkness. I guess he thought he was going home. The instructors found him the next day, sitting next to a tree in eighteen inches of water. The temperature had dropped below freezing that night, and they had to break the ice around his chest to get him out.

The killer's track linked up with the main trail and disappeared, just like I thought it would. Jerry and I searched the pack trail and the adjunct track that cut across the plateau, but we didn't find another step-off, only a deep gouge left by a truck veering off the road. Heavy horse, foot, and wheeled traffic obliterated any sign in the hard-packed gravel.

"Sheriff Tatum, come in," came Jenny's cheery voice over my radio.

"Go ahead, Jenny." I avoided call signs.

"FBI is here."

"Say again?" I asked.

"Some FBI guy is here in the office," she said. "He wants to talk to you."

"What about?" I had never met anyone from the FBI. Not too much organized crime or interstate kidnappings in Belmont.

"Didn't say," she said. "He likes your coffee, though."

"I'm on my way."

I looked at Jerry and jerked my head downhill. We rode together in silence.

By the time we hit the final descent into town, the storm had swept into the valley. Tiny, dry snowflakes sandblasted our faces. I pulled down the brim of my Resistol and squinted into the wind. I could barely see the trail. Pancho knew the way, taking each switchback with little guidance from his master.

The box canyon that held Belmont looked like a miner's jack had drilled it into the San Juan Mountains. Two streams, Willow and East Willow, carved deep draws into the rock, converged in the center of town, and dumped into the Rio. Mammoth, Bachelor, and Bulldog Mountains towered over the village but provided no protection from the first icy blast of winter.

Not one living soul moved in Belmont. Main Street ran straight up the center of town and split the canyon to the north. Shops lined Main, then houses and cabins flanked the little business district. The worst part of town lay at the tail end of the canyon—trailer parks and run-down shacks squatted near the new softball field. Nicer cabins climbed the gradual steppes of the west ridge, and Dana Pratt's new development spread out on the foothills behind them. You could fire a cannon down Main Street and not hit anybody.

The new snow would blow through like a dust storm and leave the valley cold, dry, and empty. Skiers and snowmobilers went elsewhere, north to the other side of the divide, or east to Wolf Creek Pass, where the snow stayed thick and powdery. Once the hunters left, only the residents and the cold would remain, and Belmont would close for the season.

Jerry and I walked through four empty blocks to Main Street. The taller false fronts of the shops, galleries, and restaurants on Main sheltered us from the stinging shards of snow. All the businesses had their OPEN signs on, squeezing that last drop of commerce out of hunters and winter travelers. The restaurants opened early and altered their menus to suit carnivorous appetites. The owners of the Hungry Miner had erected two large cabin tents on their lot and hired every available woman in town to serve pancakes in the morning and steaks at night. The bed and breakfasts doubled their beds to accommodate large groups of hunters unconcerned with privacy. The hardware and sporting goods stores brought out their inventories of hunting clothes and ammunition. Even Mandy Lange, Berkeley graduate and former peace activist, turned her front counter into a gun cabinet at the Weminuche Wilderness Experience, the WWE. Her husband, Jeff, would have been appalled, but he was dead now, and Mandy was always the shrewd businesswoman.

The municipal building housed the county as well as the town offices, and we all shared the space like good neighbors, which we were in real life. My sheriff's station occupied nearly all of the back end of the building, along with the coroner's office.

A green government sedan was parked in one of the department slots.

The place was a furnace. Jenny had turned up the thermostat way too high, like she always did when I was on patrol. I spun the wheel back down to sixty. Next to Jenny's yellow parka hung a dark blue winter overcoat and a short-brimmed felt hat. I hung my ice-crusted Resistol and coat on the next peg.

Behind the front counter sat three desks, two of which stood empty. I had taken over my dead predecessor's office in the back corner. I didn't like the windowless space, but the sheriff can't sit in the front with the riffraff. Jenny usually stayed in the radio room or leaned on one of the empty desks to watch CNN or the Weather Channel, like she was doing right now. A small man with a gray head sat at my old desk. Neither of them turned when we walked in.

I looked up at the TV mounted high in the corner and expected to see the Colorado radar map, but instead saw a live shot of a smoking building, or what was left of one.

"Did they get another hospital?" I asked.

"Looks that way, Sheriff," said Jenny, eyes still fixed on the set. The gray head didn't move. Jerry sat down at his desk and stared at nothing. He still wore his coat and hat. Water collected in little puddles on his blotter.

"Where was this one?" I asked.

"Fort Leavenworth," said the gray head.

The reporter spoke off-camera, giving the audience a full-screen shot of the latest horror show. Every one of these bombings looked like an eerie echo of the Murrah Federal Building in Oklahoma City—half the building had slid away from the structure and settled in a dusty pile of twisted steel and concrete. The camera flashed from the rubble to the first responders. Medics, firemen, and military police struggled inside the golden hour to recover survivors. I turned my head when I saw the first limp body.

I walked around the desk and stood between them and the television. "You must be Agent . . ." I extended my hand.

"I'm sorry, Sheriff. That's what I'm here about." He nodded at the television. "This latest incident is just coming in." He stood and shook my hand. "My name is Special Agent Ritter, Federal Bureau of Investigation." He showed me his credentials.

Agent Ritter looked more like a coffee shop owner than a federal agent. Instead of a suit, he wore a rag wool sweater with a high collar, jeans, and winter boots, like a local. He had a small frame and delicate hands. His grip was firm in mine, but it felt like a sparrow in my hand. If I gripped too hard, I would crush the tiny bones beneath the soft, thin skin. He hadn't changed his hairstyle since the late seventies—the thick gray hair feathered over his ears and parted in the middle, making his narrow face look even smaller. His mustache looped below the corners of his mouth and over the upper lip.

"Where's your partner?" I asked. "I thought you guys always traveled in pairs."

His smile remained pinned to his face. "Not today, Sheriff. My partner is covering another part of the region, doing the same thing I am."

"Which is?"

He closed his mouth and let out a little puff through his nostrils, but never dropped the grin. "Is there somewhere we can talk, Sheriff Tatum?"

"My office. Is there any coffee left?"

"Yes, Sir," said Jenny. "Fresh cup is on your desk. Should be cool enough by now."

Jenny Lange was a shorter, happier version of her older sister, Cynthia, granddaughters of the man who owned the Halfmoon Ranch.

"Jenny, you're a treasure," I said.

She blushed and scurried into the radio room, her long black hair trailing out behind her.

I led the way into my office and sat down. "Please close the door, Agent Ritter."

He did, took the chair I didn't offer, and looked around. I sipped coffee and decided I would try to be nicer to my fellow law enforcement officer.

"Nice office," he said. "Spartan. No pictures, no awards, no 'I Love Me' wall."

"What brings you all the way to Belmont, Agent Ritter?"

"I understand you're busy, so I will get right to the point," said Ritter. "We are investigating these bombings at military bases."

Every month for the last six, a new Army post would blow up. After four years of tight homeland security, someone was making a successful run at domestic terrorism. It drove the FBI crazy.

"Posts," I said.

"Excuse me?"

"In the Army, we call them 'posts,' not 'bases'," I said. "I don't recall any Air Force bases blowing up."

"I'll have to remember that," said Ritter.

"These guys are real bastards," I said. "Why do you think they're targeting hospitals?"

"Pure terrorism," said Ritter. "They're showing us they have no conscience, that they'll kill anyone—mothers, children, old veterans. It's barbaric, but it's opportunistic as well."

"Opportunistic?"

"Hospitals are soft targets, lightly secured," said Ritter. "Most of our security efforts in the last few years have focused on high value military targets—ammunition depots, aircraft hangars, barracks, command posts. No one ever thought about securing the hospitals."

"Sounds like some rag-head group doing this. They bomb hospitals in Jerusalem, too."

Ritter screwed up his mouth and set his cup on the edge of my desk. "That's what we thought, too, at first, but we were wrong. Dark skin and a Middle Eastern accent stand out in the heartland. Think about the all-American boys and girls guarding our nation's military bases. They stop anyone who looks the least bit Arab and give them a very personal search. The Army doesn't give a rip about racial profiling. It's not Al-Qaida, or any other foreign terrorist. We think these boys are homegrown."

"Militia?"

"Maybe. The militia movement really went to ground after Oklahoma City. After nine-eleven, most of them found someone else to hate besides Bill Clinton and Janet Reno. We also took down more than a few of them."

"Then why are you here in Belmont?" I asked. "Not exactly a hotbed of terrorism in Mineral County."

He rubbed his hairy upper lip. "To be frank, we're getting desperate. That's why I'm here. This group caught us with our pants down, and we're still running around trying to pull them up." He waited for me to laugh. I wasn't in the mood. He cleared his throat and continued, "We're running down every reported explosion in the last three years. I came across a report from the DEA about an explosion just upriver last year. Would you know anything about that?"

That made me laugh.

"What's so funny?" asked Ritter.

"That explosion wasn't terrorism," I said. "That was a drug war."

"A drug war?"

"You said it was a DEA report, right? Probably filed by Agent Gallagher."

Ritter nodded.

I continued, "Believe it or not, Agent Ritter, two summers ago my little town was in the middle of a drug war, a shooting drug war. The former sheriff and a former deputy ran one side, the winning side, for a time. They blew up their competition and nearly took me out in the process."

"But you're the sheriff, now," said Ritter. His sparrow hands fluttered in confusion.

"They were not on the winning side for long," I said.

"What happened?"

"We found their meth lab up in the mountains, and the deputy came after us. She was a damn good shot with a rifle. Proved it a few times. We had bodies all over this valley."

"She?"

"Deputy Sheriff Martha Three Stones. Grew up on the Ute Mountain Reservation southwest of here."

"What happened?" asked Ritter.

"I'm a better shot."

"And the sheriff?"

"Jerry killed him. Saved my life," I said.

"Jerry?"

"My deputy, Jerry Pitcher. He was at his desk."

"I missed him," said Ritter.

"Most people do."

Ritter turned his head and stared out the window I didn't have.

"Did either of them have a background in demolitions or explosives?" he asked.

I chuckled. "I doubt it. Sheriff Dale grew up here. Marty's past was pretty vague, but I'm pretty sure her grandfather didn't teach her anything about mercury switches or det cord."

Ritter tented his hands and fixed me with his eyes as he spoke. "Where do you think a small town sheriff and his Native American deputy would have gotten explosives or the knowledge to rig them?"

The real investigator sat on the other side of my desk.

"That is a very good question, Agent Ritter," was the best answer I could muster. "You think they had help?"

"Yes."

"You think they're still here? Whoever helped them?"

"Wouldn't you?" asked Ritter. "One thing we can predict about these domestic terrorists is that they choose remote places to go to ground. You said yourself that the county isn't a hotbed of terrorism, but it's a perfect place to hide out. You have I-25 a couple hours to the east, US 50 to the north." He let me absorb that, then continued, "Fort Carson was first, then Fort Collins, both in Colorado. Catch I-25 and you're there." He ticked off the targets on his porcelain fingers. "Then they shifted south, Fort Huachuca in Arizona and Fort Bliss in Texas. Now they're working their way down I-70, hitting Fort Riley last month and Fort Leavenworth today."

All of a sudden, my little county became the center of the domestic terrorism universe.

"Did you collect any real evidence at the scene of the explosion?" asked Ritter.

"I sure didn't. I was flat on my back," I said. "Sheriff Dale was still in charge then. He covered it up as an accident. You know, meth labs are prone to blowing up. They had a leaky propane tank full of ammonia. I don't think the DEA thought any differently."

"But you did," said Ritter.

He was right. I knew that Dale or Marty set me up. I just never gave it another thought after we killed them.

"Can you show me the site?" asked Ritter.

"That will be difficult," I said. "A local developer bought the property and turned it into an RV park. The site is pretty much graded and paved by now."

"Did you happen to save any debris? Maybe a vehicle?"

"Come to think of it, we did. My Bronco is still in the municipal compound. We didn't need a new one when the sheriff and Marty gave up theirs, so I just left it."

"I would very much like to get some experts out here to see it. We might be able to pull residue," said Ritter.

"No problem," I said. "I can take you out there now, if you like."

"No, not yet," said Ritter. "Would you suspect anyone in town, knowing what you do now?"

His rapid transition caught me off guard, and my face must have given away my thoughts.

"Who is it?" asked Ritter.

"There is one guy in town who is an outspoken critic of the federal government," I said, putting it lightly. Denver Petry loathed the federal government, didn't pay income tax, and had taken himself off the grid years ago.

"Does he have a military background, maybe in explosives?" asked Ritter.

"He's a former Marine. Decorated in Grenada. I don't know about the explosives part."

"Sounds like a match," said Ritter. "I need to interview this man. Do you have a name?"

"You didn't mention these guys were in the military," I said.

"Well, we have reason to believe that they're former members of the armed forces, yes. Maybe event current members."

"I can't help you if you're selective on the information you give me, Agent," I said.

"I will keep that in mind, Sheriff." Ritter waited for my answer.

I hated doing this, but I knew Denver wasn't the man. I sighed. "His name is Denver Petry. Lives in a little shack down the street, but it can't be him, Agent."

"Denver Petry." Ritter committed the name to memory. Throughout my interview, he had taken no notes, held no government-issue pen. "Why is he the wrong man?"

"He's in a wheelchair," I said. "He doesn't even own a car."

Ritter's hands took flight again. "That doesn't matter. These guys work in small groups. This man, Petry, could provide leadership and guidance."

Three knocks on the cheap door echoed in the room.

"Enter," I said.

Ritter turned. I expected Jennifer, but Mike Stanford's balding head came around the door, followed by the rest of his broad frame.

"Oops, sorry Sheriff. I didn't know you were in—had someone in, I mean," said Mike.

"What's up, Mike?" I asked. "Make it quick. The FBI's here."

Ritter didn't get up, and I didn't introduce them.

Mike's eyes flicked to Ritter as he said, "Hello," then back to me. "I didn't expect the FBI to get here so quickly over Mr. Pitcher's murder."

"What can I do for you, Mike?"

"I just wanted to thank you for letting me escort Mr. Pitcher down the mountain today," said Mike.

"No problem," I said. "Does the Doc have him?"

"I guess so. That's where we took him."

"Okay, Mike."

"Thanks again, Sheriff Tatum."

"Okay, Mike." Mike shut the door.

"Michael Petry." Ritter kept staring at the door.

"No. Mike Stanford. He's a CPA in town."

"His name is Michael Petry." He turned back to me. "I have a thing with names."

"I'm sure you do, but that man was Mike Stanford," I said.

"Who's 'Mr. Pitcher?' " asked Ritter.

"Thomas Harding Pitcher. Big man in town."

"He was murdered?" I was proud of Jenny for not telling him.

"I found him in the mountains this morning," I said.

"Pitcher," said Ritter. "Your deputy's father?" I had underestimated this man. I wondered how many steps he was ahead of me.

"That's correct," I said.

"You need any help?"

"We can handle it," I said. "It's not my first murder."

"Will you keep me informed on the details of the case?"

"Of course," I said. "Will you?"

Ritter smiled. "As much as I can." He stood. "Now, when can I see Denver Petry?"

Five

I STEPPED OUTSIDE, AND THE MELTED ICE ON MY coat froze with the first gust of wind. I stared at the purple wall of Ben Jones's tobacco shop and wondered why he had painted a massive gold G on the side.

"You have a Masons' Lodge here," said Ritter.

"What?"

"The Freemasons," said Ritter. "That's their symbol—a G with the compass and square."

"I knew that," I said. I hadn't.

"How far is it?" asked Ritter. "Walking distance?" Agent Ritter zipped his parka to his chin. The collar of his coat nearly touched the brim of his felt hat. Out of the fluorescent office light, the hat was dark green, with a narrow, multicolored band and a little feather on the side. He looked like an Austrian noble out for a *volksmarch*.

"Everything is walking distance in Belmont," I said.

On a bright, sunny day, Denver's home was a cottage in the green valley, but in the gray light of early winter it was really a shack, like the rest of the shacks along the west wall of the canyon. Chain link surrounded a patch of brown grass. An ancient snowmobile under a ragged blue tarp hunkered in the overgrown tracks next to the house, but no truck. The leaning ramp to Denver's front door looked ready to collapse. I opened the metal latch on the front gate.

"Watch out for Larry," I said.

"Who's Larry?" asked Ritter.

I pointed to a BEWARE OF DOG sign on the screen door.

"Got it," said Ritter, and led the way across the dead yard.

"You better let me go first, Agent Ritter," I said.

"Because Larry knows you?"

"No, because the last time I was here, Denver greeted me with a loaded shotgun."

"Got it," said Ritter, and he stepped aside.

I opened the screen door, careful to keep its hinges attached to the dry rot, and pounded on the door. "Denver! Denver Petry! It's Sheriff Tatum!"

A few startled woofs came from inside, then the whole top half of the door pushed into my face as Larry slammed his big front paws against it. His nails clattered against the fiberboard, followed by a steady stream of deep barks.

"Goddamnit, Larry! Get your ass down!" The clicking on the other side stopped. "Come in, Sheriff!"

I turned to Ritter. "Wait here." He didn't move. I took off my hat, opened the door, and stepped onto the cracked gray linoleum of the entryway.

"Hey, Denver," I said, "sorry to bust in on you like this." I talked into a dim corner, where I knew Denver sat in his wheelchair. I looked for the two shiny rings of his double-barrel shotgun. The room smelled of mold, dog, and gunpowder. My eyes slowly adjusted to the yellow light coming in through the cheap blinds, and there sat Denver Petry, right where I knew he'd be. The shotgun leaned in a corner. Larry sat obediently next to him and let out a little woof of greeting.

Denver folded back the corner of one blind. "Who the hell did you bring with you? Looks like a fed."

I knelt down. "C'mere Larry."

Larry glanced up at his master, who nodded. Larry bounded over to me. He sat down and offered me a paw. I shook it and rubbed his ears.

"You have an uncanny sense for the federal government, Denver," I said. "That man is from the FBI."

"And you brought him here, to my house," said Denver, dropping the blind. "I thought you were a local man."

"I am a local man, Denver," I said. "But I am also a law enforcement officer. Agent Ritter just wants to ask you a few questions. He's not here to arrest you."

"I got nothin' to say to the federal government," said Denver. "I do not recognize their authority."

"I know, Denver, and I respect that." Denver voted in every local election. I wasn't stupid. I liked my job. "I already told him he was wasting his time, but this is the best way to get him off your ass."

"There are other ways," said Denver. He wheeled across the matted carpet and through the swinging kitchen door. "Don't expect me to make coffee." Larry gave me a lick and followed his master.

I beckoned Ritter off the front porch, and we went into the kitchen.

Denver Petry reloaded bullets for a living. He made custom loads for all the members of the Halfmoon Gun Club and sold shells to Orville's clients. The wealthier ones still ordered Denver's loads even when they didn't hunt the ranch. He shipped boxes of them all over the country. The rest of Denver's income came from disability checks.

The kitchen doubled as his work area, lit up as bright as his living room was dark. The room had no table or chairs, just loading benches bolted to the walls, stacks of reloading supplies, and boxes of finished product. The only elements that made it a kitchen were a refrigerator, a microwave, and a stainless steel sink. A black-and-white television broadcast the latest military hospital bombing.

Ritter and I stood near the door, dripping hats in our hands. Denver dug in at the opposite corner. He wore a black T-shirt that said, "I'll only give up my gun when they peel my cold, dead fingers from it." He crossed his overdeveloped forearms over his massive chest and scowled at Agent Ritter. Larry let out a little growl. I tried not to laugh.

"Hey, Denver, you been working out?" I asked. Denver's arms had always been ripped, but the chest was a new development. His wrinkled face had lost its indoor pallor and had been replaced by tan skin. He'd been getting out. Denver's gray eyes twinkled at me through his vintage military-issue horn-rimmed glasses, but he didn't answer.

"Do you need to see my identification?" Ritter reached into his blue parka.

"Don't mean shit to me," said Denver.

"Here it is anyway," said Ritter. He held out his credentials and shield. Denver remained motionless. Ritter replaced the leather wallet in an inside pocket.

"Do you mind if I turn this off?" asked Ritter. Denver didn't respond. Ritter moved toward the television, but paused. The shattered military hospital filled the screen. Broken water pipes and twisted rebar lay exposed where the building had collapsed, like the entrails of a dead elephant. Hospital linens fluttered in the cold Kansas wind.

"What do you think of these hospital bombings?" asked Ritter. He snapped off the image and turned.

"I think their targeting is misdirected," said Denver.

"Why would you say that?"

"Soldiers do not kill women, children, and old people."

"Whom do soldiers kill?"

"Enemies of the Constitution," said Denver.

"And who would that be?"

"Anyone who threatens to forsake that document," said Denver.

" 'All enemies foreign and domestic?' "

"That's correct," said Denver. "Some people in this country still believe in those words. A lot more than your government thinks."

"My government is your government, Mr. Petry," said Agent Ritter.

"I don't think so," said Denver. "That wasn't a question, so if you're done, get out."

"I will not take much more of your time, Mr. Petry," said Ritter. "What was your military background?"

"You can look that up in my personnel file," said Denver.

"I'd rather hear it from you," said Ritter. "You were in the Marines, right?"

"I was an infantryman, not a demolitions guy, if that's what you're thinking."

"Did you have any explosives training?"

"Nothing more than pulling the pin on a frag grenade."

"What about your Marine buddies, any of them capable of blowing up a hospital?"

"My buddies are dead, look like me, or are still in the Corps," said Denver.

Ritter set his green felt hat on the microwave and leaned against the counter. "You fought for your country, gave your legs. Why do you hate it so much?"

Denver smiled. I knew he liked these kinds of questions, and Ritter had just pitched him a softball.

"I love my country, Agent Ritter. I swore to support and defend the Constitution of the United States. Still do. But our founding fathers never intended to have a bloated, lazy federal government like we do now. It's the mess in Washington we hate."

"We?" asked Ritter. He was good.

"I mean, people like me," said Denver.

"Are there more in this town?" asked Ritter. "People like you?"

"Of course there are," said Denver. "Why do you think we all live out here in the mountains? To get away from you people."

"Do any of you get together and talk about these things?"

"First Amendment gives us that right."

"So, you have little group of patriots in town," said Ritter. "You all gather and bash the federal government. Give commentary on the latest hospital bombing. Like a club."

"Or a militia," said Denver. "That what you're getting at, Agent Ritter?"

Ritter shrugged.

"The militia movement is dead, Agent Ritter," said Denver. "You all killed it ten years ago."

"Dead, or hibernating?" asked Ritter.

"Whatever you want to think, Ritter."

"Who else is in your group?" asked Ritter.

"Who said we were a group?"

"You did."

"Are you going to arrest me, Agent Ritter?" asked Denver.

"Should I?"

"If you're not going to arrest me, then get off my property. I've had just about enough of this shit."

"Thank you for your time, Mr. Petry." Agent Ritter smiled and put on his hat.

"Fuck you very much, Agent Ritter," said Denver. He glared at me. All I could do was shrug. Denver didn't see us out.

RITTER AND I WALKED BACK TO THE OFFICE, STRAIGHT into the stinging ice and wind. It didn't seem to affect the federal agent. He held his face into the storm. His cheeks and neck had already pinked with cold.

"Okay, that went well," I said.

"Yes, it did," he said. He walked briskly, as if out for a post-meal stroll. "Were you aware of his activities?"

"What activities?"

"You heard him. He has a group of malcontents, subversives who hate the government."

"Half the folks between here and Utah hate the government, Agent Ritter," I said.

"He said they have meetings."

"A few guys get together at a bar and bitch about their taxes. Does that constitute a militia movement?"

"Maybe," said Ritter.

"You guys really are desperate."

AGENT RITTER LEFT HIS CARD AND SAID HE WOULD return with his partner and a team of explosives experts. I was thrilled. At least he was gone, so I could get back to my murder.

Jerry hadn't moved from his desk, hadn't taken off his coat or hat. A cold cup of coffee rested near a puddle of melted snow.

I leaned on the door frame to the commo room. "He been like that the whole time?" I asked Jenny.

"Yes, Sheriff," she said. "I brought him some coffee and asked if he was okay. He didn't even look up. It's like he's in a trance or something. It's so sad." Tears welled up in her brown eyes and spilled down her soft cheeks. So different from her older sister, Cynthia. "I know how he feels."

Jennifer's father, Jeff Lange, was the victim of one of Marty Three Stones' high-velocity sniper rounds—two, actually. I didn't miss him.

"Do you need to go home, Jenny?" I asked.

She wiped her eyes with the heel of her hand and pushed a lock of black hair behind an ear. "No, Sheriff. Gosh, I'm fine. I just haven't thought about my dad in a while."

"Is Dr. Ed still around?"

"I think so. I haven't checked. I really don't want to go back there and find out."

"I don't blame you. Why don't you grab some lunch? Take a long one. Go see your sister at the WWE."

"I think I will." She waited for me to move away from the door, then scooted out of the office. Jerry and I were alone.

I stood in front of my deputy. He didn't acknowledge me, or Jenny's exit. I put both hands on the desk and leaned in close.

"Hey, bud. What are you still doing here? Go home to your wife and mother, before someone else tells them about it."

Jerry stood and shuffled into the storm.

I found Dr. Ed in his coroner's office, down a short hallway from my little department. I opened the door to harsh surgical lights and a stainless steel table full of dead, naked Thomas Pitcher. I gripped the edge of the table to keep myself from turning around. At least Ed hadn't cracked the dead man's chest open yet.

Dr. Ed still wore his hunting clothes. His coat and hat lay crumpled in a corner. He had simply rolled up the sleeves on his quilted flannel shirt and went to work on the body. His white eyebrows stood out against his red scalp. He glanced at me over the top of square magnifying glasses.

"Coffee," said Dr. Ed, turning back to the autopsy.

"I'm not your servant. Get some yourself." Maybe belligerence would cover my squeamishness.

"No, no, no," said Dr. Ed. "Coffee is what Mr. Pitcher had to drink for the last two days. It's spilled down the front of his jacket, and I can smell it in his urine. Can't you?"

"All I smell is formaldehyde," I said.

"Well, here." Dr. Ed tossed me Pitcher's hunting pants. I cringed, but caught the damp clothing. The distinct smell of coffee mingled with acrid urine.

"Yes, thank you. I smell it just fine." I looked around for a place to set the stinking wool pants.

"His jacket is not so unpleasant—it only has the coffee. But what fun is that?" said Dr. Ed. "Here, I'll take those."

I stood there, holding up my damp, smelly hands in the air.

"The sink is behind you, Sheriff. You had best get used to bodily fluids. You didn't encounter them in the Army?"

"Just blood, usually the enemy's." I washed the stink off my hands. "Jeez, you think it's hot enough in here?"

"Councilman Pitcher did not seem to mind," said Dr. Ed. "I was cold."

"Did you find anything else?" I asked.

"No, just confirmed what we found at the scene. Because you were a witness, we can approximate the time of death to within a few minutes. If it weren't for that fact, I would make the mistake that he was killed much earlier."

"Why is that?"

"Well, his core temperature was so low, the tables are useless. He hovered at the edge of hypothermia for hours. Throws everything off."

"Cause of death?" I asked.

"Big hole in his head," said Dr. Ed. "I did not recover any of the bullet. The .45 slug went straight through his skull and out his cheekbone. You might have to return to the scene and find it, if you think that's necessary."

"Where were you hunting this morning?"

Dr. Ed turned and looked at me from over the top of his glasses. "Am I a suspect, Sheriff Tatum?"

"All of you are, until I can prove otherwise."

"All of us?"

"You, Jerry, Emmet, Orville, and Mike," I said. "You were all within minutes of the crime scene. Kind of strange, having all you guys close by on a four-thousand-acre hunting ranch."

"If I am a suspect, why are you allowing me to work on the evidence?" asked Dr. Ed, waving his hand over Pitcher's body.

"What choice do I have?" I asked. "We don't have the funds for a mobile crime scene unit." I didn't tell him that I was pretty sure the killer rode a horse to and from the scene, something I was certain Dr. Ed would never do.

"Very well, Sheriff Tatum. I will do my best not to tamper with the evidence."

"I appreciate that," I said.

"So, whom will you talk to, first?" asked Dr. Ed.

"Well, I'm talking to you."

"I assure you, Sheriff Tatum. I did not kill Councilman Pitcher," said Dr. Ed. "If I did, I certainly would not let you figure it out."

"Did you hear any shooting this morning?" I asked.

"That is what drew me to the scene."

"No, before that. In the southwest quadrant where you were hunting."

"I heard nothing until the shot from the southeast quadrant," said Dr. Ed. "I was cold. It was good to get up and move around."

"Did you see Mike hunting up there?"

"I have never seen Mike Stanford while hunting. The man keeps to himself," said Dr. Ed. "Of course, my eyes aren't what they used to be. I can rarely see beyond fifty yards without binoculars." No one could confirm Mike's story. No one could confirm Dr. Ed's, either.

"What do you know about the Freemasons?" I asked.

Dr. Ed furrowed his white eyebrows and went back to

the body. "I believe George Washington was a Freemason."

"Yes, I knew that," I said. "What about in Belmont? Every time I walk out of the building, I see their emblem painted on the wall, but I never made the connection."

"We have a few of them in town," said Dr. Ed. "They are quite active, but discreet."

"I never knew."

"Well, they would not be a very good secret society if you knew everything about them," said Dr. Ed.

"I've lived in this town for over four years, Dr. Ed."

"And you think you know everything."

"I should know everything," I said. "I'm the sheriff."

"You can live in this town for forty years and still be surprised."

"Did Pitcher's murder surprise you?" I asked.

"No, not particularly," said Dr. Ed. "What surprised me is that he lasted this long."

"So, who are Freemasons in town?" I asked.

"Councilman Pitcher is a former member. Henry Earl Callahan will probably become the next worshipful master. He is the senior member now."

"So, the entire town council is made up of Freemasons," I said. Pitcher, Callahan, and Mike Stanford made up the town council. Mike was a recent addition. He took Becky Noonan's seat when we elected her mayor last fall.

"That is correct. Does that disturb you?"

"It just seems a little weird."

"I would not be concerned," said Dr. Ed. "They only manage your budget."

"Who else?" I asked.

Dr. Ed looked up at the ceiling. "Chuck Dinnerstein and Max Toliver. You never see one without the other." Everyone thought they were brothers, products of a sixty-year-old scandal.

"Are there others?"

"The four horsemen have been members for a long, long time," said Dr. Ed. "Mike Stanford was the first new member in a decade."

"Uh-huh. What about you?" I asked.

"What about me?"

"You ever think of signing up?"

Dr. Ed scowled. "They asked me years ago. I chose not to join."

"Why not?"

"I prefer fly-fishing to social clubs."

"You seem to pay attention, though."

"Someone has to," said Dr. Ed.

"What's their agenda?" I asked. "World domination?"

"Hardly," said Dr. Ed. "On the contrary, their philanthropy often goes unnoticed, except by those who receive it."

"Philanthropy?"

"Good works toward our fellow man."

"I know what it means, Dr. Ed. What have they done?"

"You are full of questions."

"You're full of answers," I said. "How about it?"

"Remember when Joe Bender's cabin burned down?" he asked. I nodded. "You notice how quickly the new one went up, and better than the original? When was the last time you saw any building go up with alacrity in this county? The Masons goosed the contractors to get it done before the first snow."

"Goosed?" I asked.

"You know what I mean," said Dr. Ed.

"What else?"

"Every year, one artist or another has a bad season. The

Masons help him through it. And the Repertory Theatre. You think that place makes money?"

"It's a popular attraction."

"Not popular enough to afford the quality of actors we see each season," said Dr. Ed. "The company hemorrhages money on a regular basis. The Masons keep it afloat."

"You seem to know a lot about them," I said. "You sure you don't want to be one?"

"I do enough philanthropy as this county's only physician," said Dr. Ed. "I've been compensated with watercolor paintings, elk venison, and handmade bamboo fly rods. I also teach the local sheriff basic forensics."

"Very funny." I squeezed my nosy coroner for more information. "Are there others?"

"What others?"

"Are there any other members?"

"Am I your informant now?"

"You seem to know a lot about the people in this town, Dr. Ed. Maybe I should come by more often. Give it up."

Dr. Ed sighed and looked at the ceiling again. "That loud, fat man who works the counter at the Trout House."

"Lenny? Lenny Leftwich?"

"I believe that is his name."

"I guess you don't have to pass an IQ test to get in," I said.

Dr. Ed straightened his glasses and put his hands behind his back.

"Well, let me know if you find anything else," I said. "When can I expect your report?"

"Tomorrow morning, Sheriff, but you know its contents already."

As I turned to go, I thought of one more question for my new informant. "Hey, what's the deal with Mike's wedding band? I've never seen a wife."

That got his attention. Dr. Ed perched his magnifiers on his pale scalp and rubbed his eyes, then leaned against the desk and let out a little sigh. I guess he was ready.

"I don't know much about Mike's personal life," he said. "He does not share it with many people. Not anyone at all, for that matter. I have no idea why he wears a wedding ring."

For the first time since coming to Belmont, I felt like Dr. Ed had just lied to me.

Six

I PULLED DRAUGHTS OF FRIGID MOUNTAIN AIR INTO my lungs and tried to clear them of urine, formaldehyde, blood, and death. The last dark clouds stormed through the valley. I watched them punish Wagon Wheel Gap then disappear over the La Garita Mountains to the southeast. A light, crystalline dust covered everything. The evergreen Snowshoe Mountain gleamed across the valley, despite the gray light. Snow devils swirled down the street. I followed them, but I didn't know exactly where I was going.

Emmet had painted the false front of his gallery periwinkle blue with cobalt trim. Not exactly the colors you would expect of a cowboy-sculptor, but it stood out from the other shops flanking it. I grabbed two cups of fresh coffee from the Mountain Grown Coffee Shop next door and entered Emmet's indoor world.

I felt as though I'd stepped into a Manhattan art district. Of course, I'd never been to New York. Emmet had extended the blue theme into the space. Blues and grays in various hues decorated the room, from carpet to walls. The décor disappeared, however, and became only a background for Emmet's art. Track lighting and spotlights illuminated his bronze sculptures.

The display was a curator's nightmare. Instead of arranging the sculptures according to theme, Emmet spread them around the room at random. Some sat on pedestals of various heights, others in groups along low shelves. Cowboys rode hard next to grizzlies standing on their hind legs. Elk trotted on the same ledges where eagles roosted. The effect made each work distinct from the others.

I stood alone amid the bronze menagerie. Emmet had left ten years of hard work worth thousands of dollars sitting around unattended. No one minded the store while Emmet worked upstairs, but you could do that in Belmont.

Something soft and strong bumped into my leg. I crouched to pet Roger, Emmet's orange tabby. Roger was fifteen pounds of muscle and scar tissue. Emmet had found him a couple of winters ago, half frozen, missing an eye and an ear. The local dogs had given him a beating. Emmet had nursed him back to health, and Roger brought him dead mice in exchange. He also brought revenge to his tormentors, teaching them the art of stealth, surprise, and sharp claws.

"Hey, buddy. What's that you brought me?"

The old cat laid a limp, gray parcel at my feet. Roger honored me with my own dead mouse, slightly chewed. He purred like my Bronco while I scratched his good ear, then he returned to his place at the window. I went up the narrow staircase.

Emmet's studio was all white plank and bare light. Emmet had knocked out the walls on the second floor and turned it into a single, large room. He whitewashed every surface and cut multiple skylights in the roof. The sun lit the studio with direct and indirect light. Workstations of various craft lined the perimeter of the studio—benches and torches, racks and tanks, metals and ceramics. If you didn't look in the center of the room, you would mistake the place for an industrial shop. Four feet of white planking separated the artist from his tools, like an invisible barrier between art and industry. Only a small cast-iron stove heated the open space. It squatted in the middle of the room. A neat stack of split wood in a brass rack waited next to the black stove. A single skylight illuminated Emmet's latest work—a wounded bull elk facing a pair of large wolves. Emmet sat on a high stool and worked bits of clay into the sculpture. He had his back to me.

"You just goin' to stand there with that coffee?" asked Emmet.

"It's cold as hell in here, Emmet," I said.

I crossed the threshold. As I approached, the air warmed from the stove's heat.

"When I'm workin' with clay, I just need my little buddy here." He tapped the stove with a boot. "It keeps the clay warm. I only work in the fall and winter, you know. Fewer interruptions." He didn't take his eyes off the work. I set the coffee down on the floor and walked slowly around his sculpture.

Emmet held a grayish-brown wad in his right hand, against his hip. His left hand pulled bits of warm clay off the lump and smoothed it into the elk's haunches. His rhythm didn't break with my interruption, his mouth set in a firm line under his cowboy mustache. His eyes could sculpt the bronze with their intensity alone. The wire rims seemed to focus his concentration. Locks of unwashed dirty-blond and gray hair, parted in the middle, were plastered against his skull, held tight over his collar with a leather thong.

He wore a yellow cowboy shirt, complete with the snaps and stitching, sleeves rolled above his elbows, no T-shirt underneath. He had the forearms of a blacksmith, not an artist—thick veins rolled across corded muscle. Faded blue tattoos painted both forearms. A pair of arrows crossed the back of his sculpting hand.

He worked fast, hardly pausing to smooth the last speck of clay before adding the next. His left hand flew between hip and model, as if he needed to hurry before the image in his head vanished forever.

"How long you been working on this?" I asked.

"Started it at the tail end of winter last year," said Emmet. "Picked it up again when the streets got quiet. I might have it done in another couple a days or so. Then the real work."

"Then what?"

"Then I make the master mold. I cover these guys with rubber supported by a plaster shell, over there in the corner." He angled his head toward one of the stations. "Then I take out the clay and fill the space with hot wax. Called a wax positive. Once it cools, I pop it out and make it look just like the finished product, even better maybe."

"How do you, uh, lose the wax?" I asked. I knew it was called the "lost wax" process, but that was it.

"Well, that's the whole deal," said Emmet. "I add gates to the wax positive—like little tubes of wax stickin' out from it—then coat the whole mess in ceramic to make another mold."

"You do that here?"

"Yup. See that oven over there? Two thousand two

hundred degrees Fahrenheit. I heat the ceramic and the wax melts out. Ta da—lost wax."

"When does the bronze come in?"

"I pour hot bronze into the ceramic mold. It cools, and I hammer off the clay, leaving the bronze. Then I grind away for a few weeks until it's done."

"It's probably more complicated than that," I said.

"Yup."

He thumped the wad of clay on the pedestal and hopped off the stool. He wiped his hands on his jeans. He looked at them, still dirty with clay, shrugged, and extended his right hand to me. I shook it. It felt like a tire tread. Ugly scar tissue made up most of his right hand, rippled pink across the back and palm.

"I thought you were done with me, Sheriff," he asked. "You're not here to arrest me, are you?" He smiled under his mustache.

What am *I doing here?*

"Well, your place was closer than any of my other suspects," I said. "And it's cold outside."

Emmet chuckled. He had an easy laugh. I examined his sculpture.

"You find a bull like this up on the mountain?" I asked.

"Sure did."

"Wanna tell me where?"

"You do your own scouting, Sheriff," said Emmet.

"It was worth a shot," I said. "That boy is a monster. He's real, huh?"

"Yes, Sir."

"How'd you get that scar on your hand, Emmet?" If I caught him off guard, Emmet didn't show it.

"You don't know?" he asked. "I thought everyone in town knew about my evil hand."

"Your 'evil hand?' "

Emmet held up his right hand and examined it, turning it like a foreign object.

For the first time, I got a good look at the hand, and, sure enough, it was evil looking. The thumb, fore, and middle fingers were shortened by a knuckle. The thumb was merely a flexible stump, like the tail of a Doberman pinscher. The healed webbing between his fingers had fused them together to the second knuckle.

"Lucky for me, I'm left-handed," he said.

"What happened?" I asked.

Emmet dropped the hand and placed both of them behind his back. He looked not at me, but through me.

"A long time ago, I wasn't a sculptor," he began. "Instead of creating things, I blew them up."

A light clicked on in my dim brain. "You were an Eighteen Charlie, an engineer sergeant."

His stare snapped back to me. "Very good, Sheriff Tatum. A complete misnomer, my job title. Engineers build things. I just blew them up. Seventh Special Forces Group, First Battalion, Alpha Company."

I should have figured this out years ago. The crossed arrows on the back of his left hand were a dead giveaway, at least for someone smarter than me. Crossed arrows were the branch insignia for the Army's Special Forces, the Green Berets.

"Maybe we were at Fort Bragg together," I said.

"Doubt it," said Emmet. His eyes went out to distance again. "I left in 1990."

"I see. Well, what's the story?" I asked.

"A device I had placed went off prematurely," said Emmet.

"You're lucky to have your hand," I said.

"I suppose. It wasn't the whole device, just the blasting cap, but it did the trick," said Emmet. "Can't use it much, 'cept to hold clay. It's about as useful as one of those hooks they put on guys' arms. Not much prettier, either."

"Is that why you left the Army?" I asked. "Disability?"

"That was part of it."

"What was the other part?"

Emmet paused before answering. "Can't tell you all my secrets in one visit, Sheriff," said Emmet. His voice echoed in his cold studio. "So, you catch Pitcher's killer, yet?"

I shook my head and took a sip of coffee. I wasn't here to answer questions.

"You know, it's a damn shame he's dead," said Emmet. "He was a real patron of the arts."

"Really?"

"Damn straight," said Emmet, "If he wasn't buyin' art, he was payin' the rent for one starvin' artist or another."

"What about you?" I asked.

Emmet smiled. "I never needed Councilman Pitcher's patronage. Now, I can say there were times when it would have helped, but no, never took any money from him. Prefer to get by on my own."

"You've had some tough years?"

"The art market changes like the weather," said Emmet. "Actually, it changes like the economy. Art's the first thing people cut when they're short on cash, whether it's learnin' or buyin'."

"So the last few years have been pretty good for you," I said.

"Yessir," said Emmet. "Folks have money to spend, and I am more than happy to take it from them. I get to stretch my limits a little with economic freedom."

"Like this piece?" I nodded to the elk and the wolves.

"Yup. Had that one in my head for a long time. Took me a while to get it right. I think I can sell it to that new Cabella's store in Denver."

"I didn't think we had any wolves in the San Juans," I said.

"Now, don't go ruinin' it," said Emmet. "Told you I was going to push the boundaries a little. Get outside your head for once."

"We don't have wolves up here, Emmet," I said. "Maybe you should turn the elk into a caribou."

"Not going for strict realism, here, Sheriff. It is art, you know."

I raised my eyebrows.

"Ain't like it's Salvador friggin' Dali, watches melting all over the place. Don't be so literal."

"All right, Emmet, I'll try."

"You just stick to sheriffin'. I'll do the sculpture." Emmet picked up his lump of clay and returned to his stool. "Thanks for the coffee."

LOW CLOUDS SCURRIED EAST ACROSS THE BIG SKY, but orange light in the west hinted at clear skies once again. The wind didn't care. Steady gusts raced through town. I had to get Pancho out of the cold street and into his warm barn.

We picked up a trot near the south of end of town. The west ridge of the Belmont box canyon encroached on Highway 149 until the big turn by the airport, then the Rio Grande valley opened wide in both directions. The first snow had dusted the top of Bristol Head, off to the west. The snowshoe patch of bare rock on Snowshoe Mountain had turned white, but the wind had erased most of the snow from the lower elevations. In the wider valley, the wind had more options, so its intensity diminished, but it still hummed in my ears, ever-present.

I crossed the airport bridge and fought back a shiver from the drop in temperature near the water. Even Pancho shuddered in the cold. The Rio Grande flowed unchecked by ice toward the Gulf of Mexico. The riverbed seemed to have as many rocks and bare patches as stretches of water. The drought and the winter had stolen its robustness.

Pancho and I took the dirt road toward Deep Creek. He chugged happily up the cut formed by the river. Tall spruce lined the one-lane track. A gap opened between the trees, and the Rio Grand Valley played its fanfare. Taking a deep breath of Rocky Mountain air, I looked back across the Rio at Belmont. Cabins and shops sprinkled the rocky gash in the San Juan Mountains. It sure beat Iowa.

The roar of eight cylinders turned my head. Front wheels and big grill bounded over the crest of the hill and rushed toward me. Horse and truck could not share the road, and I jerked Pancho off the trail. The cut dropped off rapidly toward the waterline. Pancho slid most of the way down the slope. I prayed his foot would not lodge in a hole or wedge behind a piece of deadfall.

We made it to the bottom in a cloud of cold dust. Pancho tossed his head and stamped his feet.

"Easy, boy," I said, "we're okay, now." I patted his thick neck and let him walk it off. A red Ford pickup ground around the corner, throwing dirt and gravel across the road. The driver found purchase on the blacktop and gunned it across the bridge.

"Lenny Leftwich," I said. "That son of a bitch damn near ran us over. You want me to go get him, bud?" Pancho snickered.

Lenny's off-road tires had left scars in the frosty gravel

of Deep Creek Road. I followed them to my driveway. He had gouged deep ruts at the entrance as he burned out. Reckless driving *and* trespassing. I was looking forward to bracing him.

I put Pancho away, warmed up my other Bronco, and drove into town, looking for Lenny Leftwich.

Seven

L ENNY HAD PARKED HIS TRUCK NEXT TO BEN Jones's Granite Tobacco Shop. The Masons' Lodge occupied the second floor, right next door to the municipal building. I vaulted up the back stairs to the Freemasons' lair.

Another Masons' emblem decorated the solid, windowless door at the landing. I tried the knob, and it turned, so I went in. In retrospect, I probably should have knocked, but my mind wasn't on police procedure or good manners. I was pissed off.

The interior of the lodge looked like any other place where men gathered and women didn't. The men had divided their space in half—one half for official meetings, the other half for carousing. The bar took the front, or the back, from my perspective. Dark wood paneling, straight out of the seventies, lined the walls of the long room and sucked the light out of two beer lamps and a Broncos clock. A few sagging couches hunkered around an old RCA and a coffee table covered with drink rings and cigar burns.

Compared to the tacky shabbiness of the bar and sitting area, the immaculate space where I stood was a temple.

Black and white tiles checkered the floor, buffed and waxed to perfection. I had spent many hours behind a floor buffer, so I would know. Simple, wooden chairs lined each side of the checkerboard. To my right, a small raised platform held a wide desk and single leather chair—I supposed that was where the worshipful master sat. Behind the dais, a wooden triangle with what looked like Hebrew letters hung between a hand-carved sun and moon. Two decorative pillars stood on either side of the desk, made of the same wood as the sun, moon, and triangle. An ornate J had been carved into one, a B on the other.

I felt like I had just received a full-on jolt of Freemasonry. I focused my attention on the far end the clubhouse.

Henry Earl Callahan stood behind the bar. He held a shot glass and stopped in mid-wipe when he saw me walk through their sanctuary. Two lit cigars burned in a white porcelain ashtray on the bar. Lenny's wide backside covered one of the barstools. His blue flannel shirt hiked up his back and exposed a half-moon of white flesh.

"Hey, clown boy. You damn near ran me over," I said. "Just say no to crack, by the way."

Lenny spun around in the stool and hiked up his pants. He looked like a little boy whose tree house had just been compromised by the girl next door.

"You shouldn't be here!" said Lenny. "You cannot cross the threshold!"

I kept walking toward the bar. "Yeah, whatever, Lenny. Next time, you better just run me over."

"You must leave," said Lenny. His head was one size too small for his body, or his gut had outgrown his skull. His shaved scalp only emphasized his diminutive cranium. Air hissed in and out of his flaring nostrils.

Henry Earl set his hands on the bar.

Lenny's expression shifted, and his face lost some color. "Where's your Bronco?"

"It's parked downstairs, and I'll leave when we're finished talking," I said. I stood at the edge of the bar area, just outside the dim arc of light. I would have plenty of time to react if Lenny got stupid. I kept my eyes on Lenny's shoulders—the shoulders always telegraphed physical intent, whether it was boxing or dealing with riled up fat guys. I paid attention to Henry Earl's hands, too. I didn't want them to disappear under the bar and come up with a shotgun. Henry Earl Callahan was a good old boy who owned the only gas station and grocery store in Belmont. He was closing fast on seventy years old and never had a harsh word for anyone. I didn't think Henry Earl had it in him, but it was better to be alive wrong than dead right.

"What's your business here, Sheriff?" asked Henry Earl. "We really don't favor non-members coming in uninvited, but I think we can make an exception for the sheriff, right Lenny?"

Lenny wiped the sweat and spittle from his lips. He jerked his head around and glared at the older man, then snapped back to me. The redness left his face and colored the tips of his ears.

"Roger. I suppose," said Lenny. "Whatever you say, Brother Henry."

"That your red Ford pickup parked down there, Lenny?" I asked.

"Roger, Sheriff."

"Were you just traveling east on the Deep Creek Cutoff, near the Airport Bridge?"

"Roger, Sheriff." Lenny's thin lips turned white as he pressed them together.

"Did you even see me when you came over the top of the hill?" I asked.

"No, Sheriff."

"You sure about that? I was the guy on the horse."

"I didn't see no one," said Lenny. He crossed his arms. I was surprised he was able to get them across his body.

"Bullshit, Lenny. I looked right at you, right before we jumped over the cut."

Lenny leaned forward on his toes and stuck out his three chins. "You callin' me a liar?"

"Yup."

"You gonna arrest me?"

I sighed. "No, Lenny. I'm not going to arrest you for reckless driving. Maybe trespassing, though."

If it were possible, I would have sworn the fat man's cheeks drooped even more. His pig eyes grew to the size of quarters, and I even saw a little white around black irises.

"I wasn't on your property!" he squealed.

"Never said you were." I waited for him to catch up. It would be a long wait.

"You can't prove I was there."

"Well, it sure wasn't the mailman who burned out of my driveway."

Lenny blinked. *There you go, fat boy.*

His voice dropped an octave, and his eyes shifted left and right. "You can't prove a goddamn thing."

"Next time you stop by for a visit, give me a call. Maybe I won't shoot you. You know how we ex-military guys are, Lenny." I turned to leave. "And slow down on Deep Creek Road." My anger had dissipated, and I still needed all the votes I could get.

"You sure you can't stay for a drink, Sheriff?" asked Henry Earl.

"Sorry, Henry Earl," I said. "I'm on duty."

"Just a Coke, then." The old man drew me away from his fat companion with the intensity of his invitation. Henry Earl really wanted me to stay.

Lenny didn't take his beady pig eyes off me. "He ain't one of us, Henry Earl. He needs to go."

"I was just leaving," I said. "Watch your driving, Lenny. You're too fat to ride a horse."

"Thanks for the tip, Sheriff," said Lenny.

"Can I get out this way?" I pointed behind the bar.

"Sure can, Sheriff," said Henry Earl. "Just follow your nose. Watch the stairs, though, they're a little steep."

I walked around the bar. A short, dark corridor led to a door. I opened it. The sweet smell of blended tobacco rose up the interior stairwell.

I shut the door behind me and felt for a light switch. Finding none, I reached out for the handrail. I came up short again. *Fine, I'll just open the door and keep my eye on my six.* I tried the knob. Locked from the inside. This was great.

"Nice one, Sheriff," I said to myself.

I refused to sacrifice my pride and call out to Henry Earl and Lenny. I got myself into this, so I would get out of it, too. I stood frozen at the top of the stairs and tried to remember how steep they were. When that didn't work, I waited for my eyes to adjust. Yeah, right—the stairwell was as dark as a . . . well.

I started breathing heavily, as if the air had no oxygen. My constricting throat didn't help much, either. Damp palms slid down the eggshell-painted walls. I felt light-headed, like I'd spent too much time at altitude. I had never experienced claustrophobia before, but here it was, big as shit.

"You okay in there, Sheriff?" I heard Lenny's voice from behind the door.

"I'm fine," I lied.

"Take care, Sheriff." I couldn't tell if he was chuckling at my predicament.

Luckily, the narrow staircase allowed me to touch both walls, so I leaned forward and tripped my way down. The old stairs had shifted with the building over the years, and their irregularity increased with my descent. I missed the last four steps and thumped onto the door at the bottom.

I grabbed the knob and cranked it open as hard as I could, but the cold brass didn't budge. Suppressing my desire to break down the door, I wiped my hands on my trousers and tried the knob again.

Ben Jones was unpacking a case of Nicaraguan cigars and setting them in racks when I burst into his shop. The door at the bottom of the stairwell exited into his walk-in humidor. I felt the pressure change slightly inside the climate-controlled room

"Hey, Sheriff," said Ben, "you going to be a Mason?"

I tried to recover from my newfound phobia. "No, Ben. Just visiting. I guess I was a little disoriented," I said. "I didn't know you were one."

"I'm not," said Ben. "I just let them rent the top floor. They're good customers, too."

"They smoke a lot, huh?"

"You got that right. I give them a little discount, and they buy the place out when they have their meetings."

"Good business decision," I said. "They meet every third Monday, right?"

Ben pulled the half-smoked cigar out of his mouth and gazed at the fragrant boxes. He looked like an old offensive lineman. He wore a white, short-sleeved shirt that was bigger than a bedsheet. His head nearly touched the low ceiling of his humidor.

"'Cept this last one, couple days ago. They didn't have their regular meeting," said Ben. "But they have more meetings, off and on. Seems like there's always someone up there, like now. It's like a little clubhouse for them, I think."

Dusk had been fleeting. With the sun went its meager warmth, and I was unprepared for the drop in temperature. Ben's humidor felt like a warm spring day in Florida. The dry, cold air of Colorado autumn snapped me back to reality.

I hadn't eaten since breakfast, and my stomach was a shrunken knot. Even my horse got to eat before I did, which was normal.

The lights shone happily from the windows of the Belmont Hotel. The rest of Main Street lay dark and uninhabited. I could go back to my cold cabin and cook up some frozen venison, or I could walk across the street and have a real steak from Eunice's kitchen.

Not only was it bright and cheery inside the Belmont Hotel, Eunice had the fireplaces roaring as well. More than likely, she ordered Darryl to get them roaring. I shucked my coat and hat and hung them on the rack with twenty other heavy jackets. Hunters filled the bar and the two adjoining dining rooms.

The character of the Belmont shifted during hunting season. Country music replaced classical and jazz. Eunice put the wine in the basement and stocked up on beer and whiskey. Darryl pushed the tables closer together, so he could seat more customers. Eunice adjusted the menu to suit tired men hungry from the cold—lots of steak, hamburgers, and other red meat. You could get a salad only if you didn't mind getting laughed at. The superheated, noisy hotel felt like a lumberjack dining hall. I didn't see one woman in the place, except the waitresses. They scurried about, carrying platters laden with meat and potatoes or pitchers of beer, weaving among the big field boots sticking out from under tables. I wondered where I would sit.

Eunice materialized out of the chaos and stood in front of me, hands on her hips. I am not tall, but Eunice still has to crank up her neck to look at me. I thought she had shrunk another half inch in the last year, but she didn't slow down one step. She had drawn her pewter hair into a tight bun at the back of her head and wore a blue, long-sleeved gingham pioneer dress and white apron. If I didn't know Eunice, I would think it was a costume, worn to match the western mining-town décor of the Belmont, but Eunice always wore the same dress. Her waitresses wore jeans and T-shirts.

A cigarette dangled from the corner of Eunice's mouth. Another advantage of the seasonal change at the Belmont Hotel was the smoking. A cloud of cigarette and cigar smoke hung just below the ceiling. If you didn't like it, you could go to your room and eat canned chili.

"Sheriff Tatum. What brings you here?" asked Eunice.

"Starvin' like Marvin, Ma'am," I said.

"Skipped lunch again, didn't you?"

"Yes, Ma'am." I tried to look pitiful. That wasn't hard.

"Well, we're pretty packed tonight, and I got no free handouts for you, Sheriff. These boys clean their plates."

"Come on, Eunice. Just squeeze me in. I'm sure one of them would be happy to share a meal with the town Sheriff."

She sucked in a long drag on her Camel and squinted at me, adding more wrinkles to her face. "I got just the group." She spun around. Her skirts dragged on the dirty floor.

Eunice led me to a table filled with four middle-aged white men. They all looked like bankers or lawyers—their boots new, hunting clothes shiny, faces beet red from windburn and alcohol. One of them wore a bright orange Denver Broncos sweatshirt. Two half-empty pitchers of beer and nearly a dozen shot glasses littered the table. The men talked loud and laughed louder. These boys had spent little time in the woods.

"Move over, gentlemen," said Eunice, louder than any of them. "Make room for the Sheriff. He's your guest tonight."

"Hey, Sheriff," said Sweatshirt. His bulk stretched the orange material to its limit. He wiped the beer foam off his red upper lip and held out his hand. "Haf' a seat. We were just getting started." I reluctantly shook his damp hand and sat down. He smelled like a ballpark after the seventh inning.

The other three men smiled blearily. I was glad they didn't try getting up—Eunice and I wouldn't be able to catch all of them.

"Haf' a beer, Sheriff," said Sweatshirt, pushing a mug over to me. "Oh, I'm sorry. You're prob'ly on duty." He slid the beer back to himself.

"Aren't you all staying at the Halfmoon Ranch?" I asked.

"Thas' right," said Sweatshirt, now the spokesman. "Beau'ful lodge. We come up ev'ry year. You a member?"

"Why, yes I am," I said. "Say, why don't we order?" These boys could use some food in their ample stomachs.

"Good idea!" said Sweatshirt. He slammed his open palm on the table. His buddies jumped. "Steaks all 'round. You got that, Eunice?"

"You just eat what I bring you," said Eunice. She smiled at me and swished away.

"So, why don't you all eat up at the Halfmoon?" I asked. "Philippe cooks a damn good steak. Near as good as Eunice."

"Too many goddamn rules up there," said Sweatshirt. I figured I would get his name eventually. "Orville, that old bastard, cuts us off too early, so we come down here to loosen up."

"He is serious about hunting," I said. "His family has owned that ranch for over a hundred years. Three, going on four, generations."

"Yeah, yeah, I know the whole story," said Sweatshirt. "We just need a good toot once in a while."

"Who's driving you back up tonight?" I asked. They all stared at me like I'd asked them their favorite color.

"I guess thas' me," said Sweatshirt. The others nodded.

"Well, then, you better cut it off, Mr. . . ." I said.

"Langley. Porter Langley." Mr. Langley looked like I'd just told him the Broncos were moving to Reno. His companions smiled and all took a slug of whatever they were drinking. Porter shoved his beer to the middle of the table.

"So, how's the hunt going, Mr. Langley?" I asked.

"Terrible. Haven't seen an elk yet." His speech had already improved.

I doubted any of them would, but at least they were having a good time. "That's too bad. How much longer is your stay?"

"We'll be here another coupla days," said Langley.

"Then back to the grindstone, I'll bet. What business are you in?"

"Construction," said Langley. "I run a general contracting firm in Denver."

"Nice. Work on anything I've seen?"

"We built the Rosario Bank Building last year."

I let out a low whistle. "You must have made a bundle off that one."

"Can't say in present company," said Langley. "That's Ed Rosario right over there." He nodded to a glazed-over Hispanic gentleman across the table.

"Say, didn't you all have to blow up the old post office to make room for that project?" I asked. I remembered the footage of the demolition. The old gray building had collapsed like a bad wedding cake.

"Damn right, we did," said Langley. "Took us six months to pay off enough bureaucrats and politicians to get that one to go through. Petey here laid the demo himself."

Petey put his hand on his chest and did a little bow. His bald head almost smacked the table.

"Did you guys see that last bombing on TV?" I asked. Their faces were stony.

"Yeah, we saw it. Fuckin' bastards," said Langley. We observed a moment of silence. I watched them all for a reaction other than anger, like remorse. They were either good drunks, or better actors.

"Hey, Sheriff," said Langley, "what's this I hear about a murder up on the ranch?"

"Depends on what you've heard," I said.

"Well, I heard that it was a member of the town council that got it. Said his own son killed him."

"Who said?" I asked.

"Wendy, that cute little girl who runs the lodge," said Langley. "She said the boy stalked his own father and blew him away, made it look like a hunting accident."

"What else did she say?" I asked.

"She said the boy did it for the money. Turns out, this councilman is the richest guy in town, owns damn near all the real property in Belmont, and left everything to his son."

"Wendy seems to know a lot," I said.

"She can get a doorknob to talk," said Langley. Then he smiled. "When she ain't polishin' it." They all snickered. Petey snorted beer out his nostrils.

"I see. I will have to make an effort to speak with Miss Wendy," I said.

"Well, you have fun, Sheriff," said Langley.

Eunice and one of her waitresses carried in five plates of sizzling rib eye.

"Here you go, gentlemen," said Eunice. "I hope you like 'em medium rare."

Eunice knew my preference, and I didn't think the boys from Denver cared. They ignored their drinks and their company for a few minutes. All I heard was the clinking of steak knives against their plates. I let them eat, but not finish. I needed to extract more information from them before whatever blood was sloshing around in their brains dropped into their stomachs.

"Are you going to be okay, driving back up the mountain tonight?" I asked. "I could take you myself, drive your truck."

"You know, that's mighty kind of you, Sheriff," said Langley through a mouthful of cow. "We might just take you up on that." To solidify the deal, he reached for his neglected beer and took a long pull. I had just become the designated driver.

"You know, I can drive up that mountain wi' 'bout six beer in me, mos' of the time," said Langley, his speech returning to its previous state. "You wouldn't think you'd run into anybody so late up there."

"What do you mean, Mr. Langley?" I asked.

"Porter!" Langley slammed his palm on the table again. Only Rosario jumped this time. "Call me Porter. Only my janitor and my secretary call me Mr. Langley, and I don' think you want their jobs, if you know what I mean, Sheriff."

"You said you ran into someone, Porter," I said.

"Right, Porter, there you go."

"Porter, whom did you run into?" I asked. I was losing him.

"Now, don' you fret, Sheriff, I didn' run into anyone for real," said Langley. "Almost did, though."

"How did it happen?" I asked.

Langley set his beer on the table and blinked at the ceiling, as if he were doing square roots or trying to remember the capital of Lithuania. The rest of the men kept eating, oblivious to our conversation.

"Guy on a horse," said Langley.

"What's that?" I asked.

"Guy on a horse," repeated Langley. "Damndest thing." He unglued his eyes and tore into his steak.

"I don't understand," I said. I'd had more luck with the meth heads two summers ago.

"Guy on a horse." Langley shoved what seemed to be a quarter of his steak into his mouth and moved to slurp his beer. I put my hand over the top of his mug and thunked it on the table. That got his attention.

"You want to elaborate, Mr. Langley?" I asked.

"Yeah, sure thing, Sheriff." Langley pulled his beer out from under my hand. "We were on our way back to the Halfmoon, two nights ago, almost there, too, and we almost ran over some guy on a horse."

"At night?" I asked.

"Yeah, can you b'lieve that? Guy's up there in the freezing cold, riding around in the pitch dark. It ain't like those animals have taillights or anything."

"Can you remember what time it was?" I asked.

"When does the San Juan Tavern close, Ed?" Langley asked Rosario, the banker.

Rosario was at a loss for words.

"It closes at two," I said.

"Prob'ly about two thirty, then," said Langley.

"What did he look like?" I asked.

"Big, brown ass. Four legs, 'bout seven feet tall." Langley lifted the beer up to his lips. I made a move for it, and he quickly set it back down. "Just kidding, Sheriff. I didn't get a good look at the guy. I was just tryin' to keep it on the road and not hit a tree."

"But he was heading downhill, toward town?" I asked, checking his memory.

"No, Sheriff, I told you. All I saw was a big horse's ass. He was going toward the ranch, same as us."

"How about when you got back to the lodge?" I asked, "Did you see him come in?"

"Hell, no," said Langley. "We went straight to bed. Had to get up and go huntin' next mornin'."

"Can you remember where you saw him?" I asked.

Langley gave me a stupid look. I simplified it for him. "Were you on a steep part, or a flat part?"

"Flat part," said Langley, "close to the ranch, I think."

I extracted the location of their SUV and its keys from Langley before he became completely incoherent. They weren't falling-down drunk. Well, yes they were. It was going to be a long, cold ride up to the ranch.

I had only my thoughts to keep me company. The four men slept the dead sleep of the drunk and well fed. They barely stirred, even when their heads bounced off the windows on the bigger bumps in the road.

Porter Langley's off-color remark about Wendy rattled around in my head during the drive up the mountain.

Wendy was the concierge at the Halfmoon Ranch, but Orville didn't call her that. She played a bigger role. If you wanted to know something about a guest at the Halfmoon, you went to Wendy. She knew the habits and desires of everyone who walked under the massive elk mounted in the foyer. If you liked your coffee black and eggs over hard, Wendy made sure Philippe made them that way. If you got up to take a piss at three in the morning, Wendy put out your slippers. If you walked out to your elk stand four hours before sunrise, Wendy had the coffee thermos ready.

I would get stuck at the Halfmoon Ranch tonight. I didn't mind. I was a member. Wendy would feel sorry for me and find me a place to sleep, and it gave me a good opportunity to continue the investigation. The Halfmoon Ranch was the center of gravity for the case.

We crested the Wason Plateau a couple of miles from the ranch, and the terrain flattened. The truck's headlights hardly penetrated the deep mountain night. The new moon hung like a black hole in the western sky, but the stars made up the difference. At ten thousand feet, they had no streetlights to compete with them, and their brilliance comforted me.

The sleeping hunters from Denver snored and farted, forcing me to open all four windows to provide relief. Their drunken heads hung out into the cold night, and the fresh, biting air filled the interior of the truck. The cold was a better alternative.

I had an idea. I stopped the truck, walked around to the passenger side door, and opened it. I caught Porter Langley before he toppled to the hardpan.

"Hey, Porter." I stood him up. The cold brought him around, or it might have been the slap I gave him. "Wake up. I got a question for you."

Langley blinked his eyes and took a few deep breaths. "Are we there yet? It's so dark."

"No, we're not there, yet, Porter. Look around and get your bearings. Is this about where you saw the horse and rider two nights ago?"

Langley walked to the front of the truck. He stood in the headlights and looked up the road.

"Nope," he said.

"Are you sure?" I asked.

"Yeah, I'm sure," said Langley. "There was a trail coming in from the right. There's no trail here."

I smiled. "That's what I thought. Let's go up the road a piece."

"Okay."

We got back in the truck and went farther up the mountain. I left the windows open. Porter got more lucid with every deep breath of mountain air.

I stopped the truck about one hundred meters from the intersection with the pack trail. I wasn't going to drive him right to the spot—his memory was bad enough. My leading him would taint whatever dim recollections came to him.

Langley stood in front of the truck and peered into the arc of light created by my headlights.

"This ain't it, either," he said, but instead of getting back in the passenger side, he got behind the wheel. I hopped in next to him, and we drove slowly up the road. As we approached the side trail, Langley brought the truck to a crawl, then stopped. He said nothing, just looked out the windshield, back two days to another late night.

"This is it," he said, finally. "I remember that low ground over there."

Jerry and I had come this way in the morning, following the well-traveled horse trail left by his father's killer.

"Are you sure?" I asked.

"Yeah, I'm sure," said Langley. "It's starting to come back. It was right here. I had to put two wheels into the shoulder on the left side, going around him. I think we got a flashlight somewhere in the back."

"Don't worry." I got out and pulled my mini Mag-Lite from my duty belt. I turned it on, then looked at it, as if it were a strange tool in my hand. Why hadn't I thought of my own flash when I was flailing around in the stairwell at the Masons' Lodge? Panic did weird things to your head, I guessed.

"What'sa matter?" asked Langley.

"Nothing." I shook my head, forcing away the residual memories of my new fear. "Show me where you swerved off the trail."

If I had any doubts about Langley's story, they disappeared. The shoulder dropped off sharply into a draw. Two deep swales gouged the gravel lip and along the shoulder.

"You were lucky to bring it back on the road," I said.

"I'd been drinking, but I wasn't drunk, Sheriff," said Langley. He was practically sober, now. He just looked tired.

"Do you remember anything else about the man you saw? What was he wearing?"

Langley looked up the trail into the dark. "He had a hat on."

I waited. Things were getting clearer for Porter Langley.

"He wore a cowboy hat, a light color, like gray," he said.

"Did he wear a coat, like mine?" I held out both sleeves of my sheepskin.

Langley looked at me. "No."

I dropped my arms and waited for his memory to kick in.

"No, this guy had a red coat," said Langley. "Definitely red."

It took about one second for me to make the connection—brown horse, gray hat, red coat—Jerry Pitcher. I was getting better at this. I wasn't going to jump to any conclusions, but things weren't looking good for my deputy.

Eight

LANGLEY HAD FALLEN BACK TO SLEEP BY THE TIME we crunched into the gravel lot behind the Halfmoon Lodge. The lodge stood three stories over an alpine meadow and looked like a Viking castle during the day. At night, it turned dark and gothic. Lake Madeline, named after the reluctant wife of the James patriarch, lay black and still on the downhill side of the structure. A single lamp shone above the grand main entrance. All the other lights in the big A-frame lodge were dark, except one—Wendy's office light in the east wing.

When I stopped the vehicle, Langley stumbled out and shuffled inside the lodge, leaving me with his three comatose companions. Great.

"Come on, boys," I said. I opened the back doors. The two hunters on the ends turned toward their buddy in the middle, away from the annoying voice and cold air. They slept harder than drunk paratroopers.

I thought about leaving them, but they would freeze to death in the cold. I could leave the truck running, but they would probably die of carbon monoxide asphyxiation. Maybe if I drove around with the doors open, they'd fall out. Decisions, decisions.

"You need some help, soldier?" came a sweet voice from behind me. If I didn't know better, I would have thought it was an angel, but angels don't scare the piss out of you. I tried to recover.

"You are a cat, Wendy," I said. The young concierge of the Halfmoon Lodge stood behind me, wrapped in a Hudson's Bay coat with a hood.

"Looks like you have your hands full," she said.

"Got any ideas?"

"You just have to get 'em movin'," she said. "Just like calves."

She brushed by me and reached inside the SUV, grabbing the lapels of the nearest drunken hunter.

"Come on, honey," she said, "let's get you to bed." The older man must have outweighed her by one hundred pounds, but she heaved his bulk out of the backseat like a sack of flour. Wendy leaned him against me to stop his swaying. She gripped the middle guy's coat and hauled him out. She pushed him against the side of the truck and walked around to extract the last one.

"You take those two." She led her charge toward the lodge entrance. "Just follow me. We can come back later and shut the doors."

"You've done this before," I said.

"You got it, soldier."

I chucked a shoulder under each arm and made a

controlled fall into the lodge. "I hope their rooms are on the first floor."

ONCE THE HUNTERS WERE NESTLED ALL SNUG IN their beds, Wendy led me back to the foyer. Somewhere in the lodge, a clock pealed out ten bongs. She stopped suddenly and I almost bumped into her. She didn't move from within my personal space.

She had shucked her coat, and only a thin veneer of pink sweater separated us. I could smell her perfume, barely noticeable after a day's work, but it was enough to remind me of a girl I once knew in junior high. The first girl I'd ever kissed.

"I wish you could stay, hon'," she said, then paused. Her pretty smile widened. "You have to stay. You don't have a ride down the mountain."

"Nope," I said. "I was hoping you'd put me up for the night."

"How wonderful," she said. "But it's early. You don't have to go to bed right away, do you?" She pushed her short blonde bob out of her eyes, imploring.

I did have a lot of questions for her.

"Come on, Bill, the children are all asleep," she said. "Let's us go sit and have a nice chat in the living room."

"Make me some coffee, and we can talk all night long," I said.

She nearly squealed with delight. I followed her out of the east wing and into the main hall.

I loved the grand hall of the Halfmoon Lodge. If I ever made it to Valhalla, this was what it would look like. Three granite pillars stood like sentinels, holding up the rough-hewn timber roof, three stories above our heads. The embers of whole logs glowed in the hearths at the base of each pillar. Our heels tapped on the cold slate floor and echoed off the unfinished wood. Bodiless glass-eyed elk and deer stared at us as we walked to the massive plate windows at the south end. In daylight, the San Juan Mountains lay like obedient pets on Orville's doorstep. At night, it was a void. She sat me down on one of the sofas.

"Now, you sit tight, hon', and I'll be right back with the coffee. You sure you don't want anything stronger?"

"No Ma'am."

She spun and flitted toward the kitchen. Wendy's tiny feet made quick steps across the long hall. I watched her go and admired her backside. How did she stay warm in this drafty old lodge with just a tight cashmere sweater and tighter jeans? Constant movement, I guessed, or maybe something more artificial. Her high-octane level of energy hadn't changed in the last eighteen months, but everything else about Wendy Schnuck sure had.

Wendy whisked through the hall ten minutes later carrying a silver coffee service.

"I brought some adult beverage, too, in case you need to warm up your coffee," she said.

"The coffee's fine," I said. "You know, just a mug would have been okay, too. You didn't have to go through all the trouble."

A frown rippled across her lightly freckled face. "I thought you'd like it." She pouted, standing there holding the tray.

"No, no, it's fine," I said. "Please sit, I have some questions for you."

She set the tray on a nearby coffee table and poured us each a cup. I rarely drank coffee this late, but it had been a long day, and I would need the shot of caffeine to fend off Wendy's unrelenting advance. She recovered from my horrible comment and plopped down in a leather arm-chair across from me. I was relieved she didn't join me on the sofa.

"You want to talk to me about Tommy Pitcher, don't you?" she asked. She ran her fingers through her curly mop. I took a long pull of scalding coffee and got out my notebook.

Only Orville referred to Thomas Pitcher as "Tommy." Everyone else used titles of authority and respect—"Councilman," "Brother," "Mr.," or "Dad." Where did a girl thirty years his junior get the right to use such familiarity?

"Not just yet," I said. "Let's talk about you."

"Me?" She batted her eyes.

"How was rehab?"

Her batting stopped. "I'm out, and I'm clean."

"Are you?" I asked.

"Yes."

"You sure lost a lot of weight in the last year or so," I said. "What's your secret?"

"Well, it ain't crystal meth, if that's what you're thinking. That's what everybody thinks."

"They have reason."

"I stopped taking meth the day Marty shot Jacob in the street," said Wendy. "That stuff'll kill you, more ways than one."

Jacob Stackhouse used to run the stables at the ranch and a nice crystal meth operation on the side. He and Wendy sold it to the guests and shared the product. Jacob had gotten on the wrong side of Marty Three Stones and the business end of her rifle.

"Did you meet any other meth users in rehab?" I asked.

"Yes, a couple."

"You still keep in contact?"

"You mean, do we hook up and score crank, now that we're out?"

I raised my eyebrows. "Crank makes a great diet pill, if you live long enough."

"You sound like my counselor. I thought you wanted to talk about Tommy."

"You might have been the last person to see him alive, Wendy," I said.

"Well, the second-to-last, right?" she asked. "The guy who killed him would have been the last." She seemed relieved to change the subject. That was the idea.

"Who said he was murdered?"

"Tommy would never kill himself, Bill. He loved bein' councilman, bein' the richest man in town, bein' the 'worshipful master.' He liked bein' called that the most."

"I heard you're telling folks that Jerry did it," I said. No use beating around the bush, although I think Wendy had that in mind.

"Who told you that?" she asked.

"The same old boys we just brought in," I said. "Why would you go spreading that rumor around?"

"Who said it was a rumor?" she asked.

"You didn't answer my question."

"Call it intuition, Bill." She smiled at me. "It does make sense, doesn't it?"

"They don't pay me to speculate," I said. "I put facts together and make conclusions."

"Haven't you ever just gone with your gut, Bill? That little ache in your loins tellin' you what's right?"

I was trying to ignore that ache right now.

"When was the last time you saw him?" I asked.

She closed her eyes. "Would have been two days ago.

He got up at his usual time—two o'clock in the morning. I was ready for him, as usual, with his oatmeal and his tea."

"Tea? I figured the councilman to be a coffee drinker."

"I would never make coffee for Tommy Pitcher," she said.

"Why not?"

"Because Tommy had an ulcer and a heart condition," she said. "The acid in the coffee tore him up, and Dr. Ed took him off caffeine years ago. I always made him a thermos of decaf green tea. He hated it, but it was the only thing that kept him warm."

"Do you get any sleep at all?" I asked.

"I get more now that Tommy's gone," she said, and smiled.

"When did he return from hunting?"

"Long after dark," said Wendy. She closed her eyes again. "He would come in after the kitchen was closed, but I always had something prepared for him. He would take it in his room, eat, and go to sleep."

"This was all pretty regular?" I asked.

"The man was as regular as Metamucil and spartan as a monk, at least when he was hunting."

"Weren't you concerned when he didn't come back?"

"To be honest, Bill, I thought he'd left," said Wendy. "He doesn't bring a change of clothes or anything else with him on his hunt. Leaves nothing in the room. He pays extra for the bed all season long, so he comes and goes as he pleases."

"But Jerry was still up here," I said. "Didn't they drive up together?"

"Sure, but Jerry has his own horse, and Tommy doesn't. I figured if Tommy needed to get down the mountain in a hurry, he'd take the truck and leave Jerry up here. He's done it before."

"Does Jerry ride around at night?" I asked.

Wendy cocked her head and gave me a puzzled look. "That's an odd question."

"It's not a hard one, though."

"I wouldn't know. Why do you ask?"

"Two nights ago, those hunters from Denver were coming up late from town," I said. "One of them said he almost hit someone on a horse down by the pack trail. Did you hear about that?"

"Maybe."

"Come on, Wendy. It's just you and me sitting here in the dark lodge. Give it up."

"I remember them talking about it when they came in that night, yes."

"All four of them?"

"No, just Porter," said Wendy. "The others came in falling down, like tonight."

"Porter said the rider was heading downhill, toward town."

"Really? That's not what he told me," said Wendy. *Why did that always work?*

"What did he tell you?" I flipped through my notebook as if I had misplaced Langley's report.

"Porter and his boys came in close to three in the morning, said they almost ran someone over. Some guy on a horse heading up toward the lodge," she said.

"What were you doing up?"

"Doin' what I always do, takin' care of my guests."

I checked my dates. "That would have been the last night you saw Thomas Pitcher, right? That would explain why you were up."

She frowned. "No, the last time I saw him was the day before that."

"But you said two days ago."

"The days and nights get mixed up in my head, I guess. Maybe it was three nights ago when Tommy left for good. Yes, definitely three, not including tonight, of course."

"Okay, that seems to check with their story." I turned back the pages in my notebook. "What are Jerry's habits when he's hunting up here?"

"Poor Jerry," said Wendy. "He always seems so lost when he's on the ranch."

"Lost?"

"Well, not literally, I guess. I only see him when he's in the lodge." She sighed. "He's such a shy boy. Has no one to talk to. He completely ignores me." Once again, my deputy was just a boy. Married, respectable job, new child of his own, but still a boy.

"He *is* married," I said.

"When did bein' married have anythin' to do with anythin'?" she asked. "Jerry tried so hard to reach his father. That's why he started hunting last year. Poor boy didn't know that the ranch was the last place to reach Tommy Pitcher. He'd have better luck in his office downtown."

"How did he spend his days up here?"

"Jerry and his father would come up together, but that would be the last time they saw each other until Jerry needed to rotate with you. Sometimes he'd leave the truck for Tommy, other times they'd ride back down together. Depended how well Tommy was hunting."

I kept my mouth shut.

"Jerry always wanted to hunt with his father, but couldn't manage the wake-up. Even Orville gets up later than Tommy. But this week, he did it."

"Did what?" I asked.

"Jerry got up when Tommy did, first day of their hunt.

He scared the dickens out of me, coming into the kitchen while I was making Tommy's tea. He looked like death warmed over, but he was up. I actually felt proud of him."

"Did he say anything?"

"No one says anything that early in the mornin', hon'," said Wendy.

"And he did this all week?" I asked.

"Yup, without fail. I guess he just got in the cycle, like his father. He'd even stay out until after dark, though not as long. He didn't have to walk, like Tommy did."

"So, could it have been Jerry riding up the trail that night?" I asked.

"How should I know?"

"If you were up when the guys from Denver came in, you must have seen the rider come in, too."

"What makes you think he came to the lodge?" she asked.

"Where else would he go? The Halfmoon has the closest stable for miles. I doubt he rode up here from town, in the dark."

"Maybe he likes to ride in the moonlight."

"There hasn't been more than a fingernail for the last five days," I said. "Come on, answer the question."

"I didn't stay up waiting for the midnight horseman, but I guess it could have been Jerry," said Wendy.

"What does Jerry wear when he's hunting?"

"He wears a hat just like yours, and a coat like his father's. I think Mrs. Pitcher got them matching outfits for Christmas last year."

"Red wool?"

"Red wool," she repeated. "Jerry's mama wants them to be safe while they're hunting, and Tommy's too old-fashioned to wear blaze orange."

"Did you see Jerry come in the evening before, or go out that morning?"

"I can't recall. Maybe," she said. I had the feeling "maybe" meant "yes" for this woman. "Like I said, the days and nights get mixed up. I had guests to attend to."

"What 'attending to' do they need at three in the morning?" I asked.

She just smiled at me over the silver rim of her coffee cup.

"You do more than just make their beds, don't you, Wendy? Do you warm them, too?" I already knew the answer, but I didn't expect one from her.

She looked out the cathedral windows at the black shadows of the La Garita Mountains. "The men get lonely up here. There's hardly any women guests during hunting season, not like the summer, when their wives and girlfriends come to ride our horses and mountain bikes. We take care of our guests."

"We?"

"I'm not the only working girl in the lodge, Bill," said Wendy. Her pretty blue eyes slid back over, and she peeked at me from under her curly blonde bangs. She used to call me Deputy Tatum. Ever since she got back from rehab, I was Bill.

"Did you ever 'attend' to Thomas Pitcher?" I asked.

"I'll never tell."

"So, you run a regular brothel up here during hunting season," I said. "Where's the red velvet, Madam? What do you charge?"

"Who said we take any compensation?" said Wendy, smiling. "That would be illegal, Bill."

"Does Orville know about your activities?"

She rolled her head back and laughed at the high ceiling, doing her best Grace Kelly impression. " 'Activities'—

that's funny. Orville spends most of his time out in the field. He lets me run the inside operation."

"What about Mandy?" I asked. Mandy Lange was chief financial officer of the Halfmoon Ranch and Gun Club. She was also Orville's only daughter and mother of my dispatcher.

"What about her? What she doesn't know won't hurt her."

"The wives in town would come up here with torches and burn this place down if they ever found out about your operation."

"Who's going to tell them, Bill, you?" she asked. She faced me and leaned forward. Her v-neck opened, and she gave me a full shot of deep cleavage. She hadn't lost any weight down there.

"You don't have a girlfriend, do you, Bill?" she asked.

"Nope."

"Do you want one?"

What happened to this girl in rehab? "No, Wendy, I'm okay. I'm here to conduct an investigation, nothing else."

"It's Jenny, isn't it?" she asked, falling back on the leather chair.

"Jenny?"

"Jenny's your girlfriend. That's why you have her working dispatch. You keep her nearby, call her into the office when you need it, right?"

"Uh, no," I said. "Why don't you let me ask the questions?"

"Sorry, Sheriff," said Wendy. She snapped up straight in the chair and primly placed her hands in her lap. The position squeezed her breasts together and pushed them toward me, stretching the thin cashmere so tightly, I could see the lace pattern of her bra underneath. Time for me to leave. I didn't want to get any dirt on me.

I stood. "Tell you what, Wendy. Let's finish up in the morning. I'm getting pretty bleary. It's been a long day. Can you put me up?"

"I got a queen-sized bed in my room."

"No thanks, Wendy, really," I said.

"Orville won't let you stay in one of the guest rooms without paying." Wendy pouted, then brightened. "But you can crash on the couch in his office. It's comfy, and it fits two. I can vouch for that."

"Sounds great," I said, ignoring her barrage of propositions. "As long as you wake me before Orville comes in. I don't want the old sniper to see me racked out on his furniture."

"Sure thing, Bill." I was Bill again. "If there's anything else you need, I'm just down the hall."

WHEN I WAS A YOUNG SERGEANT IN THE EIGHTY-second Airborne, I spent a few nights on duty at Brigade Headquarters. The colonel had a big corner office with black leather couches and chairs. The duty sergeants and I took turns sleeping in there while the others manned the phones and kept an eye out for the old man. I was scared shitless that he'd come in unexpectedly, so I didn't sleep a wink. That's exactly how I felt now, sitting on Orville's brown leather couch in his spartan office.

Even though I was the sheriff, and Orville was my friend and mentor, I couldn't just lie down on the old man's sofa like the lodge was a boarding house and I was some vagabond. I sighed and walked over to the stone fireplace that dominated one wall. A stack of dry split kindling sat neatly in stone holder set into the hearth. Maybe a fire would take off the chill and make me more comfortable about sleeping in Orville's sanctum. The office had no door—none of the administrative rooms in the lodge did. Alpine drafts filtered into the room unabated. I could almost see my breath.

The wood flared to life, the result of storage in a dry climate. The fire snapped as pine pitch deep inside the grains heated and burst. The orange flame lit the room. I sat in one of Orville's armchairs near the hearth, hoping I wouldn't fall asleep in it, knowing I would.

The alpine wind hummed through the old timbers of the lodge. The ancient wood creaked with each gust and contracted in the cold. The hidden clock pealed twelve times. The fire's heat slowly rippled out of the fireplace and pushed the cold behind me. I heard someone cough.

Someone cough?

I sat up and turned my head toward the open door. The outer hall was black. Someone was up. Probably one of the guests going for a snack, or a quickie.

Then I heard the urgent tone of men's voices, trying hard to be quiet and failing miserably. Time to eavesdrop. I had to take advantage of my position.

I slipped out the doorway and followed voices and shadow through the main hall. I wished for the soft crepe soles of my regular boots as I toe-heeled across the cold slate. Nonetheless, I knew no one would hear my footsteps, even in the silent lodge.

Sergeant Richter picked me as his gunner for one reason, and it had nothing to do with my ability to shoot a rifle. *I can teach any fool can pull a trigger. Even a fuckin' hayseed like you, Tatum. But if you don't know your feet, you're gonna get me killed.*

I smelled Lenny before I saw his fat ass. I doubted he bathed during the cold months of the year. What the hell was that fat fuck Lenny Leftwich doing up here? The Masons might be desperate enough to let that clown into their club, but Orville had banned him from the ranch for life.

I had arrested Lenny for poaching three years ago. I caught him standing over a bull elk in full velvet, gutting him in broad daylight one spring. I found evidence of over a dozen other animals in his cabin, taken well out of season. The sheriff's department really didn't have a mandate to stop poachers, but Lenny pissed me off enough to take him down. I acted on a non-anonymous tip from Orville. I took all of Lenny's guns away and sold them at an auction. That had been fun. I'd bought one of them myself. Lenny really hated me.

Needless to say, he was not welcome in the Halfmoon Lodge.

I crept through the foyer and down the opposite hall in the east wing. It led to the other administrative offices, the kitchen, and the dining hall. Dim light spilled out of the doorway to the dining hall. Murmurs and the occasional raised word did, too. I slid up next to the frame and listened.

"Yes, Sir. Yes, Sir. Roger, Sir." Lenny made no attempt to lower his whining voice, but whomever he groveled to kept his voice to a vibration.

"Negative, Sir. Negative, Sir. I didn't think of that, Sir." I'd never heard Lenny call anyone "Sir."

"Wilco, Sir. Wilco, Sir," said Lenny.

Wilco? I hadn't heard that word since the Army. It meant, "I understand and will comply."

It was time for me to go in and surprise them. I turned the corner and ran right into Lenny's big gut.

I am not a large person. I never played football in high school. I don't know if Lenny did, either, but he sure laid me out flat in the hallway. I cracked my head on the stone floor.

"Sheriff Tatum?" asked Lenny. He made no move to help me up. His big, stinky frame filled the doorway. He wore a bulky brown hunting coat over his blue flannel. "What are you doing up here?" He said it loud enough for his boss to hear.

"I was going to ask you the same question." I stood and rubbed the back of my head. Lenny glanced quickly over his shoulder. I stepped toward the door. He leaned his bulk to block my way.

"Did you drive your truck up here, Sheriff?" he asked, still very loud.

"Lenny, I'm right here," I said. "You don't have to shout. You'll wake the guests."

"I didn't see your truck out front."

"I got another ride," I said. "Who were you talking to?" I tried peering around him. He sidestepped again to prevent me from seeing into the room.

"No one," said Lenny. *Wrong answer, Clown Boy.*

"Come on, Lenny, let me by." He didn't budge. I started getting riled up. "You know, Orville's gonna have your ass on a stick if he catches you up here. Now get out of my way." I shouldered past him. Then he did something I never would have expected.

The smelly fat man put his arms around my waist, picked me up, and carried me back into the hallway. He plopped me down on the tile floor and returned to guard the door. His eyes were wide and his chest heaved with the effort. He stood there like an offensive lineman protecting the quarterback. I was no linebacker, either.

"What the fuck are you doing, Fat Boy?" I stepped toward him. He straightened both arms and shoved me up against the wall. I bumped a large, oval mirror adorned with elk antlers.

I'd had about enough of this. The moment he stepped away from me, I let him have it. One quick left jab broke his nose. A right to the windpipe dented his larynx. He stood there, wheezing and bleeding like an angry bull. That should have clued me in.

He dropped his shoulder and drilled me into the wall. My head smashed against the mirror. I never got to see who it was in the dining room.

Nine

W AS THAT A SHOT?
    I would have jolted upright, but my neck must
have cranked over and calcified, my ear permanently fused
to my shoulder. Eye crud glued my lids together.

"Serves you right, fallin' asleep in my chair."

I knew that voice. I heard another shot, and realized it
was just the loud clap of cold wood on the colder hearth,
then the scrape of cast iron against rough stone.

My nose felt like my horse's, only colder and snottier,
but it detected the blessed scent of morning coffee.

"You ain't that mad," I croaked.

"What makes you say that?" Fresh wood clunked in the
iron grate. A crack of sulfur in the air.

"You brought me coffee," I said.

"Don't be so sure."

I rubbed the sleep out of my eyes and forced my head into an upright position. I thought I could feel my vertebrae cracking. *When did I get so old?*

A Hudson's Bay blanket covered me. Wendy might be a whore, but she sure knew how to take care of you.

I pried my eyes open. Orville stood between me and the hearth. The old man watched the new flames overcome the dry tinder, then the kindling, then spread across the split, twisted chunks of local spruce. The fire released evergreen like burning incense.

"That was a stand-up thing you did, bringin' my guests back to the lodge," said Orville. "Now they can pay their bill. Maybe that's why I brought coffee."

" 'To protect and serve,' " I said. "Gave me an excuse to come up here."

"You need an excuse?"

"Good point."

I rubbed the back of my head and winced. Dried blood matted my hair and stained the back of Orville's chair.

It all came back to me in a flood of memory—the late-night encounter with Lenny, slamming up against the mirror, losing consciousness. I bolted upright.

"How did I get here?" I asked.

Orville handed me the cup of coffee. "I thought you knew." He sat down on the couch and began lacing up his hunting boots. "You drove the Denver party up here."

"No, how did I get in this chair?" I asked.

"Beats me. That's Wendy's blanket."

"What time is it?"

"Close to four a.m. I slept in a little, now that Tommy's not gettin' up. Some of the boys are in the kitchen. You want a little breakfast?"

His nonchalance confused me. Did it all happen? Did Orville see the blood?

"Yeah, sure," I said. "Let's go."

The fireplaces in the main hall already blazed. The place would have been cheery, were it not four in the morning.

We walked down the east hall toward the dining room. I heard the sounds of early breakfast coming from the kitchen. The warmth and aroma of cooking filled the hallway.

"Boys don't eat much before dawn, unless they're going to be out 'til dinner," said Orville. "Most of them hunt the morning, then come back in for a late breakfast. Philippe pretty much cooks all day."

I stopped where Lenny had slammed me against the wall. "The mirror," I said. It was gone, and no glass littered the slate floor.

"What mirror?" asked Orville.

"There used to be a mirror here," I said. "Lenny and I crashed into it last night. That's how I got the blood on my head. It was the last thing I remember, before waking up just now."

Orville grabbed my shoulder and turned me. The old man was half a head shorter than me, but powerful. His rough fingers gripped the back of my neck.

"Nice one," he said. "You better let Dr. Ed take a look at that." He released me. "As for the mirror, I never liked it much anyway. I wouldn't've noticed, if you hadn't said anything. Ain't my seven years."

I was still trying to clear my head when we walked into the dining hall. A few hunters sat around a circular table. Orville had his guests sit together, which made it easier to serve them and fostered camaraderie.

Chuck and Max, the brothers who weren't, sat together.

Too early to bicker, they tore into their steak and eggs like old farmers.

Henry Earl Callahan chose coffee and a cigarette for his breakfast. He sat far from the table and stared at the honey jar, hunting hat pushed back on his head. A tuft of gray chest hair that matched the grizzled stubble on his chin sprung out from his unbuttoned long johns. He wasn't quite among us, yet. A congealing bowl of lonely oatmeal pondered its fate.

Only pepper flakes and a yellow swirl of egg yoke remained on Dr. Ed's plate. His pipe poked out from under his white mustache and his arms folded across his chest. I was surprised to see him at the lodge. He spotted me from across the room and nodded to an empty place next to him.

None of the Denver party joined the early morning ritual. I doubted they ever did.

I got a tandem "Sheriff" from Chuck and Max, and Henry Earl blinked at me in acknowledgment. Philippe dropped a hot plate of scrambled eggs and bacon in front of me.

"Thanks, Philippe," I said. "You got any coffee?" He looked pissed. Wendy usually served.

"There's a fucking pot of Folgers in the kitchen," said Philippe, "but no coffee."

Orville grabbed my cup and followed his grumpy chef through the swinging door.

Orville returned alone with our warm-ups. His hunting guests filled the table, so he leaned against the wall and waited for them to finish.

Dr. Ed scraped his chair away from the table. "What happened to your head, Sheriff?" He pushed away the matted hair and exposed the wound with his large-animal-vet fingers. In the process, the new scab that had formed over

the laceration split, and a fresh trickle of blood ran down
the back of my neck.

"Jesus Christ, Doc!" I dropped my fork. "Let me finish
my breakfast before you go pokin' at me." The other
hunters stopped and watched the show.

"You require stitches," said Dr. Ed. "Fortunately for
you, I brought my bag with me." He really meant it—he
was going to stitch up my head in the middle of the dining
room. Dr. Ed kept manipulating the skin on my sore head.
He dipped his napkin in a water glass and cleaned away the
dried blood. Tiny glass fragments abraded my scalp. My
eyes watered.

"There is glass in the wound," said Dr. Ed. "How did
this happen?"

"I had a run-in with Lenny last night," I said. I did my
best to scan the group for reactions, which was difficult
with my face on the table.

"I thought he wasn't welcome on the ranch, Orville,"
said Dr. Ed.

"Can't be everywhere, all the time, right Sheriff?"
asked Orville. "You wanna do that somewheres else, Doc?
My guests are tryin' to eat." Only Chuck and Max were still
eating, and my head wound didn't slow them down a bit.

"Certainly." Dr. Ed wiped the blood off my neck and
patted my shoulder.

"What are you goin' to do about Lenny?" asked Orville.

"I'm going to arrest his fat ass as soon as I get down the
mountain," I said. No one reacted to my bravado. Angry
with the pain or lack of sympathy, I glared at them. They
ignored me.

"Do any of you know what he was doing up here?" I
asked the group. None of them answered. "He was right in
here, in the dining room, talking to someone. Called him

'Sir' about a dozen times. Lenny call any of you gentlemen 'Sir?' " I would have had better luck talking to a herd of elk.

I wanted to ask Dr. Ed if he was finished with the autopsy on Thomas Pitcher, why he was up here hunting, rather than doing his job as coroner. I wouldn't ask him in front of everyone, however, so I kept my mouth shut, except to drink coffee or shovel eggs and bacon.

I was angry, and I felt like everyone's stupid nephew. My status as a junior member of the Gun Club and my youth in general seemed to diminish the authority that went along with the Sheriff's badge. I didn't know if it was the weeness of the hour, guilt, or lack of respect that closed their mouths, but I would not measure my dick with these men at the breakfast table.

Orville sipped, Chuck and Max clinked, Henry Earl stared, and Dr. Ed puffed. No one asked me about the investigation. No one asked me how Jerry was doing, or his mother, not that I would know. None of them seemed interested in finding the person who had tortured and killed a man they had lived and hunted with for the last forty years.

"OUCH! WHAT ARE YOU USING BACK THERE, DOC? A knitting needle? Something out of your tackle box?"

"I believe Wendy has a staple gun in her office, if you would prefer," said Dr. Ed. Orville chuckled around his cigarette. Smoke filled the tiny space of Orville's personal lavatory. Orville manned a tray of stitching supplies and swabbed where Dr. Ed directed. Ed had already clipped away the matted hair and exposed enough of my split scalp to clean the glass particles and crusted blood from the wound. Now he tugged and poked my inflamed skin with what seemed to be an eleven-gauge needle and braided fishing line.

"Now the butterfly closures, Orville," said Dr. Ed to his attendant. A final pinch of flesh, and my tormentor was finished.

"I would be careful putting your hat on," said Dr. Ed.

"I'll keep that in mind," I said.

Dr. Ed washed his hands in Orville's sink. Orville stood there and smoked the rest of his Marlboro.

"Where the hell is Wendy?" I asked.

"Don't know," said Orville. He pulled on his cigarette and eyeballed me.

"Isn't she usually up at this time?"

"Yup."

I'd have to take notes if I wanted to keep up.

"Maybe she's sleeping in, now that Pitcher's dead." I thought that would get a rise out of him. It didn't.

"Are we done here, Doc?" asked Orville. "I have guests to attend to."

"You are relieved, Sergeant," said Dr. Ed. Orville left without a word.

"Unless you require any other treatment, Sheriff, I was hoping to get on with my hunt," said Dr. Ed. "This seems to be a tradition. Someone gets murdered, you split your head, I sew you up."

"I'm fine," I said. "What about your ATV? Orville didn't give in, did he?"

"Not in the least. Now that he knows my secret, that option is no longer viable. I must walk or ride a horse to my stand. That is why I am up staying at the lodge. The walk from town would be too tedious for me."

"No chance on a horse, huh?" I asked.

"No."

"Done with your autopsy, already?" I leaned on the bathroom counter and crossed my arms.

"The full report is on your desk," said Dr. Ed, then he left as abruptly as his attendant.

The main hall stood dark and empty, but a gray promise whispered behind the La Garita Mountains to the southeast. The generous fire in the nearest hearth warmed my back as I looked out the tall glass. Given the choice of venturing out into the cold morning and staying inside the warm lodge, I was tempted to curl up on the couch. My closed-mouthed breakfast companions had dispersed to all four quadrants of the ranch to seek big game, leaving me with no Bronco—hoofed or wheeled—to get around. I walked out the back door.

I stood on the wide deck and filled my lungs with frost. Gray light lit the edges of the eastern mountains. I jammed my fingers into fur-lined leather gloves and set my hat low in the front to avoid the fresh stitches in the back. When the stiff inner band brushed the swollen flesh, I winced and reconsidered my course of action.

What I saw when I opened my eyes would keep me out in the cold for hours.

Two sets of human tracks marred the crusty layer of snow on the deck. They started at the back door and moved off the deck to the southeast. I knew there were two, because one set was booted, and one was barefoot.

Barefoot?

I leaned over and inspected the footprints, disbelieving. Certainly a bear or some other large animal had made them, looking for scraps or a warm place to sleep. The footprints told a different story—they had the high, delicate arch and slender taper of a woman's foot. Her toes kicked up little tufts of snow—walking fast, but not running. They looked like footprints on a bleach-white coastline.

The boot prints had destroyed many of the barefoot tracks—he had walked behind her, driving her into the bitter night.

Ten

I CROSSED THE DECK AND DROPPED TO THE FROZEN turf. The short alpine grass crunched under my boots. The tracks disappeared for a few dozen meters, obliterated by the wind, but I followed their line until they picked up again at the edge of the trees on the south side of the ranch.

She had stumbled twice in the tree line, her body crushing the delicate frost, imprinting her plight.

I knew this path. They had walked southeast, toward the dawn, along the path that Thomas Pitcher took every morning. Every morning until someone tied him up in his own elk stand and kept him in a near-hypothermic state until shooting him in the back of the head.

"Jenny, this is Tatum," I spoke into my radio.

"Yes, Sheriff, good morning." Prompt as usual. "Are you calling yourself in for duty?"

"Roger, Jenny," I said. "I'm up here at the lodge. I'm headed back to the scene, on foot. I'm following a pair of tracks."

"Hoofed or booted?" she asked.

"One booted, one shoeless."

"In this weather?"

"Looks that way."

"Okay, Sheriff. Where's your vehicle?"

"Long story."

"Is Jerry with you?" Jenny asked.

"Negative. I take it he hasn't reported in yet."

"No, Sheriff. Haven't seen nor heard from him since yesterday."

"Roger, out." I clipped the radio back on my belt and kept walking.

When I hit the gravel pack trail that led to town, I lost the tracks and walked for about a mile until I found the little feeder stream. The sun had edged close enough to the tops of the mountains for me to see the tire gouge where Porter Langley had swerved to avoid hitting Jerry—or at least to avoid hitting someone *who was dressed like Jerry*.

Nearby, I found the east-west trail where Jerry and I had followed the killer's track the day before. The trampling of our horses made tracking easy. The woman's bare feet made round heel prints in the metal-shod hoof gashes in the earth.

I stepped off the pack trail and into the cut formed by the feeder stream. From a horse, this draw seemed shallow and unremarkable. On foot, it was a trench. The low ground and denser vegetation trapped the dampness of the creek and penetrated my layers of warmth. The shaded draw trapped the snow from yesterday as well. The sun couldn't touch the white dusting on the banks of the stream, and new frost had locked the snow in place. As gray morning bled light and color into the day, I noted the snow had filled our horse tracks from the day before, but the footprints lay empty of snow.

I had walked nearly four miles across the frozen earth. How could a barefooted woman make it this far? Just the thought made my toes go numb.

Quiet cold pressed on my ears. I stopped and held my breath. The strand of juniper and Engelmann spruce marking the stream looked like an Ansel Adams photograph. I removed my hat and continued the listening halt. I tuned my ears to the undercurrent of sound in my surroundings. Nothing. I waited. Still nothing. I gently placed my sheriff's hat on my head and followed the draw.

After another mile, the faint pack trail diverted from the stream and turned northeast, toward the divide, but the feeder stream ambled southeast, as did the sets of fresh prints. I stayed with them and closed on Thomas Pitcher's final stand.

Farther down the mountain, the draw deepened. The sides rose in a sharp vee, and taller spruces concealed the top in places.

I gained the ridge overlooking Pitcher's deer stand and saw open space for the first time in five miles. I stood at the edge of the Wason Plateau and looked down into the wooded canyons formed by Bellows Creek, and beyond it the flat valley of the Rio Grande. The La Garita Mountains had released the sun, and it painted the cold western slopes bright morning yellow. The faint heat warmed my face. I stood with my eyes closed at the top of the world. It was good to be alone.

I suddenly felt exposed.

What was I doing out here without my rifle?

Where's your weapon, Ranger? Sergeant Richter would ask when he caught me leaning my M24 against a tree to take a piss. *You ain't shit without it, and things'll turn to shit quick as death as soon as you let it go.*

So, here I was, walking around without a rifle in an area where everyone else had a rifle, including, probably, the person who killed Thomas Pitcher. What was I thinking?

I wasn't thinking. My head hurt, and I was pissed off. Pissed that Lenny Leftwich had knocked me down and knocked me out, pissed that I had no wheels or stirrups, pissed that the old men sitting around the breakfast table that morning paid no attention to me, pissed that I had no clue who the murderer was and how to proceed with the case. I was the sheriff, for God's sake. These things only happened to deputies.

Shake it off, Ranger. You could be barefoot, or tied to a tree.

I sought the nearest concealment—the strip of evergreen that terminated in Pitcher's deer stand at the cusp of the spur. It was too late to recover from my mistake. The next best thing was to hide. I didn't feel much safer in the thin line of juniper and Engelmann spruce, but it was enough to keep my mind off my stupidity.

I found lots of footprints at the scene. The cloven-hoofed tracks of deer and elk mingled with the booted and barefoot prints of man and woman. The pair had walked right through the crime scene and out the downhill side. I would follow them later.

I also found the stuff I forgot. One of these days, I would start acting like a law enforcement officer, instead of a retired Army sniper who likes to ride a horse, wear a cowboy hat, and carry a gun. I didn't even have the right gun.

I recovered Pitcher's hunting stool where it lay at the

base of the Engelmann spruce. In my haste to follow the killer's horse tracks the day before, I had left it. It was more than a stool. It had a foldout backrest, a carry-sling, and a small zippered compartment underneath the cloth seat. The compartment held a small silver thermos, still full. I unscrewed the cap and sniffed at the contents—hot tea. Well, it wasn't hot anymore, but it must have been the tea Wendy made for the councilman the morning he disappeared.

I focused on the Engelmann spruce where Pitcher had been tied up. The ligature burns on the bark remained, but I didn't find any other sign of human activity. I thought there should have been more.

Working through the sequence of events on the morning of Pitcher's murder, I decided that if I had surprised him as I came up Farmer's Creek Trail, he had certainly handled it smoothly. I had interrupted him at the climax of his plan, and he still managed to kill Pitcher, cleanse the scene, and get away.

I wiggled my toes in the killer's boots.

I stand behind a hypothermic Thomas Pitcher. He is barely alive, tied to the tree. His hands are swollen with frostbite, blue fingertips. He is stripped to the waist. I grip the cold flesh of his bare right shoulder and hold the .45 against his head. The trigger pull is stiff in the cold. I hear a horse snicker down the slope. Someone is coming. Too late. It has to be now. I can make it. I pull the trigger. Pitcher's head jerks sideways and slumps against his chest. I toss the Colt on the ground in front of him. I slit the old man's bonds and release the body. It flops lifelessly to the turf. I put Pitcher's coat back on and rip the duct tape from his mouth. Checking the scene one last time, I stuff the tape and rope in my pocket and disappear over the ridge.

This guy was a decision-maker. He had to make a quick

decision when he saw me—kill Pitcher or hesitate. He didn't hesitate, even in the face of imminent discovery.

Not only did he make quick decisions, he had planned his egress as well. I hadn't stayed down very long. I came right out of the draw and moved up the ridge, waving my hat, but he slipped away undetected.

I knew I'd missed something. After leaving the hunting stool out here for over twenty-four hours, that wasn't too hard for me to believe. Something else was here, right in front of me, but I couldn't place it.

Going back to the footprints, I followed them to the edge of the pine grove, then stopped. The barefoot and booted tracks tempted me to emerge, but I would have to cross a large open area with a commanding ridge above it.

Where's your weapon, Ranger?

I pulled the radio of my utility belt. Utility belt—I always think of Batman when I pull something off my belt.

My vantage point had a line-of-sight shot to the radio repeater on top of Snowshoe Mountain, across the valley. "Jenny, this is Tatum."

A warped return answered my call. I jerked my ear away from the noise. The squeal echoed through the still air. Jenny must have knocked over her microphone.

"Yes, Sheriff."

"Ouch."

"Sorry, Sheriff."

"Any sign of Jerry?" When would he become Deputy Pitcher?

"No, Sir."

"All right. Well, I'm back at the crime scene."

"Are you coming down, or going back up?" Jenny asked.

It was a fair question. I had walked far enough down the

mountain to be as close to town as the Halfmoon Ranch, and Belmont was downhill.

"Don't know yet."

"I can come pick you up at the Farmer's Creek Trail-head if it'll help," said Jenny. "It must suck to be out there without your wheels."

"Jenny, you're a treasure," I said.

I could feel her blush through the police band spectrum. She didn't respond.

"Anything else going on?" I asked. "Any word from our favorite federal agent?"

"Negative, Sheriff."

"Okay, then. Thanks, Jenny."

"You're welcome, Sheriff."

Well, I couldn't stay in the trees forever, so I found a little fold in the ridge and hoped it would provide enough defilade to protect me from rifle fire.

Hope is not a method, Tatum, Sergeant Richter used to tell me. I got sick of the phrase, probably as sick as Richter had been hearing *I hope* from me, as in:

I hope our target comes out, soon, or: *I hope my zero is good on my scope.*

Unfortunately, hope was all I had five miles from sanctuary and my own rifle.

I moved quickly though the field of fire, following the contour of the slope to the sharp draw carved by the east branch of Farmer's Creek. I gained the low ground without being ventilated. The footprints went down the trail.

When the rocky draw came up around me, I breathed easier. Blue spruce and Engelmann defied the bare rock and steep grade. Their roots sought and found water in the dry bones of the mountains. Their height and girth challenged reason, but their dominance in the valley was undeniable.

Gravity brought water to this place, and the mountain ever-greens flourished on its offerings. I almost felt safe.

Only a light dusting of snow lay under the thick spruce canopy. The barefoot and boot prints stopped. The thin layer of new snow had swirled with dirt and gravel as they struggled.

My guts turned over. Something bad was coming. I threw off my gunbelt and dropped my trousers just as a shit-storm blew out my backside. Having no paper, I had to cut off my underwear and use it. I thought Philippe's eggs had looked a little runny, the bacon a little underdone. I buttoned my pants.

Where's your weapon, Ranger?

Pretending not to hear Sergeant Richter, I looked over the edge and into the deep ravine of Farmer's Creek—a few more degrees of grade, and it would be a cliff. A fresh drag-mark slashed across the crusty snow and dirt toward the bottom.

Then a moving bullet snapped by my head.

I felt the round break the sound barrier next to my ear, then the cold crack of the rifle followed immediately behind it. Things began to happen very fast.

I dove over the edge and tumbled ungracefully down the wash. I must have slammed against every rock and tree, but the rough descent comforted me at a subconscious level. Not only was I a moving target, I was getting low, seeking defilade. My inner soldier was happy.

My outer sheriff was getting beaten up. I tumbled, rolled, and slid to the bottom of the draw, then settled in silence. Pebbles and loose dirt followed me, but no second rifle shot. That was a good thing, because I couldn't move. I lay on my back in the dry creek bed and wondered if I'd been hit or if I could get up at all.

Eleven

G ET UP, RANGER.
    Get up, Ranger, before he has a chance to relocate and take your ass out.

I lay at the bottom of the draw, next to the tiny vein of Farmer's Creek and its corresponding trail, hatless and . . . gunless.

"Son of a bitch," I croaked out loud. I'd left my .45 at the top of the wash. It would have been a frail comfort, but at least I'd be armed.

Relocate, Ranger, relocate.

Taking a deep breath, I got ready to move. A knife pain in my right side brought cold tears to my eyes. I wasn't going anywhere.

I'd broken my ribs before, on a long fall under a parachute. It was on a mass tactical jump in the Eighty-second

Airborne—hundreds of stupid paratroopers coming down in the middle of the night over Normandy Drop Zone. One cherry jumper—I swear it was that prick Haines—stole my air. Stealing air happened when one jumper drifted underneath another. The top jumper's canopy collapses for lack of air to keep it open and gravity takes over. If it's high enough, the canopy will reinflate, but when Haines stole my air, we were about two hundred feet from the ground. My parachute had no time to catch air, but it slowed me down a little. I hit the sandy soil and could have sworn I bounced back up six feet. I got away with a concussion and three broken ribs. Sergeant Richter had been more concerned about the damage to my M24 sniper rifle than my body.

You'll heal, Ranger. Let's go check your zero.

I should just rest awhile. I drifted in and out of consciousness and my limbs turned to wood. The cold became a blanket, if not warm, at least a comfort, a soothing haze over the pain.

My shooter saved me from hypothermia.

A bullet pinging off the rock next to my head brought me around. My sniper had gained a new position and pinned me down while I daydreamed about Fort Bragg.

What're you gonna to do now, Ranger?

As I rolled to the unbroken side of my ribs, Wendy's dead face looked right back at me.

She lay flat on her stomach, her head turned a lot too far to the left. The grotesque angle of her chin resting on the back of her left shoulder made me want to throw up, or it might have been the exit wound blossoming out of her right cheek. Her lips were the same dusky color as Pitcher's on the morning I'd found him, her bare skin the same blue death tone. Snow, dirt, and pine needles matted her fine hair. Red abrasions and massive black bruises covered her naked body. Her eyes were wide, locked in an eternal expression of fear and despair.

Panic waited in the wings. I beat it back. I had about three seconds to decide what to do—the amount of time it takes to cycle a bullet into a bolt-action rifle.

Somewhere in the eternity of three seconds, a thought struck me—if this guy couldn't hit me sitting still, he sure as hell wouldn't hit me if I were moving. Wendy was already dead. I could do nothing for her now.

I shouted in pain as I rolled over my broken ribs, but found my feet and scuttled down the trail. I sought anything that would stop a bullet or obscure my movement. Moving hurt, a lot, but at least I was moving. A massive charley horse crippled my left thigh and both ankles felt sprained, but I was moving. I made short bounds from rock to tree to gnarled juniper. I tried my best to fall on my left side, away from the searing pain in my right chest.

Every three seconds, another shot ripped through the canyon, snapping on the trail or mangling a tree trunk, but as long as I was moving, I knew he couldn't tag me. Not very good, for a sniper. Any Army or Marine sniper worth his boots would have put ten rounds in me by now.

Every fifth round, there was a long pause in the shooting, almost a full thirty seconds. He was reloading his five-shot magazine. After the next four rounds, I waited for a fifth shot. It snapped by my head and I bolted down the trail. I stayed low, legs churning down the rocky path away from my shooter. As I stumbled down the narrow track, I watched him in my mind's eye push five more rounds into the magazine. When he worked the action home, I found my next patch of cover.

After twenty-five rounds, he stopped firing. Did he run out, or was I out of range? I brought up a mental topographical of the Farmer's Creek canyon. He had fired from the east ridge, which ran to the southeast, away from the trail. He couldn't maintain a superior position from the ridge as long as I moved down the trail. I had run away from my shooter.

I ran down the path in a controlled fall, thankful that downhill was my avenue of escape. My hands were freezing, so I tucked them into the pockets of my jacket while I jogged, which didn't help my balance. I could do nothing about my head. My ears tingled, burned, then disappeared from my tactile senses. My nose did the same, followed by the skin over my cheekbones. I'd have frostnip, at the very least, by the time I walked back to town. Each gust of wind sent thin tendrils of pain through my exposed skin.

"Damn, that wind is cold," I mumbled to myself.

Suck it up, Ranger. It ain't the wind that's cold, it's just you.

Jenny Lange leaned against her Bronco at the Farmer's Creek Trailhead, smoking a cigarette and staring off across the valley toward Snowshoe Mountain. I let her drive Marty's truck—my old partner and drug-ring sniper wouldn't be needing it anymore.

We should really get Jenny a uniform. She wore jeans and a bright yellow jacket. Her blue knit ski hat had earflaps, dangling tassels, and the words "Wolf Creek" stitched in white across the crown.

Maybe I wasn't ready to deputize another woman. The last one hadn't gone so well.

She tossed the cigarette into the brush when she saw me crest the last rise in the trail. Then she reached into the truck and grabbed the mike on the Bronco's radio. I wondered if the elk would hear her, back up on Farmer's Creek Trail, where my own radio lay. I sure as hell didn't. She kept trying, bringing the handset up to her mouth, then looking back at me. She hung it back on its bracket, put a fist on her hip, and waited for me to explain why I wouldn't acknowledge her transmission.

"You shouldn't smoke," I said. I tried to hide the limp and bury the grimace over broken ribs. "Cynthia would kill you if she found out."

"She's not my mother," said Jenny. "How the heck did you see me, all the way up the trail?"

"I have great vision," I said. "Former sniper, remember?"

"Anyway, you smoke."

"A habit I wish I could break." I opened the passenger door, painfully, with my left hand, keeping my right arm tucked against my side to support my ribs, and got in. I melted into the seat.

Her petulance turned to concern, but then she remembered being ignored. She followed me around the truck.

"Why didn't you respond to my call?" Jenny asked through the window.

"I lost my radio." I closed my eyes. I wasn't ready to tell her about Wendy.

"You lost more than that. Your utility belt is gone. Your hat, too."

"Very good, Boy Wonder."

"You don't want to drive?"

"No, Jenny. Please, just drive me home and see if you can get a hold of Dr. Ed. I think my ribs are broken."

"Your ribs are not broken, Sheriff," said Dr. Ed. "They just feel that way. You must have struck something on the way down the wash. The cartilage between your three lower ribs has separated."

"I struck about ten things," I said. I sat in my bed and winced each time Dr. Ed wrapped another turn of Ace bandage around my rib cage. "I can't breathe."

"That's good. We need to keep your ribs immobile, so the tissue can re-knit." He paused. "One day, I'm going to ask you about these scars."

"But not today," I said.

"No, not today."

He finished the wrap and walked into the kitchen. "You need to get up and move around. You are not hurt badly enough to stay in bed all day, and I think you have some law enforcement work to take care of."

I growled, but put my shirt back on, and followed him. He had filled the pot with water and was loading coffee grounds into the filter.

"Make yourself at home. Shall I make you an omelet?" I asked. I gently lowered myself into one of the two kitchen table chairs. The wood-burning stove in the corner warmed my little kitchen.

"No, thank you. The coffee is fine."

He plugged in the percolator and walked over to the kitchen table. Instead of sitting down, he turned me in my chair and looked at my head.

"I don't think I hit my head." I blinked at his penlight.

"Didn't you say you lay there for a while before getting up? Can you recall if you lost consciousness?"

"No," I said. "How 'bout some pain meds?"

He turned my head. "Your stitches held up remarkably well. A testament to the surgeon. Let's clean them up a bit."

He dabbed at the laceration with an alcohol swab from his black bag while the new coffee bubbled.

"Pain meds, Dr. Ed."

"You don't need any, big tough ex-paratrooper like yourself."

I grunted and wondered where I'd left my bottle of Advil. "How did you get down here so fast?" I asked. "Weren't you on foot? Hunting on the ranch?"

"As Mineral County coroner, I am required to be on call. Your dispatcher knows how to get a hold of me."

"Yeah, I know that, Dr. Ed. I'm the one who implemented that policy, remember? How did you get down the mountain so quickly?"

"Jenny drove up and found me," said Dr. Ed. "She is a very capable dispatcher, and I carry a radio."

"Yeah, I knew that, too." This made sense. Many things were making sense again.

"Who is our new sniper?" he asked. He threw the bloody, dirty swab into the trash can and washed his hands in the sink.

"You can hardly call him a sniper. He fired twenty-five rounds at me, but never connected. Even you can shoot better than that."

Dr. Ed flicked the water off his fingers and looked around for a towel. I gestured at the roll of paper.

"Maybe he didn't want to hit you," he said.

I opened my mouth to give another smart-ass answer, then wisely closed it again. The man had a point. The percolator hissed its completion, and Dr. Ed filled two thick white mugs.

"Maybe you did exactly as he wanted—left the area," he said. "Maybe that is why he did not pursue. He could have easily taken you down the trail—you were injured and unarmed."

"Maybe."

"Think of the risk involved, shooting a county sheriff.

From what you described, I'd say you surprised him during his return to the scene. If he had planned to shoot you dead from the beginning, he had plenty of opportunity to do so. You don't just go off and shoot the sheriff without planning."

"Sounds like you've thought about it some, yourself," I said.

"Once or twice." Dr. Ed sat down across from me. "Your shooter was either very bad or very good—placing his rounds just close enough to make it believable, but far enough away to keep you uninjured."

"I can't imagine what he was after," I said. "I checked the scene thoroughly. There was nothing left. Well, just about nothing."

"Just about?"

"I forgot Pitcher's stool up there yesterday," I said. "I brought it down the trail with me."

"But it's still up there, with your hat and belt, no doubt. Did you recover the forty-five bullet?"

"Oh, shit!" I threw my arms up in the air. The item nagging my subconscious back at the crime scene—I knew I'd forgotten something. I'd have to go back there again.

"I found something else up there," I said.

I didn't like talking about it, but I was the sheriff now. These things weren't supposed to bother me. Dr. Ed waited.

"I found Wendy Schnuck."

"She was dead," said Dr. Ed.

"Graveyard dead. Someone walked her down the mountain last night—five miles naked and barefoot in that bitter cold. Looks like he shoved her over the drop-off on Farmer's Creek Trail. Broke her neck. Then he came down and shot her in the back of the head to make sure."

"You didn't remain at the scene?" asked Dr. Ed.

"I was getting shot at, remember? I didn't take the time to secure the body," I said, "but I'll have to go back up there today and find her."

"Don't forget your rifle this time."

Twelve

Dr. Ed gave me a ride to town in his coroner-mobile—a converted black hearse with the words MINERAL COUNTY CORONER stenciled in white block letters on both sides.

"Have to take the old girl out once in a while." He maneuvered the boat down the narrow gravel trail from Deep Creek. It lumbered around the sharp turn onto the airport road, and Dr. Ed pointed it toward Belmont. "From the way things are heating up around here, I might have to put her to official use very soon."

We parked behind the municipal building, right next to the yellow emergency generator and the green outer door to the body locker. In the daylight, the locker looked like a kiln or a pizza oven. At night, the happy green door turned black, and I imagined the locker looked like a different oven, like one at Auschwitz. I was glad it was daytime.

"You coming, Sheriff?" asked Dr. Ed. He caught me staring at the heavy door.

"Yeah, my head is cold." I broke my trance. My uncovered head was getting to me.

Sergeant, my head is cold. Richter made me circle the block and repeat that any time I walked out of the barracks without my beret. You'd think I would have remembered after the first time.

I headed straight for my office and opened the locker where I kept my extra gear—hat, belt, and weapon. I kept a Beretta 9mm in a lockbox on the floor. None of these items were there, not even the Beretta. I scowled and walked into the radio room. Jenny ate her lunch out of a brown paper bag and read from the FBI Web site on the desktop.

"Jenny, where's my extra gear?"

"I don't know, Sheriff," she said. She wiped her mouth and spun away from the monitor. "I checked your locker, after dropping you off at your cabin. I thought I'd bring them out to you, but they weren't there."

"Shit." I sat down on the edge of the radio counter. Jenny got up and brought me a cup of coffee. She sat back down and made a little frown of concern.

"How are you feeling?" she asked.

"Okay, I guess, for a few separated ribs and a split head." *And a dead Wendy Schnuck.*

"Poor baby. Dr. Ed give you something for the pain?"

"No. You got any Advil?"

"Drawer under your legs. Help yourself," she said. "Ben Jones called from next door. He wants you to move your Bronco."

"I better move it." I started for the door.

"Jeez, Sheriff, I almost forgot." Jenny moved some papers around her tiny work area, then brought out a yellow phone message. "Agent Ritter called this morning. He's on his way back out."

"Does he want me to call him?"

She checked her scrawl. "No. He'll come by when he gets here. Later this evening."

"That's it?"

"That's it."

"Well, I can't wait around for him. I'm going back to the cabin to get my extra gear."

I sat in my truck but didn't turn the ignition. The return to Farmer's Creek to look for Wendy's body did not appeal to me. I cut myself a little slack—I'd just been shot at. Did I really want to go back up there, alone and uncovered? I turned the key and heard nothing but a staccato series of muted clicks.

"Son of a bitch," I said quietly and tried the key again. The clicks mocked me. Maybe it just needed a new starter.

Not that I would know. I knew nothing about cars. I knew where the key went, I knew where to put the gas and the windshield wiper fluid. I knew to change the oil every three thousand miles, which I had Henry Earl's nephew do for me. I was a mechanical midget.

"Got a problem, there, Sheriff?" Emmet's grizzled mug appeared in the driver's side window.

"Truck won't start," I said.

"Battery?"

"Maybe."

Emmet held my hat and my duty belt in each hand.

"Well, I was wondering if you wanted these back," he said. "Glad I caught you before you took off, but it looks like that ain't happenin' any time soon."

"Where did you find them?"

"Farmer's Creek Trail. Just sittin' there, like you went off to take a dump and forgot 'em."

I stepped out of the truck and looked at the items in amazement, then I closed my gaping mouth. I took my hat from him, confirmed the sheriff's star was still intact, and set it on my head. The stitches reminded me of my earlier wound. I ignored them. I turned the belt over in my hands—not a thing was missing. My .45 was still snapped into its holster, full magazine, extra clips waiting. Pepper spray, flashlight, everything. Emmet had even snapped my leather gloves to the little D ring.

"I was surprised to find them," said Emmet. "Good soldier like you, leavin' his hat and his weapon behind. Somethin' happen up there?"

"Something like that." I buckled the belt around my waist and my little world realigned itself. "Did you find a hunting stool?"

"Nope, just your stuff."

"Nothing else?" I asked. *Like a body?*

"Nothin' Sheriff." He eyed me. "What are you gettin' at?"

"What time was this?"

"Couple hours ago. I was up there, doin' my artist thing. I think my model's dead, though."

"Say again?"

"My model, my big bull elk. Someone shot him and left him up there to rot."

"You found an elk carcass?"

"Yup. A few days old," said Emmet. "Looks like someone shot him and didn't bother to track and recover him. He just lay down and died."

"Where?"

"Up in the southeast quadrant. About a mile northeast of Pitcher's stand."

I placed the spot in my head. "Could you take me there?"

"Sure, anytime."

"Did you see anyone else in the southeast quadrant this morning?"

"Just Jerry."

My heart thumped alive in my chest. "How do you know it was Jerry?"

Emmet frowned. "We had this conversation before, Sheriff. I just assumed it was Jerry—you know, red coat, gray hat . . ."

"Right, right. Well, thanks a lot for recovering my stuff, Emmet." We looked at each other.

"Want me to take a look?" he asked

"At what?"

"Your truck—it won't start, right?"

"Can't hurt," I said.

Emmet walked around to the front of the truck. I joined him. We stood there for a moment, looking at the big Mineral County sheriff's star painted on the hood.

"You wanna pop the hood for me, Sheriff?"

"Oh, yeah." I returned to the driver's side and reached under the dash. The release popped with a loud clunk.

Emmet raised the hood and we peered into the automotive mystery that was my truck's engine. Emmet stared at it for a full minute. I waited for his diagnosis, for his hands to move over the V8 and fix whatever was broken. He didn't move. His mangled right hand remained tucked under his left arm and his other hand gripped his whiskered chin. His mouth pressed a tight line under his drooping mustache. I thought I saw the skin on his knuckles go white.

"That's not a starter," said Emmet, very, very quietly. So quiet he scared the shit out of me. "Sheriff, why don't you just clear out of here, maybe go in the bomb shelter under the municipal building."

"What's going on, Emmet?"

"You have a . . . device . . . attached to your starter."

"A device?"

"Sheriff, please. I know what I'm talking about. You seen the TV lately? Fort Leavenworth, Fort Bliss? Truck bomb like this could level our whole downtown.

Truck bomb. Those two words were used in other countries, like Israel or Iraq, or at least in big cities, like Oklahoma City or New York. Not in Belmont, Colorado, population 756, elevation 8,966 feet. We were safe here, tucked away in our deep notch in the San Juan Mountains. Terrorism and fear stalked other parts of the world and left us alone in little Belmont.

Not anymore. I had a device attached to my starter.

I had lived with hatred, fear, and violent death for four years as an Army sniper, taking lives, delivering my country's justice with a bullet. I had come to Belmont to escape it, but it had followed me here. Maybe this was my penance, maybe it was just irony.

Maybe you better suck it up and drive on, Ranger.

"Hey, you found your stuff!" Jenny called from the radio room as I wandered by.

"Jenny, you better get Dr. Ed and get downstairs," I said, but I went into my office and stood in the center of the room. The thought of huddling in the dark cellar of the municipal building seemed worse than having the ceiling collapse on my head. The cold sweat on my back renewed itself with the new fear. Maybe I could crawl under my desk.

"What's going on, Sheriff?" Jenny stood in my doorway.

"Just do it, Jenny," I said. I pushed papers around the surface of my desk. "Let's just call it a tornado drill." She probably had no idea what I was talking about. I did tornado drills all the time, growing up in Iowa, but I doubted she'd had them at Belmont's public school. Avalanche drills, maybe.

I turned to tell my dispatcher to get moving, but she had transformed into Emmet Springer.

He grinned beneath his droopy mustache. He held an object made of wires and gray plastic.

"Pretty amateur stuff." He turned the device over and pulled at the wires. I froze. My eyes must have looked like headlights.

"Don't worry, Sheriff. If this thing had a chance to go off, it would have blown you up as soon as you turned the key. It's inert, now. We used to burn C4 to heat our C-rations. I could start it up with my lighter, right here in your office."

"Please don't," I said. "C4?"

"Yup, U.S. Army issue. Pretty new, too. You've seen this stuff, I suppose, in the Airborne."

I had seen it. I had received minimal demolitions training as a paratrooper, just enough to know I didn't want any part of it. I preferred a nice, clean sniper kill.

"What do you want me to do with it?" asked Emmet.

I pulled a paper evidence bag out of a desk drawer. In Belmont, the sheriff's department used brown bags from the Rio Grande Grocery.

"Put it in here." I held out the open bag. Emmet lay the

explosive gently in the bottom. I rolled it up and stowed it in the empty gun box at the bottom of my locker.

"I checked the rest of your truck for other devices. It's clean," said Emmet. "Thought I'd be rusty, but it all came back to me. Once an Eighteen Charlie, always an Eighteen Charlie, I guess."

"You think it's safe for me to drive it?"

"Well, I started her up and parked it in your spot," said Emmet. "I heard Ben was gettin' pretty hot over you parking in one of his slots." He dropped my keys on the desk.

"You moved it?"

"Sheriff, you feelin' okay? You're kind of slow on the uptake this afternoon."

I rubbed my forehead, then screwed my hat down on my tender scalp. "Nothing that a little time in the saddle won't fix. Let's get out of here. I want you to show me that carcass."

Emmet led the way back up Farmer's Creek Trail. I followed the brown and white haunches of Emmet's paint, Henry.

"What does Henry Earl think of being your horse's namesake?" I asked.

"I don't even think he knows," said Emmet. "Henry Earl's not much of a horse guy, kind of like the doc."

The stiff wind from the valley blew against my back. I turned up my collar and shivered, not from the cold, but from the memory of being shot at along this same trail. What choice did I have? I could not sit in my office and do nothing.

"My rifle and my badge, they comfort me," I muttered to myself, but they did. I rested my hand on the stock of my Ruger No. 1 and boldly scanned the ridgeline ahead of me.

* * *

BACK AT THE TRIGGER POINT OF THE KILLER'S
ambush, I peered down the wash. I could see the path in the
dust of snow and turf where I'd tumbled into it, but I didn't
see Wendy at the bottom.

"Elk's over this way, Sheriff," said Emmet.

"I'm looking for something else," I said. I pulled my rifle out of the scabbard and handed it to Emmet.

"What's this for?" he asked.

"Cover me. You know how to work a breechloader?"

"I can fire about any weapon you give me, Sheriff, including an M1 tank. You got any more rounds for this
thing?" I unclipped the leather pouch of ten .30-06 rounds
from my belt and held it out.

"Where you goin'?" He rested the stock on his hip. He
looked like an old cavalry scout with a long Springfield.

"Down," I said. "Cover me. Keep your eyes up the draw."

"Roger that, Sheriff."

I sidestepped down the slope and struggled to stay upright. The wash became nearly vertical at the bottom. I ex-
ecuted a controlled fall and planted my feet hard in the turf.

I didn't like being down here again, even with Emmet
up top. Something about getting shot at in the same place
triggered my psyche.

I wouldn't need to stay long. The churned-up snow and
dirt was recent. My sniper had cleaned up. He had moved
Wendy and left no trace of her.

Had I seen her at all? Maybe I had hallucinated her
body after bouncing my head off one too many rocks. I followed my movement down the draw, but found nothing. No
extra prints, no drag-marks. My shooter was lucky Wendy
had lost all that weight. He'd carried her out.

I scrambled up the draw with some pain and difficulty.

"Where is the elk from here?" I asked, breathing hard.

"What were you looking for down there?" asked Emmet. He cleared the rifle and handed it back to me. I replaced the single bullet in the breech, safed the weapon, and put it in its scabbard.

"Something that isn't there anymore. Maybe it was never there. Where was the elk, again?"

"'Bout a mile from here, opposite side of the spur." Emmet pointed to the northeast, over the top of the ridge. "You wanna take the trail up and over?"

"No," I said, "let's follow the spur around to the south."

"You're the sheriff." Emmet clicked at Henry and turned east off the trail. "I go this way a lot, especially this year. Our big boy lorded over this valley."

I looked up the ridge toward Pitcher's last stand. "Isn't this where you saw Jerry?"

Emmet followed my gaze. "Yup. Or someone who dressed like Jerry. You know the story."

We came around the eastern side of the spur. To our right, the terrain plunged into the sharp valley carved by West Bellows Creek. The southern exposure and nearby water source made this section of the ranch thick with green pine and yellow aspen groves. Emmet found a game trail and we entered the green silence. Tall spruce banished the incessant wind. Not to be denied, the wind shook the tops of the trees, but could not reach the forest floor.

"Hold up," I said. He stopped.

Pancho sensed the death in the clearing. He stomped his hooves and jerked back his head. "Easy there, big fella," I whispered to him. I got out of the saddle and patted his rippling neck. Pancho took that as a dismissal and turned

back down the trail. I knew he would not go far. Emmet
didn't dismount.

The ivory-colored tips of the elk's antlers emerged behind a low granite shelf like an irregular picket fence. I approached, but smelled no hint of decay. The cold weather
must have slowed the process.

A thick line of trees and gray rock obscured the cliff to
our right. I walked to the edge and peered down the sudden
drop to the gorge that held Bellows Creek. I thought I could
hear the whisper of the stream, hundreds of feet below, but
it might have been the evergreens.

The size of Rocky Mountain elk always shocked me, regardless of how many I saw or killed. This bull must have
weighed at least nine hundred pounds. Six sharp tines bristled on one antler, seven on the other. He looked like a
sleeping dragon, only with light brown hair instead of
green scales.

He had walked as far as he could down a familiar trail
that had provided sanctuary in the past. Weakened by
blood loss from the bullet, he lay down, stretched out his
neck on the frozen turf, and died.

The hunter who ended his long life had not claimed his
prize, but the coyotes had. His right hindquarters and ab-
domen lay red and savaged against the gray and green.

When I saw the red mass of tangled hair and flesh behind his front shoulder, something came over me that I
guess real law enforcement officers called a hunch.

"Help me turn him," I called over to Emmet. "Bring
Henry."

Emmet slowly nudged his young paint over to the
dead elk.

"You got a rope or something?" I asked. Emmet tossed

me a length of climbing rope. I tied it to the right legs of the elk and Emmet cinched the other end to the pommel on his saddle. Henry backed up like a good horse, unlike mine, and I helped him haul the bull onto its back. Joints cracked and flesh ripped from the frozen ground.

I took off my gloves, coat, and hat, and rolled up my sleeves. The decomposition process was evident when I cut into the soft white flesh of the bull's belly. I clenched my jaw and kept my knife moving. Emmet held the legs. When gutting out an animal in the cold weather, the only benefit is that it keeps your hands warm. That only works, however, if you have recently killed it. Not only did the animal smell like an abandoned slaughterhouse, his wet insides were as cold as a well. With both hands, I removed what little entrails the coyotes had left behind, including a frozen chunk of coagulated blood the size of a football. I reached into the chest cavity and felt around for the entrance wound in the elk's rib cage. I found it and traced the path of the bullet through the lungs, past the heart, and into the other side. The bullet did not exit. Instead, it mushroomed almost flat and lodged in the elk's broad left scapula. I withdrew the mangled bullet and held it in the gray afternoon light. I tucked the bloody chunk of lead and copper in a small paper evidence bag the size of a playing card and buttoned it up in my shirt pocket.

"Now, why did you go and do that?" asked Emmet. He looked at me like I had lost my mind. That would not be a stretch. Rotting elk blood painted my chest, hands, and forearms. I looked like a crazed butcher. I did my best to wipe my hands on the sparse, ground-level vegetation. After a minute of fruitless chafing, I just rolled my sleeves back down over red forearms and put on my gloves. Out of sight, out of mind. I could shower later. I had been filthier before.

"Call it a hunch," I said. "Not certain if I know what one is, but I have a feeling Thomas Pitcher shot this animal. I wanted to retrieve the bullet as evidence."

"Evidence of what?" asked Emmet. "Killing a beautiful animal and leaving it to the coyotes?"

"Maybe."

I found Pancho impatiently pulling up dry mountain grass with his teeth. He didn't like the way I smelled.

"Sorry, bud, you'll just have to deal with it," I told him. He blew out a loud snuff from both nostrils. Emmet laughed so hard he nearly fell out of the saddle.

He sobered up immediately, though, as if someone had dropped a lead curtain on him. He looked back at the ruined animal, gutted and eaten.

"What do you want to do with him?" I asked.

Emmet sighed and rubbed his long mustache. "Meat's no good, 'cept for coyotes." He paused.

"We could cape him ourselves, pack him out," I said. "I'll do it. I'm a mess already."

Emmet thought about that. "No, Sheriff, we shouldn't leave the old man up here without his head. It's bad enough that his insides'll get ripped out. No, he needs to stay in this canyon. It's his, anyway."

We only had a few hours of daylight left, and I had one more bullet to recover. Emmet started on a dead reckon for Pitcher's stand.

"Hold up." I dismounted and peered at the game trail we'd followed. The afternoon sun still provided enough light for me to backtrack the elk's last walk along the canyon edge.

"What're you doing?" asked Emmet. "Crime scene's that way."

"If my hunch is right, it's this way, too." Emmet didn't answer.

"Just humor me," I said.

"You're the sheriff. I'm just a crazy artist."

Finding the bull's tracks among the multiple deer and elk prints proved very simple. Not only were they the largest prints, by far, but they had a marker, as well. The entrance wound in his side bled down his right leg. Each step had left a drop of blood in the brown alpine grass. I led Pancho by the reins to keep him from marring the prints. When we emerged from the trees, his track diverged from the game trail. The elk had crossed the open area on the southeast side of Pitcher's stand, running from the gunshot and the flash of pain in his chest.

I felt a twinge of panic, exposed on the downhill side of the spur. I half expected to see my sniper on the ridge, drawing a bead on my nose. I shook it off and returned to my track. I knew I wouldn't see him. I'd just have to deal. It wasn't like I hadn't been here before, at the wrong end of a rifle scope. I crossed the open area, straight for Pitcher's last stand. I tried to think of other things besides a bullet in the face.

Why hadn't Pitcher claimed his prize? The bloody marker on his hoofprint made tracking easy. Jenny Lange could have followed this trail, in the dark, with a candle. Any tracker worth his boots would have recovered the trophy bull in less than an hour.

This was unlike him. Not only was Thomas Pitcher an avid hunter, he was a successful businessman, as well. A workaholic who spent many days away from his office would expect results for his effort. A hunter with Pitcher's discipline and focus would never leave such a magnificent animal to scavengers.

But when it was time to recover his trophy, he did not. *Why?*

Because he was tied to a tree.

No one knew exactly where the councilman hunted, and if the killer performed a thorough search, his actions might reveal him, or at least draw suspicion. The murderer had masked his activities by hunting—he belonged on the ranch, and no one would suspect that he really hunted Thomas Pitcher.

Why the elaborate staging at Pitcher's stand? Why didn't the killer just take him out on the trail and disappear? A simple ambush of the councilman would have been easy to set up. Like most successful men, Pitcher used routine and habit to maximize his productivity, whether in the field or in the office. He walked five miles to get to his deer stand early in the morning, then five miles back in the evening. I could think of three places along his route to kill him quickly and get away cleanly, but the killer had other plans. He wanted to kill Pitcher close up and make him suffer for a few days before the end. To do so, he would have to know the exact location of Pitcher's deer stand. He found it when the councilman shot the trophy elk.

I had seen it myself many times while hunting, saw it the day Pitcher was killed—a rifle shot draws people like a house fire. They all wanted to see the new trophy. Turns out the trophy was human this time.

Pitcher knew his tormentor. He carried a .45 on him at all times and would never let some stranger walk up on him in the middle of nowhere. The old man had accepted the killer into his sanctuary because he was a trusted comrade in the field. The murderer had then disarmed Pitcher, tied him up, and kept him alive for three days in the freezing alpine autumn.

I ENTERED THE SPRUCE GROVE WHERE PITCHER HAD died, .45 drawn, thinking like the killer again.

I stand behind Thomas Pitcher in the early light of October. I place my .45 at the back of his skull and pull the trigger. The big slug rips through flesh and bone, bursting obscenely through the old man's cheekbone. The slow projectile loses most of its energy as it smashes through the cranial wall, twice, and embeds itself in the dirt in front of me.

I looked down the barrel of my own Colt and followed the bullet's path to the base of a juniper sapling. Not taking my eyes off the ripple in the turf, I holstered my weapon and crossed the clearing. I gently dropped to my knees and peered at the ground.

Our trampling on the scene had nearly obliterated the evidence of the slug's penetration, but a fold in the pine duff and a few tiny clods of dirt revealed it.

I took off my glove and pushed my bloody fingers into the dirt. Hard, cold copper met them. I brushed the tips of my fingers on the smooth base of the projectile and knew something was wrong. I pulled it out and understood.

"That's not a forty-five," I said out loud. I rocked back on my heels and examined the bullet that had killed Thomas Pitcher.

"Looks like a thirty-eight to me, Sheriff." Emmet stood behind me. "Or a nine-millimeter. Government issue, maybe."

He was correct. The 9mm round looked like the full metal jacket bullets I'd used in the Eighty-second.

"Definitely not a forty-five," I repeated, but where was the shell casing? I had only found two shells at the scene on the first day—the .270 rifle brass and the .45 shell—both from Pitcher's weapons. The killer must have taken it with him and left the others.

Pitcher had been killed with a weapon not his own, and the murderer still had it.

Thirteen

I HAD NEVER LIKED THE DUSK, THE IN-BETWEEN time before the sun gives way to black. As a sniper, I'd slept during the day and killed at night, but the twilight was not my friend. Something primal always stirred in me, a reptilian fear of the loss of the sun. Maybe it was the shift of dominance from cones to rods in my eyes. I never told Sergeant Richter about it. I just sucked it up and waited for the dark.

I would have a long time to wait, up here at elevation. When the sun dipped behind Bristol Head on the valley floor, darkness dropped like a hammer, but higher elevations extended the twilight. I felt the night creeping no faster than we had descended Farmer's Creek Trail.

"Hey, Emmet," I said to his back.

"Yes, Sheriff."

"You never told me the story about your hand."

"You never asked."

I waited for him. He rocked gently back and forth with each of Henry's downhill steps. Emmet lifted his head to the dim band of light behind the mountains.

"You askin' now?"

"I guess."

Emmet sighed, then started talking.

"I received a bad conduct discharge from the Army in 1990."

A bad conduct discharge was actually worse than a dishonorable one. A BCD meant he'd been court-martialed.

"During Operation Just Cause in Panama, my team was performing a DA mission—that's direct action—ambushing a Panamanian Defense Force convoy. We heard The Man himself, Manuel Noreiga, would be in the procession, so it was a snatch-and-grab mission. I rigged an explosive charge to destroy the lead vehicle and block the intersection. We would then kill everybody except The Man. It was perfect— one of the only good pieces of intel we had the whole time down there."

"What happened?" I asked.

"We were all set up—locked, cocked, and ready to rock. Then an old woman came out of nowhere. She was shuffling through the kill zone when the PDF convoy pulled up. There were a lot more soldiers than intel told us—about thirty PDF goons with AK-47s and wetback attitudes. They had to stop to get her out of the way. Noriega was a prick, but he didn't run down old women. It was killing us. There they were, bigger 'n shit, sittin' in our kill zone, but nobody wanted me to set off the demo with the old señora standing there. Except my team leader."

"What did you do?" I asked.

"I refused to set the demo. The captain told me to, and I told him to go fuck himself. I even handed him the plunger. I didn't think he had the sack, but he called my bluff and grabbed it, but he couldn't figure out how to set it off. I crawled over to the demo. I managed to pull out the blasting cap from the charge and had it in my hands when the captain figured out the plunger. The cap blew up in my hand. The wetbacks heard it and went crazy. They were better trained than we thought. The whole platoon deployed on us, and we had to break contact. The captain took a bullet in the gut. He survived, but he had to leave the Army. So did I. Bad conduct discharge. "Big chicken dinner"— that's what my Army lawyer called it, the little prick. Spent a little time in Leavenworth. It was not a high point the annals of the Special Forces."

As long as I was prying, might as well go all the way. "I heard about an incident at the San Juan Tavern a few years back."

Emmet chuckled. "That would have been Master Sergeant Gerald Humphries, my old team sergeant."

"I heard you put him in the hospital," I said.

"He kind of let himself go after retirement."

"Emmet."

"What?"

"What happened?" I asked.

"Well, what do you think happened? The old boy either looked me up or just happened to drive through Belmont on his piece of shit Harley. He saw me at the bar and started in with the old bullshit of unexpected reunion. You know, small world and all that."

"Sounds innocent enough," I said. "Why did you nearly choke him to death?"

"Humphries was the only NCO on the team who testified

against me at my court-martial. Not that it mattered. It was my word against an officer's. Guess who won?"

I said nothing.

Emmet was getting riled up. "You see, Humphries didn't have to say anything, but no, he wanted to get his shots in, kick my ass on the way out. He'd been passed over for command sergeant major three times, and was just spiteful."

"I bet it felt good to hurt him," I said.

"No, it didn't," said Emmet. "I saw him, said a few nice things, then tried to leave. I was pretty tanked. Well, I was pretty tanked most of the time back then, but I knew I had a good one goin'. He got through the pleasantries and started in on the incident. He just wouldn't shut up."

"So you choked him?"

"He just wouldn't let it go. I came to Belmont to put my demons behind me, but one of them rides up on a scraggly fat boy and sits next to me at the bar. He yanked on my ponytail, made fun of my glasses. I wasn't in the mood for his bullshit, so I started walking out, but he grabbed me and spun me around. Back then, that was all the provocation I needed. It took three guys to get me off him. Like I said, I kept in better shape than he did. They took him to the hospital in Del Norte, and I went to AA the next day. Never saw him again."

WE PASSED THE TRAILHEAD AND CONTINUED DOWN the gravel road that ran along the northeast wall of the Belmont Valley. The sinking twilight painted the beige rock orange.

"You hear that shootin'?" asked Emmet.

"Yup." My inner lizard didn't feel like talking.

"Someone's at the public range," said Emmet. "Strange time to be shootin'."

I said nothing. We came up the rise above the public shooting range nestled in Dry Gulch. I saw a white SUV parked in the lot.

"Stanford's sightin' in his rifle," said Emmet. "Don't know what the hell he's been doin' out in the field, if he ain't confident in his shooting."

"Which is why he's down here, instead of at the Club's range, up top," I said. "Orville would yank his membership if he pulled that shit up there."

We moseyed past the rifle range. I turned. Emmet did not.

"Thanks, Emmet," I called after him. He raised a hand, but didn't look back. He coaxed Henry into a trot and disappeared over the next rise.

I found earplugs in a coat pocket and jammed them into my ears. Mike blasted away, round after round, pausing only a second or two between shots. I wondered if the animals on the ranch got spooked by the shooting. Pancho was a rock. He laid his ears back every third round or so, but did his best to look bored. He wandered off, looking for any hardy vegetation left over from the summer.

The town had built two bench rests at the end of a four-hundred-meter public rifle range. It might have been four hundred yards, but I couldn't shake my training.

Yards you mow, or walk around when you're in prison, Sergeant Richter said when he caught me saying "yards." *We shoot men at six hundred* meters, *Ranger.*

Mike sat at the nearest firing position, his rifle propped up, elbows resting on the bench. He had no sandbags to support the weapon. Spent brass littered his feet. I didn't want to startle him, so I eased up behind the spotter's scope. I looked through it and checked Mike's accuracy.

He fired at a two-hundred-meter target. Mike stopped firing and removed his big, red ear protectors.

"Hey, Sheriff. Did you drive your Bronco up here? I didn't see you pull up."

"Pancho brought me. You suck, Mike." I left my eye in the spotter's scope. "How the hell did Orville let you in the Club?"

"You come up here just to give me shit?"

"No," I said. I stood and peered out at the two-hundred-meter target, wondering if he were shooting at something else. His groups were pathetic. "But you really suck."

He set the rifle on the bench. "I told you. Pitcher has a lot of influence in this town, even all the way up there at Halfmoon."

"Had a lot of influence, you mean," I said. "Who's going to protect you from Orville, now that Pitcher's dead?"

"I can take care of myself," said Mike. "Anyway, Chuck and Max are longtime members. Put together, I think they can watch over me."

"Uh-huh," I said. "What's that you're shooting?"

"Two twenty-three." Mike cleared the chamber, safed the rifle and handed it to me. I hefted the little Ruger M77, all thick barrel and big Leupold scope. I hadn't noticed the caliber when I'd looked at it the first time, up on Wason Plateau.

"Orville lets you hunt up there with a varmint rifle?" I asked.

"I prefer the range. You see, I'm not very sneaky. I need all the help I can get."

"Uh-huh." The Winchester .223 cartridge was the equivalent of the NATO 5.56mm round, used in M16s and other military rifles around the world. He was right about the range—the .223 maintained its velocity and energy well beyond six hundred meters, but the bullet had a tendency to tumble. Tumbling was great if you wanted it to tear through an enemy soldier's chest cavity or blow up a prairie dog, but it wouldn't take down a bull elk.

I shouldered the weapon and peered through the scope. The light-gathering qualities of the Leupold turned the dusky canyon into midday. The two-hundred-meter target filled the scope as if I stood in front of it. "You don't shoot well enough to use the long-range benefits of this cartridge, Mike."

"Why do you think I'm out here practicing?" He remained seated. "You want to squeeze off a few rounds, show me how it's done?"

"Kind of late in the season to be working on your skills, don't you think?" I asked. "I mean, everybody's out hunting, and here you are, blasting away during prime hunting hours."

"Suit yourself. I was just finishing up, anyway." Mike never answered my question.

"I didn't see you this morning at breakfast," I said. "Sleep in?"

"I do not join the old boys for breakfast," he said, "and I had some affairs to attend to here in town."

"Affairs?"

"Business, not that it's any of yours," said Mike, but he continued, anyway. "I am the executor of Thomas Pitcher's estate. I had to read the will to the family."

"Jerry and his mom?"

"That's correct. Mrs. Pitcher will not receive much, though. She will receive a monthly allotment, just enough to cover the mortgage on their cottage and her considerable medical expenses. Mr. Pitcher left everything to Jerry."

I didn't know why Mike was telling me all this, but I kept my mouth shut and listened. He changed the subject.

"Was that Emmet?" he asked.

"Yes."

"I wonder what Jerry will do about his studio."

"What do you mean?"

"Mr. Pitcher was about to throw our village sculptor out in the street." He said it like "village idiot." "Emmet's markets have dried up, and he cannot make enough money teaching his meager trade to old women and poor college students."

"I thought the former councilman was a benefactor in town, a patron of the arts."

"Who told you that?" asked Mike.

"Emmet." I felt silly saying it.

"I see." His smile got minutely bigger. "Well, that's not entirely accurate. Emmet was essentially Thomas Pitcher's indentured servant, his own personal artist. Emmet owns nothing in that studio, except maybe his clothing and that sway-backed paint. Now, Jerry owns it all."

"Why are you telling me this?"

"Just making conversation. Thought you'd like to know."

Mike stood and carefully picked up his brass, one by one. I don't know how he found them all in the dark twilight. He inserted each spent shell into the foam core of the plastic bullet box. He closed the lid, then started packing up the rest of his equipment. His movements were slow and deliberate—the measured control of a meticulous personality. I guessed accountants were like that, but I doubted most CPAs had Mike Stanford's build. His broad back and thick upper arms pushed out the cloth in his canvas hunting coat. His green wool pants bunched around tree-stump legs.

"Are you just going to stand there or give me a hand?" Mike turned with his rifle case in one hand and the box of shells in the other. He jerked his head at the spotting scope. "You can put that away and bring it to the truck. Or not." He pushed by me and walked over to the SUV—a big white Chevy Tahoe.

I pulled my bloody hands out of leather gloves and dismantled the scope. Instinct, or curiosity, made me glance down to see if Mike had missed any brass. Sergeant Richter made me do one hundred pushups for every round I missed at the shooting range.

Quickest way to getting compromised is to leave shit lying around, Ranger. I learned my lesson quickly.

Mike Stanford, on the other hand, did not have the benefit of negative physical punishment to reinforce his range discipline. I slipped the spent round into my coat pocket without looking at it.

Mike popped open the rear gate to his truck. The resulting honk from the horn made me jump, but it brought to full consciousness the thought floating in the back of my head—I didn't like having my back to this man.

I stepped around the bench and finished my task facing the bodybuilding CPA. He placed his equipment gently into the rear cargo area and sat down on the bumper.

I brushed my hand over the back of the scope case and felt a bizarre scrape on the surface of the smooth plastic. Two strips of hook tape—the clingy side of Velcro—were stuck to one side.

We don't got any "Velcro" in the Army, Ranger. We got hook-pile tape.

I walked over and started to set the scope in the back of the Tahoe.

"I'll take that," said Mike. He put his hand through the

handle on the scope case and twisted it free of my grip, like he was taking a delicate instrument from a small child. I buried the pain in my hand from the rude wrenching and watched Mike.

He gently lay the scope next to a Coleman lantern case. The space around it was equidistant from every other item. They were all like that—rifle case, ammo box, cleaning kit. I noticed an old, black Motorola bag phone next to the left wheel well. It sat at perfect right angles to the side of the truck; an even one-inch gap separated it from the spotting scope. Mike would have to drive back to town like my grandmother to keep them from sliding around. Then I remembered the hook tape. I lay my hand on the plastic ammo box and pushed it. It didn't budge. I picked up one corner and heard the familiar ripping sound of dozens of little hooks detaching from their pile mates. Everything in Mike's truck was Velcroed down to the nylon fabric bed of the Tahoe.

"What are you doing?" asked Mike. I pushed the box firmly back down, reattaching the hooks, and looked up at Mike. He was staring at me as if I'd just taken a dump in the trunk.

"Sorry," I said. "I've just never seen anything like that before."

"I don't like my stuff sliding around." He rose up on his toes for the tailgate. Once he got it, he brought it down hard and fast. I had to jump out of the way to keep from being pinned in the latch. The curly pigtail antenna for the car phone almost snapped my face.

"I haven't seen a bag phone like that in years." I said, "Does it still work?" Five years into the twenty-first century and Belmont still had no cell phone service. I hoped we never would.

"Yes. I use it when I'm traveling. I like the long range

of the old models," said Mike. He wrinkled his nose at me. "You ever take a bath?" He broke away and went to the front of the vehicle.

"I've been inside a dead elk."

"Lovely. You should clean yourself up."

"Thanks." I thought of something. "Hey, Mike, now that we've gotten all personal about my smell, I've been meaning to ask you about that wedding ring."

Mike stopped and looked at his left hand on the door handle. The thin ring glistened in the twilight.

"What about it?" he asked.

"Are you married? I've never seen you with anyone."

Mike didn't take his eyes off his hand. "I still consider myself married, yes."

"Does she?"

"Maybe," he said.

"Oh, shit, she's dead, isn't she?" I asked. "I'm sorry."

"That's okay," he said.

Mike opened the door and scaled the side of the truck. The massive vehicle was too tall for him to climb into without the help of a step mounted under the side panel. He pulled the door shut with the same force as the tailgate, started the big V8, and drove away.

Pancho laid his ears back and watched the monster from Detroit spit gravel and dust.

"Sheriff, dispatch, over."

I gripped the radio and removed it from my belt. The comfort of having my duty belt back buoyed my morale. "Go ahead, Jenny."

"Agent Mulder is here to see you."

"He didn't bring Scully?"

"No, Sir. Sorry."

"Then I ain't comin'."

"You want me to tell him that, Sheriff?"

"Negative, I'm on my way," I said. "You better clear out of there, Jenny, I smell like an antelope. A dead one."

JENNY HAD TAKEN MY JEST SERIOUSLY. AGENT RITTER sat alone in the department office, sipping scalded coffee and looking prim. His red cheeks and nose spoke of drinking or windburn. Probably the latter. He wore his English professor uniform—starched yellow oxford shirt under green wool sweater under tweed jacket with leather patches on the elbows. This time, however, he held a leather portfolio in his lap—the first evidence of written material I'd seen the agent carry. I removed his hat and Lands' End jacket from my peg by the door and hung my coat in its rightful place.

"Agent Ritter." I walked by his perch. "I didn't expect you back so soon. You find the terrorists, yet?"

"Possibly," said Ritter. He stood and followed in the wake of my ripeness, but was too polite to say anything. I was too tired to care.

I avoided my desk chair, not wanting to pollute the old fabric forever with dead elk. I stood in the middle of the floor. Agent Ritter extended his hand. I pulled mine out and showed him. Crusty, black-and-crimson flecks were embedded in the skin. Ritter put his hand back on his hip.

"Leonard Jorgensen. You know him?" he asked.

"Nope. We only have one Leonard in this town, but most folks affectionately call him Lenny. I affectionately call him a fuckhead. I intend to arrest him tomorrow."

"Would that be Lenny Leftwich?" asked Ritter. Once again, he used no notes, just the ones in his photographic head.

"Why, yes it would."

"His real name is Leonard Jorgensen. Leftwich is an alias." He noted my blank expression. "More like a nickname. He's not smart enough to have an alias."

"That sounds like Lenny. What do you want him for?"

"He blew up that hospital in Leavenworth."

"*Lenny Leftwich* is your terrorist?" I asked.

"We believe he is one of them," said Ritter, carefully. "We have been able to connect him to one of the bombings, so far."

"How?"

Ritter was forthcoming. "Well, it started with an anonymous tip." He turned and paced, delicate hands stroking his thick, gray mustache. "But not the usual phone call—a fax. Someone faxed a letter to our office in Denver. A letter Leonard Jorgensen wrote two years ago. It detailed each bombing—location, date, time, method."

"Like a plan?" I asked. "Lenny couldn't plan a bake sale."

"More like an operations order." He stopped pacing and drew a folded stack of copy paper from his black leather folder. He handed it to me. "I assume you are familiar with them."

I had read dozens of operations orders in my four years as an Army sniper. They all had the same format, cadence, and intent—a precise delivery of information for the purpose of eliminating America's enemies.

Lenny's letter was an abomination of the form. Instead of typing it, Lenny wrote the operations order in longhand on narrow-lined notebook paper. His cursive script looked like a sixth grader's gone mad. It even canted to the left, a ten-degree list to the port side, my father used to say.

Situation: The enemies of the Constitution continue to forsake the sacred document, but they have weakened in their vigilance. Now is the time to strike where they least expect, at their weakest of the herd . . .

High Value Targets include the post hospitals at Fort Huachuca, Fort Collins, Fort Leavenworth, Fort Riley . . .

The enemy's most likely course of action is to protect their hard, military targets—arms rooms, motor pools, ammunition depots. Hospitals provide targets of opportunity that will maximize the effect of our flaming sword, thrusting it deep into the hearts of the enemies of the Constitution . . .

Mission: The Minutemen will destroy the post hospital at Fort Carson, Colorado, 0504150900, using remote detonation of an explosive device in order to kill as many enemies of the Constitution of the United States as possible.

"April fifteenth of this year." I looked up. "Carson was the first one." Ritter nodded.

I scoffed. " 'The Minutemen.' What a crock."

Purpose: The purpose of the operation is to kill as many of the enemies of the Constitution of the United States of America as possible. The desired effect is to strike fear and terror into the enemy's heart, show him that his bloated federal government cannot defend against the hard steel of the Minutemen . . .

Concept of the Operation: We will accomplish this task by penetrating the post boundary at the main gate, flaunting their fruitless heightened security protocol. We will then move across the interior of the post to the Army Medical Center. We will deploy a mobile explosive device on the grounds of the post hospital in the vicinity of the emergency

*room entrance. We will then extract from the area of opera-
tions, exiting through another avenue, and take up a defensive position in the surrounding area. We will then detonate
our device, perform BDA, and return to base.*

"Do you know what BDA means?" I asked.

"We have not yet confirmed that acronym," said Ritter.

"Battle Damage Assessment—confirm or deny the destruction of the target. Standard post-mission task. I used
to do it all the time."

Ritter nodded.

"How do you know this is Lenny's handwriting?" I asked.

"He signed it."

"You're kidding." I flipped to the last page. Lenny's official signature block completed the order.

*Leonard Jorgensen
Master Sergeant
Sergeant at Arms/Operations Officer
The Minutemen*

"The Department of Defense has a record of Staff
Sergeant Leonard Jorgensen's signature," said Ritter. "Even
some of his script. The comparison was simple. It's Lenny."

"He was in the Army."

"Correct."

I should have realized that sooner. Armyspeak peppered Lenny's diction—he said "Roger" more than an air-
line pilot.

"Now he's master sergeant. I guess he promoted himself. When did you get this?" I asked.

"The transmission arrived at the communications office
six days before the Leavenworth bombing."

I checked my desk calendar—six days before Ritter had first visited.

"What took you guys so long?" I asked. "Your own office had this fax while you were here all by yourself in your little government sedan. I figured you would have roared out on a chopper, warrant in hand and Special Weapons team in tow. You didn't even want to talk to Lenny."

"The document was buried in a flurry of other communications items." Ritter employed the passive voice for his explanation—a typical use of bureaucracy obfuscation to hide blame, as if the little piece of paper had eluded capture.

"Uh-huh," I said. "Did you trace the originating number for the fax?"

"The letter was sent from Thomas Pitcher's office line." More passive voice.

"Whoa. Now, there's a wrinkle. What do you think that means?"

"It could mean anything," said Ritter. "Maybe Pitcher sent it himself, maybe it was his secretary or a client."

"Or his son," I said.

"Certainly. Anyone who had access to Pitcher's fax machine," said Ritter. "That person also has the original, here in Belmont."

"Sounds like someone setting up Lenny to take the fall. The guy has "patsy" tattooed on his forehead."

"That may be true, but the handwriting analysis is undeniable—Leonard Jorgensen, former sergeant, U.S. Army. Last assigned to Fort Riley, Kansas."

"Another Junction City boy." I said, "Must be the water in the Republican River." Tim McVeigh, the Oklahoma City bomber and martyr of the militia movement, had been assigned to Fort Riley. Junction City, Kansas fed off the Army post in the middle of the prairie.

"He's not alone, you know," I said. "He answers to someone else here in town. Someone local he calls 'Sir.' " I told him about the midnight encounter at the Halfmoon Lodge.

"That's why I didn't bring the cavalry, Sheriff. We want all of them, not just their scapegoat."

"And you can't have another Ruby Ridge," I said, "because you may be wrong on this one."

Ritter just looked at me, waiting.

"You want me to go get him for you," I said.

"You said so yourself, you were going to arrest him in the morning," he said. "That is quite convenient for my partner and I. We prefer a gradual response. No need for a big, public standoff."

"Your partner?"

"Agent Vilicek is quietly surveying Jorgensen's cabin as we speak."

"Through a rifle scope, no doubt."

Ritter smiled. "No, just binoculars."

"I hope he's careful," I said. "Rat Creek doesn't get many visitors."

"He will be."

I couldn't help feeling manipulated, but it made more sense for me to arrest Lenny under the pretense of his assault. That would allow the FBI to question him quietly in my own jail or transport him to Denver when necessary. Lenny would disappear from the valley, and few would notice or miss him.

"I have something that'll interest you," I said.

He raised his gray eyebrows and waited.

"Remember the tie-in you had with the explosion last year? The demolition that brought you here?" I asked. He nodded. I squatted down and popped the quick-release on the small lockbox that held the device Emmet had pulled from my car.

When I saw what was there, I froze, out of disbelief and a desire to keep my fingerprints to myself.

"Something wrong, Sheriff?" Ritter asked. He had moved behind me with undeniable law enforcement curiosity. "You had something to show me?"

"My Beretta," I said.

"Yes, I see that," said Ritter. "What's in the bag?" The weapon lay on top of the rolled-up brown grocery bag that held the C4.

"No. You don't understand," I said. "When I put the device in here this afternoon, the lockbox was empty. I thought I'd left my nine-millimeter at home."

"Well, it's in there now." I heard the snap of latex gloves behind me. I stood and turned, looking straight through an anxious Agent Ritter.

"I need to make an arrest," I said.

"What for?"

"Murder."

"I see," said Ritter. "Well, before you leave, can you give me a little background on the device?" He politely but firmly shouldered past me and withdrew both the weapon and the paper bag. He lay them on the desk. He carefully unrolled the bag and withdrew the C4 with both hands.

"Found it in my truck, attached to my starter," I said. "Actually, Emmet found it."

"Emmet?"

"He's an artist, a sculptor."

"And he also defuses unexploded ordnance?"

"He used to be a Green Beret," I said. Like that would explain it all.

"Right."

"You got another pair of those?" I nodded at his gloves. He mysteriously drew another pair out of his tweed pocket. I pulled them on. The talcum mixed with dried elk blood.

I safed my 9mm, dropped the magazine, and locked back the slide with the familiar move Sergeant Richter had taught me. A single round flipped out of the chamber and clattered onto my desk. Agent Ritter and I both looked at the brass-and-copper object as if a tiny spaceship had landed there.

Sergeant Richter had also taught me to keep the chamber clear.

After fieldstripping the Beretta, I held the short silver barrel up to the light and peered through it.

One other thing Richter had taught me was to clean my weapon before putting it away. Flecks of powder peppered the lands and grooves inside the barrel. The barrel was a mirror when I had touched it last. Someone had fired my weapon and put it away without cleaning it.

"I need to go," I said. I jerked off the latex gloves and tossed them in the trash. I wasn't looking forward to what I had to do next.

"Are you coming back?" asked Ritter.

"Yes," I said, "and I'll have someone with me."

Fourteen

ONLY FOUR PEOPLE KNEW THE COMBINATION TO the lockbox in the sheriff's locker, and two of them were dead. That left Jerry and me, and I would never put away a dirty, loaded weapon.

It was almost as if he wanted to get caught.

Night had dropped like a bucket of black paint over the valley. The dark comforted me, but then I noticed the change in the weather. It felt as though I'd walked out the door and into another state.

I'd heard of chinook winds—dry weather patterns descending from the western side of the mountains, warming as they slid down—but I'd never experienced them before. A warm wind born from the Pacific coast drove the bone-dry cold out of the valley. We'd skipped winter and gone right to spring.

This sense of unreality continued as I walked down dark, warm Main Street. I was going to arrest another trusted member of my department. At least I wouldn't have to shoot him, like the others.

The Pitcher house lay just a few blocks from downtown, but sweat gathered underneath my sheepskin coat before I was halfway there. I opened the coat and wiped the perspiration off my forehead. The only noise in our quiet town came from my reluctant feet and Willow Creek's constant patter. I crossed the bridge over the happy Willow and quickened my step. The warm chinook pushed me along.

It had been a few months since I'd last visited the yellow house on Baker Street. It was hard to imagine five souls living in the little cottage. Of course, only four lived there now—Jerry, his mother, his young wife, and the new baby. Their patch of lawn lay brown and dormant in the warm dark.

The wheelchair ramp was new. A fresh coat of white paint shone in the moonless night. I thought of Denver Petry's dilapidated ramp. This one was just the opposite, complete with skid tape and handrails. Its presence confused me. I walked around it and rang the doorbell. No one answered. I opened the screen door and knocked three times on the six-panel oak door. Jerry's Bronco and his wife's minivan sat in the driveway. I realized I hadn't seen my deputy in thirty-six hours.

I heard the bolt slide away and a chain rattle behind it, then the door opened slowly. A gray head, bent down with effort, appeared just above the doorknob. Mrs. Pitcher rolled back the door, one hand on the knob, the other turning the wheel on her chair. The new, coordinated movement consumed her focus and energy.

Mrs. Pitcher was ill and rarely left the cottage. I knew

that much. I didn't know her physical state had deteriorated to the point of confining her to a wheelchair. The pleasant woman looked up at me, unable to speak from the strain of opening the door. I stood there like an idiot.

"Sheriff Tatum," she finally said in a breathy, delicate voice, "how good of you to drop by. It has been a while. I'm sorry it took me so long to answer the door. The children are tending to the little one."

If she noticed that I had sweat like a pig and stank like a slaughterhouse, her refined manners buried any indication.

I slowly took one step into the small foyer, allowing Mrs. Pitcher to pivot her chair and inch toward the sitting room. The house smelled of tea, pot roast, and baby wipes, just like my Aunt Rennie's. I felt eleven years old again.

"Let me help you, Mrs. Pitcher." I awkwardly gripped the plastic handles.

"I'd appreciate it if you didn't," she said. Her voice had regained some firmness. "I cannot be a burden to anyone, especially my guests. I must learn to get around on my own. The children have enough on their hands with the little one." Her head bobbed and breath hissed with each tiny push. She finished her campaign across the tiny sitting room and turned to face me. The standard wheelchair swallowed her tiny frame. Her late husband was probably too cheap to buy one that fit.

Mrs. Pitcher wore black. She had added a tasteful touch of makeup, and her blue-white hair was sculpted elegantly around her face, as if she had just come from her husband's wake. She looked at me with a pleasant smile, but her pinched chest still heaved.

I remained in the foyer, hat in hand. I looked toward the kitchen, then up the narrow stairs to the second floor. I wasn't here to pay a social call.

I noticed two-inch paths cut in the thick white pile carpet of the front room. The twin tracks circled from the dining room and out to the kitchen.

Who laid white carpet in Belmont?

"Can I get you something to drink? Some cookies, maybe?" she asked. "You look hungry. I could heat up some of the things left over from the visitation. Marjorie Dunwater made the nicest Swedish meatballs." Two generations of diluted manners and forty years in Belmont had not tarnished this woman's hospitality. She put her fragile hands back on the wheels and took a deep breath.

"No, thank you, Ma'am." I held out a hand to stop her. "You stay put. I just need to grab my deputy and head back to the station." I thrust my dirty hands into my pockets to hide the blood and unclean nails. Better to have bad posture than poor hygiene in this woman's presence.

"Nonsense," she said, "you come with me." I knew better than to argue. My mama raised me right. I reached for the handles on her wheelchair.

"Hands off, Sheriff," she said.

Eyes in the back of her head, for God's sake. Were all mothers alike?

"I said, I need to learn to get around on my own. I've grown soft in my old age. At least now, I'll get a little exercise."

The woman had spirit as well as good manners. How the hell did Jerry turn out the way he did?

Thomas Pitcher had built the house long before his wife's imprisonment in a wheelchair, so the tall kitchen counters were inaccessible to the old woman. A raised platform lifted the floor and allowed her to reach the sink and other appliances. The smell of fresh paint and new decking lingered.

"Jerry made this for me." She started up the little ramp

from the dining room. She leaned forward and strained at
the mild incline. She breathed heavily around her words,
but kept going. "Just like the ramp out front. He's such a
good boy. And an excellent carpenter. I don't know where
he learned it. His father never taught him. Thomas never
lifted a hammer or a saw in his life."

She stretched for the teapot on the electric stove and
fussed with it.

"I hope you like tea," she said. "I have green decaf-
feinated, of course, and some very old Earl Grey."

"Either is fine, Ma'am. I'm more of a coffee drinker."

"We don't have coffee in this house," said Mrs. Pitcher.
"If we have guests, I send Jerry to Marjorie's with a thermos. Thomas has an ulcer, so we make tea." She put a hand
to her mouth, then recovered, filling the pot from the sink.
"Jerry never has coffee, either. Instead he used to drink six
Coca-Colas a day. It'll ruin his teeth, I tell him. Not anymore. He stopped drinking sugared soda when he lost all
that weight. I really don't know what he drinks now."

"He looks good," I managed.

Mrs. Pitcher filled the pot and set it back on the stove.
She cranked hard on the wheels of her chair to face me.

"What brings you by, Sheriff, some criminal matter?"

I shook off the irony. "Yes, Ma'am."

"Is someone here, Mama?" Jerry's voice came from
somewhere upstairs. I walked to the front room.

"Yes, Dear," Mrs. Pitcher called from behind me. "It's
the Sheriff. He says he needs you back at the station."

Jerry appeared at the top of the miniature staircase. He
looked like he'd just woken up from a nap. He wore green
sweatpants with the Colorado State emblem stitched to the
right thigh and a matching sweatshirt. A white tube sock
hung for dear life over the landing.

"Get suited up, Deputy Pitcher," I said. "Duty calls."

"Yes, Sheriff," said Jerry. He turned and disappeared. I hoped he would come back. Mrs. Pitcher joined me in the front room while the water boiled for tea I would not drink.

"I'm sorry for bustin' in like this so late at night, Mrs. Pitcher," I said.

She waved me off. "You do not need to apologize, Sheriff. It's not very late, and this town has needed active law enforcement for years. I sleep better knowing you and Jerry are on duty."

"Thank you, Ma'am." Now I really hated myself for the deception.

We made valiant but halting attempts at small talk, then Mrs. Pitcher came to the question I didn't want to answer.

"What progress have you made in apprehending my husband's murderer?"

I couldn't lie to this woman. "I am just about to make an arrest, Ma'am," I said, but I didn't meet her pale blue eyes, the same color as her son's. *You coward.*

"That is good news, Sheriff Tatum. Is that why you need Jerry?"

"Yes, Ma'am." The hat brim whirled in my hands. The irony came back, and so did Jerry. He thundered down the white-carpeted steps. I backed up to make room for him in the foyer.

"I'm ready," he said. He didn't look ready. Face unshaven, hair uncombed, body unwashed. His uniform, however, looked better than mine on a Monday morning. It still hung loosely from his skinny body—I needed to get him a uniform that fit. Two sharp creases ran down his shirt and trousers. The work of Mrs. Pitcher, younger or older, no doubt. Then I saw his boots—a muted shine in the soft light of the front room. Jerry shined his own shoes and probably pressed his own uniform, too, just like he'd prepared his father's business outfit for fifteen years. A man of contradictions was my deputy.

"Bye, Mom." Jerry shut the door and joined me out front. I had already moved halfway down the narrow flagstone walk.

"No coat?" I asked.

"It's warm out, didn't you notice? Chinook wind, I think they're called."

"I've only heard about them."

Jerry took off his cowboy hat and smelled the dry air. "I don't think we've had one since you came to town. We're pretty high up, so we don't get them that much. Happened once before when I was just a kid. What's that smell? You smell that? Smells like something died."

"That's me," I said. "Long story. I'll tell you when we get in my office."

I turned and started walking back to the sheriff's department. I knew Jerry would follow. My inner self cringed at the deception. It seemed cowardly to use my deputy's loyalty to draw him to the jailhouse. Then I remembered Thomas Pitcher's frozen body, reeking of his own urine.

"What's going on, Sheriff?" asked Jerry. "Why won't you tell me what's going on?"

I'd said nothing for two blocks.

"Something's come up in your father's murder," I said.

"Why don't you tell me now?"

"It would be better sitting in my office. Not on Main Street."

"Who's going to hear?" Jerry stretched out his arms at the empty sidewalks. He stepped out into the middle of Main. "We're all alone, Sheriff."

"Knock it off, Jerry," I said. "Get your ass back on the sidewalk."

"Yes, *Sir*." Jerry had found belligerence, now that his father was dead. I swallowed my desire to throw him through the plateglass window of Bernie's Hardware. I just needed to keep him moving toward the department.

Jerry stopped. I kept walking, hoping he'd follow. *Hope is not a method.*

"You think *I* did it," said Jerry. His voice stopped me and I turned around. I didn't want my back to this man, boy, deputy. We stood under the balcony of the Firehouse Bed and Breakfast, dark in the dim light from the lamp on the corner. I thought I could hear the snores of half a dozen hunters sacked out in the new bunks Max had installed for the season. Shadow hid Jerry's eyes.

We need more streetlights.

Jerry stood still, feet wide, hands clenched at his sides. We were close, just a few feet away, and I could smell his anxiety. Sweat glistened on his forehead and dark moons soaked the armpits of his uniform. It wasn't *that* hot.

Jerry slowly moved his right hand to the butt of his .45.
Oh, shit.

"You're taking me to jail," said Jerry. "Why didn't you just be a man and arrest me in front of my mother?"

"Take it easy, Jerry," I said. "And take your hand off your weapon."

Jerry looked down at his hand like it was another living thing. He stared at it for a long time, like a drug addict discovering the mystery of the human digit. Then he turned and ran.

I didn't bother yelling. The rapid cadence of his stride telegraphed his panic. I leaned forward and sprinted after him. Part of me knew it would end like this, but I wished that part had been a little more vocal.

The altitude in Belmont will render most folks out of breath in less than two hundred meters, even locals, but Jerry ran like a track star. Or a madman. Or a criminal. It could have been any of them. Either way, he moved as though his father's ghost were chasing him.

He ran straight down Main Street, past Chucks Orvis's shop, past Veteran's Memorial Park, past the Rio Grande Grocery. I stayed with him, but didn't gain. Every step jarred my broken ribs, and the sharp pain and tight tape forced me to take shallow breaths. I never realized how small our town really was until I ran through it at top speed. The dark buildings flicked by.

Jerry started flagging near the softball field at the south end of town, but so did I. His paced slowed, both by adrenaline depletion and the transfer from pavement to gravel. He started bobbing his head and pumping his arms, as if moving them would help him go faster. It didn't, but the glance over his shoulder did. He saw that I was still with him. With a high, panicked moan, he ran faster.

I couldn't remember the last time I had sprinted for more than one hundred meters. I suppose most cops focus their physical training on long sprints like this, anaerobic workouts designed to prepare themselves for chasing down criminals. We don't chase down criminals in Belmont.

A year ago, Jerry would've keeled over from exhaustion when we hit Ralph Munger's Rock Shop. The new Jerry was thinner and motivated. He ran across the softball field, duty belt bouncing on his narrow hips. In a sign of desperation, he unbuckled it and dropped his equipment in the dead grass of right field. He flipped his cowboy hat from his head. I jumped over his gear and remembered my own. I shucked the sheepskin coat and hat. I brushed my hand over the buckle of my duty belt, then hesitated. As much as I wanted to shed the added weight, I figured I would need it. I had learned my lesson at Farmer's Creek.

Now unburdened by the trappings of law enforcement, Jerry ran with new strength and abandon. He hopped the right field fence and let out a screech, but regained his pace and stumbled into the rows of little shacks and trailers on the south side of town, shaking his hands. I wondered what that was all about.

I put my hands on the four-foot chain-link fence and vaulted over. As I touched the metal, a hard shock snapped up my forearms.

"Shit!" I yelled out, I hoped not as wimpy-sounding as Jerry's girly scream. I actually stopped the chase in alarm and looked at the outfield fence. Had someone electrified it for some bizarre reason? A strange image of cattle grazing on Joe Bender's manicured grass flashed into my head, then I turned and went after Jerry. My hands tingled as if I'd slept on them all night.

If it was dark on Main Street, the trailer park was a dim void by comparison. Dogs barked as we passed them on the narrow dirt lane running through the low-rent section of Belmont. Many shacks had been abandoned when their occupants had moved up to the new starter houses on the western slope above town. Only the occasional porch light or forgotten television lit our chase.

We emerged from the trailer park onto the flat watershed of Willow Creek. The town had built a walking path around the broad gravel plain that once carried mine sluice out of silver holes in the canyon. Jerry ran down the path, but I couldn't imagine that he had anywhere to go. The only destinations in front of him were the airport, the river, and Elk Hollow RV park. He would find no help at any of them. He was just running, running away from Belmont.

We had sprinted at top speed for over half a mile and Jerry's strength was fading. His head-bobbing started again, and he pushed through the pain, but it would do him no good. I was gaining. Aside from the heavy gear pounding my hips and chapping my ass, this race was familiar to me. I could stay with Jerry for hours, if necessary, but it wasn't going to be necessary. I started reeling him in; every third stride gained a step on my quarry.

What would I do when I caught up to him? Pull my weapon? Use harsh language? Something about Jerry's demeanor told me that these methods would be ineffective. I didn't have long to ponder. When I was at arm's length, I grabbed him by the shirt collar and started yanking him down. He shoved my hand away and ran harder.

"Goddamnit, Jerry," I huffed. "Stop this shit." He grunted again and kept going.

The gravel trail ran along the embankment of Highway 149. Twin sewage ponds sat black and calm to our left, still unfrozen with treated water.

I never played football in high school, but I'd watched enough Iowa State football games to know that I needed to wrap him up. I took two hard strides and caught Jerry around the waist. He threw up his arms and fell to the left. We tumbled over the bank of the larger sewage pond. My broken ribs screamed with the impact. As we fell, a small part of my mind wondered how deep they were.

About two feet to the bottom with a ten-inch layer of sludge, I found out immediately.

I struggled to regain my feet in the tepid water, but the pain in my side blinded me and slowed my recovery. I was completely submerged in sewer water and slime. I squeezed my eyes and mouth shut. Jerry was quicker and bigger. After rolling down the bank, Jerry and I reversed positions, and he ended up on top of me. Jerry put his knees on my chest and broke my grip around his waist. I tried to slither through the slime and get out from under his weight, but he didn't move. Instead, he shifted, centering his knees. His hands found my head and kept it under. Lances of exquisite pain laced around my torso. My own deputy was going to drown me.

Although I kicked and squirmed underneath him, that just made me sink deeper into the filth. He'd lost a lot of weight in the last year, but Jerry still had a forty-pound advantage over me. Tiny stars crept into the periphery of my vision. My arms and legs got heavy. I told my sinking self that it was the water, or the sludge, but it was really lack of oxygen. Soon I would pass out, then my autonomous nervous system would trigger a deep breath, drawing in two lungfuls of treated sewage water and bottom slime, and then I would die.

Fifteen

Y OU CAN STILL MOVE YOUR ARMS, YOU ASSHOLE.
Who has the gun? Or did you lose it again?

I could move my arms. My right hand slid to my hip, so
slowly it seemed to drift. I felt the rubber Pachmayr grips
of my .45. Still in slow motion, I unsnapped the release and
withdrew the weapon. Stars dominated the blackness in my
eyes, but there was gray at the edges. Hypoxia threatened.

How was I going to work the action and get a bullet into
the chamber? I would need my other hand, but Jerry's big
body still crushed my sternum. I would have to fake it.

I thrust the gun through two feet of water, guessing
where Jerry's head would be. The cool night air tingled on
the back of my hand. I felt the soft flesh under his chin and
pressed the barrel deep into it. For a sickening moment, I
thought he would call my bluff, but then I felt his weight

shift, then release. I burst my head through the turgid surface of the pond and took a massive breath, but kept the barrel of my .45 jammed in the pocket of Jerry's throat.

I blinked water, sludge, and the effects of hypoxia out of my eyes. Thrusting the barrel even farther into Jerry's throat, I wiped my face with my hand and stood. The movement and resulting head rush finally cleared the gray and black, and I looked at my pathetic deputy. He remained on his knees in the pond, head tilted back by the force of my .45.

"You son of a bitch," I said. "You were trying to kill me." My words spat particles of green slime onto his sad face.

"No, I wasn't, Sheriff." He made weak choking sounds from the press of metal against his larynx. Tough. "I just wanted to slow you down, so I could get away."

"Get away where, Jerry?" I asked. "Where were you going to run? Alamosa?"

He didn't answer. I eased up on his neck. Only his head and shoulders rose above the water. I thought about his hands and pressed the barrel back in.

"Why did you run?" I asked.

"Why did you chase me?" *Cough.*

"I needed to arrest you."

"Why?" he yelped.

"Resisting arrest, assault on a law enforcement officer, attempted homicide," I ticked off the counts, "and homicide."

"I didn't kill my father," said Jerry. He started shivering. The chinook made the valley abnormally warm, but this wasn't Flordia. The water rippled around his quivering body.

"Yes, you did," I said. "And you did it with my own Beretta. Did you think *maybe* I wouldn't notice it missing, then reappear? You didn't even clean it."

He said nothing.

I thought for a moment. "Holy shit. You killed Wendy with it, too, didn't you? That was you on Farmer's Creek Canyon this morning."

His eyes shifted rapidly back and forth. I could almost hear him thinking, but he had stopped talking. Smart of him.

I had had enough of this shit. "Get up, Jerry. You're going to jail."

"I'm not going," he said. He wouldn't look at me. "I didn't do anything."

"I said get up. I'm freezing my ass out here, and I smell like shit. I don't have time for your whining."

He didn't move. Leaving the barrel pressed against his soft neck, I chambered a round. The dull click of heavy gunmetal got his attention. His looked at me, eyes wide. Then he realized I was serious. Why did it take him this long?

He stood, arms clutched around his shuddering body, and walked out of the pond. I gave him a few steps, then joined him on the gravel trail. I kept Jerry ahead of me this time, all the way back to the station.

Agent Ritter heard us enter and poked his head out of my office door. We must have been quite a sight, my deputy and I—Jerry shivering and cowering, me loaded down with all of our gear, both of us soaking wet and smelling faintly like a truck-stop bathroom. I nodded to Ritter, as if to say: *We do this all the time, here in Belmont. I'll be with you in a minute.*

Slamming the cell door on my own deputy evoked less drama than I thought it would. I was probably just too tired to appreciate it. Jerry bypassed the neatly made cot— hospital corners courtesy of Jenny Lange—and chose the concrete floor instead. He put his back to the wall and slid down, eyes staring off at the midpoint of nothing. I left him to his shivering and his father's ghost.

"Was that your deputy?" asked Agent Ritter when I returned to my office. He sat in my guest chair. The brown bag with the explosive inside rested innocently on his lap, like a big cat. "And your murderer?"

"Suspect," I corrected him. I stood in the center of the room and crossed my arms, for warmth as much as an attempt to regain some of my dignity in front of this man.

"I see. Well." Ritter stood. "If you don't mind, I will take this with me. The lot numbers on the C4 are in the same range as the explosive residue we've found at three of the hospital bombings." This was a windfall, a key tie-in to their terrorists. Things in Belmont were about to get very busy.

"You found all that out sitting in my office?" I asked.

"Well, the lot numbers are clearly stamped into the packaging. We've already traced the lots from previous events." He probably had the number ranges memorized.

"You still want me to pick up Lenny in the morning?" I asked.

"Absolutely. This connection does not change our course of action. You will bring in Jorgensen, then we will take it from there. How does seven o'clock sound?"

"Sounds fine. For what?"

"Agent Vilicek has observed Mr. Jorgensen's sleeping habits. Our target normally sleeps until at least ten a.m. Seven o'clock will find him drowsy and unalert."

"Or surprised and agitated," I said. Ritter just looked at me.

"Seven is fine," I said.

"Excellent. I will meet you here at six, then accompany you to the arrest."

I gave him a stupid look. I didn't care anymore. "I thought you wanted this done quietly."

Ritter shrugged. "In case things go badly, we can be there to assist."

"Take over, you mean."

"We hope it does not come to that."

"Hope is not a method," I mumbled, staring at the floor.

"What was that?" asked Ritter.

"Nothing. Was there anything else? I need to get cleaned up." I walked to the door. Ritter took the hint and got up.

"See you in the morning, Sheriff Tatum." He tucked the bag with the explosive device under his arm, put on his hat and coat, and left the building.

And then there was one. I was the last official member of the Mineral County sheriff's department. Two were dead, one was in jail.

I had a long night ahead of me. I couldn't leave Jerry by himself in the cell, like a sick dog at the vet. I couldn't call in anyone to rotate shifts. I would have to stay with him all night. I leaned on the door frame and stared at the empty front office.

"You are dripping all over your waxed and buffed floor," came a voice from the darkness. "Joe Bender will not be happy."

"You're up late. Making another house call?"

Dr. Ed emerged from the shadows of the back hall, just outside my peripheral vision. I wasn't using it, anyway, and I was too exhausted to be startled.

"I saw the sheriff and his deputy racing down Main Street," he said. "I wanted to see what all the fuss was about."

"You are nosy. I was hoping no one saw that little episode."

"I miss very few things in Belmont." Dr. Ed wrinkled

his nose. "I assume you are going to clean yourself up, then tell me everything."

Unlike Jerry, I had two extra uniforms in my locker, along with an olive green Army-issue wool sweater. After ten minutes of getting peed on by weak water pressure, I stepped out of the department shower, cleaner and warmer, but still smelling faintly of dead elk and sewage. Dr. Ed pretended not to notice. I cinched my evil clothes into a blue nylon laundry bag and tossed the whole mess into my locker. The coroner's pipe smoke and my Marlboro Reds covered the odor, as did the Coors longnecks from my office fridge. I fieldstripped my .45 on the desk and cleaned the slime out of it while catching him up on the day's events.

He puffed a blue cloud of Captain Black over his head until I finished. I lit another Red off the butt of the first. Jenny wasn't around to give me trouble about smoking in my office.

"Did you find Wendy?" he asked.

"Nope."

"Do you think that her disappearance and Pitcher's murder are related?"

"I think everything in this town is related," I said.

"You consider Jerry's behavior a sign of guilt," he said.

"That's correct. Don't you?"

He puffed some more and grunted.

"You know, Sheriff." He took off his spectacles and set them on my desk, trading up for his beer. "There may be another reason why Deputy Jerry was acting so strangely tonight."

"You mean, besides guilt and fear of getting caught?"

"Yes," said Dr. Ed. "Did you notice the abrupt change in the air temperature?"

I rolled my eyes. "I know you think I'm not observant, Dr. Ed, but I do pick up on stuff like the weather."

Dr. Ed ignored me and waved his pipe stem at the ceiling. "The Snow-eating Winds, taking their name from the Chinook Indians who once lived along the Columbia River. One of three varieties of katabatic wind, which means a breeze that flows from high elevations down to lower ones. Besides the obvious physical warming effects on the environment, chinook winds cause other secondary changes. I've heard they can electrify metal objects."

I leaned my face in my hand and listened to the lecture. No point in stopping him—I had all night. At least that explained the shock I'd received from the right-field fence.

He continued, "Chinook winds are also known to cause anxiety and irritability, in animals as well as people."

"Why?" I asked.

"Who knows? I'm not a psychologist."

I sat back in my chair. "Here's what I think, Dr. Ed. Jerry gets it in his head to kill his father. They go up to the Halfmoon Ranch for a week of father-son hunting. As usual, Thomas Pitcher ignores him, but Jerry follows his dad to the deer stand. Jerry ambushes him there, ties him up, and keeps him alive for three days in the freezing weather. He pulls the trigger on his dad, sees me, and takes off, but not too far. He returns to the scene, along with everyone else, and almost gets away with murder."

Dr. Ed closed his eyes and nodded slowly. Then he opened his eyes. "What finally made you arrest him?"

"Multiple witnesses saw him in the area while his father was missing."

"No hard evidence?"

"I went back to the scene this morning and dug out the

bullet—nine-millimeter Luger, not the forty-five from his father's Colt."

"How does that tie in?" asked Dr. Ed. "Does Jerry own a nine-millimeter?"

I shrugged. "Not anymore. He didn't need one—he used my backup gun, the nine-millimeter Beretta I keep here in the office. It was missing this morning. I thought I'd moved it myself, but when I came back this evening, it was in the lockbox, fired and dirty. I sure as hell didn't take it out and put it back. No one else has the combination to the safe, not even Jenny."

Dr. Ed sucked on his pipe, found it cold, and tamped out the cake in my Iowa State Cyclones ashtray. He filled the bowl from a worn leather pouch and lit up. Satisfied with the new smoke, he asked a question:

"You were the first person to find Thomas Pitcher dead, correct?"

"You know that."

"And he was killed with your weapon?"

"I suspect so, yes," I said. "I haven't sent it off for tests yet."

"You have no witnesses to the events on Farmer's Creek Trail, the first shooting or the second?"

"No, just me."

"And you were the only person to see Wendy's body in the gulch."

"Me and whoever killed her."

He raised his eyebrows and pointed his pipe at me. "The evidence could indicate that you are the murderer."

I blinked. "You sound like Jerry."

He put his pipe back between his teeth. "But you know I am right."

I leaned forward in my chair. The old wood and iron screeched in the quiet room. "I know you're full of shit. Maybe that's what you're smoking."

Dr. Ed chuckled, shifting his pipe from one side of his mouth to the other. "Now, don't get defensive, Sheriff. I know you did not shoot the infamous Thomas Pitcher nor the vivacious Wendy Schnuck. I am just trying to show you how it could look from another perspective. You may have implicated and incarcerated the only person capable of arresting you for the crime. How convenient."

He was right, of course. Out here in this remote valley in the San Juan Mountains, Jerry and I were the only law enforcement in the county. If I wanted to kill someone, making it look like my deputy did it would be the best way to get away with murder.

"You see how it looks?" asked Dr. Ed. "Now, please understand that I am probably the only person in town with a mind devious enough to think that way about you. The residents love and trust you. You are Belmont's Boy Scout. You are a war hero. You saved them from the Belmont Sniper. You cleaned up the meth labs. You ride around on your horse and tip your hat to the ladies. You pay your dues at the Halfmoon Gun Club and shoot only mature bucks. They love you in this town. No one will think twice about your arrest of Jerry Pitcher, not even his own mother."

"But you did," I said.

"I told you, I have a devious mind. You need me to play devil's advocate."

"Do you think I have the right man?" I asked.

He tilted his head back and blew smoke at the ceiling. "In your position, I would have done the same thing. Pitcher the Younger certainly has not acted innocently of late. Given his proximity to the murder scene and access to your backup weapon, it makes sense that you arrested him."

"You didn't answer my question, Dr. Ed."

He smiled at me. The wrinkles radiated out from his eyes, but he kept his lips tight around the pipe stem.

Sixteen

D<small>R. E</small>D IGNORED MY PROTESTS AND INSISTED ON sharing the watch with me. He even took the first shift. I curled up on the tight Army cot in my office and slept for six blissful hours, rolled up in my poncho liner like a tired soldier.

Six hours?

I sat up with a start, not believing the luminous dial on my watch. The creaking cot reminded me that I had slept at the department, but slept way too long. Dr. Ed must have fallen asleep on his watch. Agent Ritter would be here in an hour.

Ill-prepared prepared to deal with fluorescent tubes at five a.m., I dressed by the gentle light of my desk lamp and stalked down the back hall to Dr. Ed's office. A layer of blue haze hovered near the ceiling.

I found Dr. Ed tying flies at his desk. Little piles of Parachute Adams, Olive Duns, and Stonefly Nymphs lay in a circle of light on the blotter. He looked up at me over the top of magnifying lenses.

"You are up. Good. I just brewed a fresh pot in the silver bullet. Not as strong as you like it, but beggars can't be choosers."

"You let me sleep too long," I said. "We were supposed to split the night."

"Nonsense. You needed your rest. I'm not the one who's going to arrest Lenny Leftwich for the FBI today."

"Is there anything in this town you don't know?"

He just smiled and snipped the last bit of elk hair from the caddis locked in the vice.

"Did our prisoner make any noise last night?" I asked.

"Nothing. But some time in the night, he decided that the floor was too cold and curled up on the bed."

"So you checked on him."

"Once or twice."

He swept each pile of flies into its appropriate box and unclamped the vice from the edge of his desk. "Well, now that you are among the living, I am off to coax some break-fast out of Eunice, then off to bed."

"Thanks again for the extra sleep, Dr. Ed."

"Think nothing of it." He waved me off. "Where are you going to put Lenny? There is no more room at the inn." We had only one cell at the department.

"They'll just have to shack up," I said. Dr. Ed chuckled all the way out the door.

JENNY LANGE ARRIVED PROMPTLY AT SIX. I TOLD HER about our newest guest in the cell.

"Jerry killed his father?" she asked.

"That's what it looks like," I said.

Her eyes went wide. "Wow, that's huge." And that was it. She accepted the new reality and took her seat in the radio room, fresh coffee, bran muffin, and microphone at the ready.

"Hey, Jenny." I leaned on the narrow door. "What do you know about Mike Stanford's wife?"

She looked up at me, slowly chewing her muffin. I could see the gossip in her emerge.

"It's so sad. They both died," she said, blinking slowly. "He's all alone now. Doesn't even try to meet anyone else."

"Both?"

"His wife and their little baby," she said. "They were trying to have one for years, and when they finally did, she died having it, the baby, too."

Mike hadn't mentioned a child and neither had Dr. Ed. "This all happen here?"

"No, no." She shook her head. "He was alone when he came to Belmont. Like he was starting over again."

"Does everyone know this story?" I asked. "I mean, is it common knowledge?"

"Pretty much," said Jenny. She turned away from me and powered up her radio system. Gossip time was finished, along with her muffin.

"Agent Ritter is waiting for you out front. He's smoking," she said.

"I like him already," I said. Jenny snorted.

I liked him even more when he handed me a hot paper cup.

"Ms. Dunwater makes a mean latte." Ritter slurped between drags on a Camel.

"I wouldn't know. Lattes give me the shits," I said. "And

if Marge caught you calling her 'Ms.' the same thing might happen to you."

Ritter laughed and sucked on his cigarette. He wore his signature green felt hat with the little feather in the band. He seemed relaxed this morning, like he was trying too hard to show the small-town Sheriff how calm and collected a federal agent could be.

"What's up with the weather?" asked Ritter. "Froze my tail off last time I was up here, but now I don't even need my jacket."

"Chinook winds," I said. I was tired of talking about our katabatic anomaly. *Okay, it's warm, let's get on with our lives.*

"I see. Are you ready?" he asked.

"I was born ready," I said. "Let's take my truck." I was eager to confront my fear about it blowing up on me. That, or I didn't want to reveal my hesitation to Agent Ritter. I walked over to the Bronco.

Ritter didn't move. "Don't you think we should take my sedan?"

I looked at him. "Don't you think *maybe* Lenny will suspect something when I step out of your secret-agent-mobile?"

Ritter pursed his lips, but said nothing. I guess that meant he agreed.

We got into my Bronco and I pushed the key in the ignition. Ritter put a hand on my arm before I cranked the engine.

"Aren't you a bit concerned, Sheriff?" he asked. "I mean, that was real C4 you gave me yesterday."

"Are you sure about Lenny?" I asked.

"Yes."

"And your man has had eyes on him all night?"

"We rotated shifts, but Agent Vilicek is conducting surveillance at the moment."

"And has Lenny left the building?"

"No."

"Then we should be all right." With that, I turned the key.
The engine turned over and started. We didn't blow up.

I looked over at Agent Ritter. I hadn't noticed how short
he was until I saw him in the truck—the crown of his hat
didn't even brush the Bronco's ceiling. He sat rigidly in the
front seat and stared straight out the windshield, knees
clamped together. He gripped his leather notebook for dear
life. His color nearly matched the silver hair on his head.
Good. Had to shake him up a little.

The chinook had driven away the clouds, and the Rio
Grande Valley lay poised for a brilliant morning show.
Already, the rounded top of Bristol Head glowed a faint
orange. At its foot, deep in the watershed of Shallow
Creek, the green rooftops of Dana Pratt's ranch gathered
the approaching dawn. We rode in silence through the
morning twilight. The day was only a hint of warmth and
light.

That hint hadn't reached Rat Creek Canyon, yet, and I
wasn't sure it ever did. The residents of Rat Creek called it
a canyon to make themselves feel better, but to me it re-
sembled a shallow trench. The narrow run dribbled south
from the continental divide and provided little moisture for
green things. Gravel, sand, and scree were more prevalent
than the sparse clumps of scrub juniper and river willow.
Homesteaders squeezed their cabins between the single-
lane road and the stream. Things hadn't improved much in
Rat Creek since the miners had left it.

"Please stop on the next hill," said Ritter. "I have to contact Agent Vilicek."

I stopped. Ritter pulled an earbud out of his jacket and screwed it in. Then he started talking to his sleeve.

"Eagle Two, this is Eagle One. We are en route. Acknowledge." Ritter and his partner used cool call signs.

"Eagle Two, this is Eagle One. Over." This went on for at least five minutes. We idled on top of a short rise in the terrain, in plain sight of at least three of Lenny's neighbors. No doubt they had already let him know we were coming. At least their communication worked.

"Maybe he fell asleep," I said.

"Federal agents do not fall asleep on surveillance."

"Right. You want me to turn around?"

"No," said Ritter. "This has no impact on your part of the operation. Proceed with your arrest."

I didn't much care for Ritter giving me orders in my own county. I drove up the trench and stopped fifty meters from Lenny's lot.

It was the last shack on the block. The east wall of Rat Creek Valley thrust out a low mound of gray slag, wedging Lenny's lot between the stream and the west wall. A few miserable cottonwoods and patches of river willow did their best to add life to the spot, but the attempt was futile. Dry rivulets of brown silt rippled through his narrow front yard. A rickety footbridge made from an old pallet lurched across the icy trickle of Rat Creek. Next to the house lay the woodpile, and it was literally a pile, not the neat stack of spilt fuel proudly displayed, cord by cord, around the valley. A young mule deer, four years short of trophy status, hung gutted from an H-frame made out of old railroad ties. His dark red gash turned toward our approach.

The cabin made no attempt to look the part. Cheap, white aluminum siding hung limply on the cabin walls, dusted gray by wind and oxidation, like liver spots. Black shingles scattered across the low, sloping roof. The front porch was a concrete block. Two shaded windows hung crooked on either side of the aluminum screen door. A weathered rack of mule deer antlers and skull were nailed above the door frame. A scalp of gray hair still clung to the white bone.

Mike Stanford's white Tahoe and Lenny's red Ford pickup were parked, one behind the other, in the space of dirt next to the house.

Ritter took a breath and lifted his sleeve to his face, but hesitated, then set his arm back down in his lap. He adjusted the earpiece, as if doing that would help him hear the reports from his silent partner.

"You didn't mention Mike Stanford being here," I said.

"Mr. Leftwich was alone at our shift change last night," said Ritter to the windshield.

"Well, he ain't alone, now. Where's your OP?" I asked.

"OP?"

"Observation Post."

"Up there." Ritter pointed about halfway up the west side of the valley.

"That's a steep climb, even for you physically fit federal agents." I craned my neck to look. "You must look straight down on Lenny's cabin. I figured you'd set up on the other side."

"Which is exactly why we chose that particular location," said Ritter. "Proceed." He extended his hand toward the windshield.

"How the hell did you guys get up there without Lenny or his neighbors knowing?" I asked, still looking up the slope. "You have a chopper hidden over in Miner's Creek?" Ritter didn't answer. He just flicked his hand toward the windshield again.

I didn't move. "This is getting complicated, Agent Ritter. We don't have eyes on the target. We don't know his disposition. And now, we have at least one other civilian on site."

Ritter stared straight out the windshield. "This is not a crack house, nor is it a hostage situation. You are the local sheriff, paying a visit to one of his miscreant constituents. Considering the run-in you had two nights ago, I assume he is expecting you."

"You assume too much, and I guaran-fucking-tee you he's expecting me, the way we just rolled up in here, stopping along the way, giving his neighbors plenty of time to call him." I pointed to the thirty-year-old telephone pole made of local ponderosa, hidden in the cottonwood stand. A single stand of wire ran up the valley and terminated at the corner of Lenny's cabin.

"And?" he asked. The man was infuriating. I put the truck in gear and approached the cabin.

But I didn't stop right in front of it.

"What are you doing?" asked Ritter, finally looking at me. "You just drove by the residence."

"I'll get there," I said, and kept going.

I drove past Lenny's lot and continued up the mountain. Once through the clusters of little shacks, Rat Creek Valley transformed into a wide, stunning plateau, as if trying to make up for its tackiness downstream. I found a spot and turned around.

"I have my reasons for not stopping right in front of Lenny's cabin," I said.

"And they are?" asked Ritter.

"First, we've already lost the element of surprise. Maybe he sees us driving by and will think we're just driving by. Lenny isn't a deep thinker—once we're out of sight, I have a pretty good suspicion that we'll be out of mind, as well. Second, I feel cramped down there. I'm more comfortable with a little standoff."

"That's it?" asked Ritter.

"No."

"What's your third reason?"

"I don't want to get out of the truck exposed to Lenny's front door," I said.

Ritter caught on immediately. "And if we're pointed downhill, I would have that honor."

"You aren't getting out, anyway, right?"

We rolled to a stop forty meters uphill from the cabin.

"Jenny, this is the sheriff," I spoke into my radio.

"Roger, Sheriff."

"I am at the Leftwich residence. Agent Ritter is with me. I am about to bring in Lenny."

"Have fun, Sheriff."

"One more thing, Jenny, for your log," I said. "Mike Stanford's vehicle is parked in the driveway. I assume he is with Lenny."

"Got it, Sheriff." Jenny signed off.

"Well, no use waiting around, give him time to bug out." I jammed on my Resistol and opened the door. "Watch your step, if you get out. Rat Creek is ice cold year-round."

"I wasn't planning on getting out," said Ritter. "You can handle this on your own, I assume."

"Now, there you go assuming again. It's not like I can call for backup. I'm fresh out of deputies, but I can handle Lenny Leftwich."

I did my easy sheriff's shuffle toward the cabin. Mike Stanford stood like a linebacker in the middle of the road, arms crossed, feet planted, waiting for me. I hadn't even seen him come out.

"What are you doing here, Stanford?" I called out. So much for being cool, keeping the situation nonconfrontational. Why couldn't I have just said, "Good morning?" or "Hey, Mike, how's it hangin'?"

I watched the shaded windows of the cabin for movement.

"Having coffee with Leonard," said Mike. "I should ask you the same thing."

"Is Lenny here?"

"He's inside." Mike stood up on his toes and looked over my shoulder. "Who's that you brought along, Agent Ritter?"

"That's not your concern. He's just along for the ride." I am a shitty liar. Mike stayed up on his toes.

"What interest does the FBI have with our little town?" Mike rocked back down on his heels and raised his eyebrows.

"He likes to see the fall color. Now let's go talk to Lenny."

"You are here to arrest him, not just talk."

"Very good, young Skywalker. You win the Rat Creek perceptive award." I moved toward the cabin.

Mike sidestepped into my path. He was quick.

"You have exactly two seconds to get out of my way before I take you down and cuff you in the dirt," I said.

Mike held up his hands, palms out. "Please, Sheriff, I am only here to keep the peace."

"That's my job, Mike. Get out of the way."

"Would you allow me to bring Leonard out and turn him over to you?"

"What, are you his lawyer, now?"

"I am just a friend. If Leonard is at odds with the law, he should stand and answer for his actions." He looked at me like my old company commander used to when he was about to pass judgment. "In addition, you have a reputation for applying deadly force in your former and current occupation. I want to ensure we all get through this alive."

"Jesus Christ, Mike, don't be so dramatic. Just tell Lenny to get his fat ass out here, so I can take him to jail."

Mike nodded. He hopped over the bridge and yanked open the screen door, disappearing inside the shaded cabin with the liver spots.

I heard a thunk behind me. Ritter stepped out of the Bronco and straddled Rat Creek. He was talking to his sleeve again, desperate to reach the partner on the ridge.

The first shot shattered the agent's wrist. The second destroyed his hand. The third and fourth exploded in his chest. The rapid rifle fire roared a single echo through the shallow canyon, then died just as quickly.

Seventeen

RITTER HELD HIS RUINED LEFT HAND AND STUDIED the red blots on the starched yellow of his shirt. His eyes drifted to the west ridge for the partner who'd failed him. Then he fell face first into creek.

I dove into the icy run, seeking the life-giving dead space in the field of fire. The shots came from the direction of the cabin, but I was uncertain if the shooter was inside or up the ridge. Didn't matter. I crawled up the rocky streambed.

The water ran red around me. I panicked and flipped over on my back. No holes in my clothing. I looked upstream. Ritter lay still in the cold flow. He bled a lot. I tried to pretend that the water wasn't a little warmer.

I scrambled up the remaining dozen meters and crawled over the agent's body. Grabbing him by the shoulders, I dragged him out of the creek, taking shelter behind the

Bronco. Bullets skipped around me. The creek had washed away most of the blood from his body, but twin trickles of fresh red renewed the stains on his yellow shirt. I checked his pulse. He was graveyard dead. Unless I could send a smoke signal to his partner on the ridge, I was on my own.

I popped the back hatch of the Bronco, yanked my Ruger No. 1 from its case, and stuffed a box of .30-06 shells into my jacket pocket. Five shots peppered my front windshield and upraised hatch, but none penetrated. I guessed Lenny had reloaded.

That was the first time I put a name to the lead. Bullets tend to have their own lives until you remember that someone has to launch them.

I considered my adversary and felt much better about my situation. Lenny was a pretty good shot—Ritter was living . . . dead . . . proof of his proficiency, but it was still Lenny. He had failed to put a bullet in me while I dawdled in his kill zone, and now I had my rifle in a covered position.

Lenny kept shooting my truck. The front grill took the brunt of his volleys, as did both front tires. That was fine with me. Of course, someone would have to give me a ride back to the station.

There was a pause in the rifle fire while Lenny reloaded. I sidled backward toward the top of the rise, keeping the vehicle between me and the cabin. Magazine full, Lenny started up again on my windshield. The safety glass fell inward, and he had a clear shot through the interior of the Bronco. A few bullets snicked at my feet, but they did nothing but increase my rate of climb. I turned and lurched in three-point scramble into the defilade, rifle cradled in one hand.

Lenny was mine. I now had the freedom of movement to reposition, pinpoint Lenny's location, and take him out.

You have a reputation for applying deadly force, Mike's words echoed in my head.

Fuck him. He ain't in the crosshairs, Sergeant Richter's voice countered.

The next round of bullets shattered the light bar on my roof. Lenny had no idea where I was, or if he'd hit me or not.

The decisive point of any operation happens when you gain the distinct advantage over your target. When you know he can do nothing to stop you and he can do nothing to keep from dying. Get to that point as quick as you can, Ranger.

This move was decisive. Now I had the advantage. Now Lenny was going to die.

Scrambling low around the back side of the slope, I found a position quartering away from the cabin. I could see the front yard and north side of the house. Knowing Lenny's simple mind, I figured he would look for me directly out front, and the sun would illuminate him perfectly in my crosshairs.

I lay in the prone and shook a pocketful of bullets into my coat. I dropped the falling block chamber of my single-shot Ruger and slid a warm brass cartridge into the breech. The familiar, comfortable movements of preparing for the shot calmed my nerves. My breathing slowed and deepened. Inexplicably, throughout the ambush, my cowboy hat remained screwed down on my scalp. I carefully removed the Resistol and set it behind me.

I felt like I was shooting in an alley. Fewer than one hundred meters separated my position from Lenny's front porch. Behind me, the terrain stretched into a broad valley, but the lower watershed of Rat Creek narrowed as it descended from the continental divide. Lenny's cabin lay at the transition point, still in the trench, but close enough to the final rise to provide a nice, but tight, field of fire. I had never been to Ruby Ridge, but it might have looked something like Rat Creek.

Lenny's lot lay still. The poached mule deer turned gently in the warm wind. Lenny had ceased his blasting of my Bronco, out of either bullets or interest. His position eluded me. The air felt close and tense.

"Lenny, Lenny, Lenny," I whispered to myself, "I got you now, Fat Boy. You should have killed me first." I considered calling out to him, but decided that would be futile and dangerous. Futile, because Lenny was an idiot. Dangerous, because Agent Ritter was stone cold dead.

You have a reputation for applying deadly force.

The irony of Mike's judgment struck me again, and my will quivered. I should just wait it out. Maybe Mike could talk some sense into him, convince Lenny to give himself up. Ever since Ruby Ridge, the FBI just surrounded their holdouts and waited. I could do that. I had the patience. I didn't have to kill him.

Then I looked at the lifeless body of Agent Ritter, at the pulp of his left hand on his bloody chest, and my backbone returned. Lenny had already chosen his fate when he pulled the trigger on a law enforcement officer. Lenny wasn't leaving this canyon alive, and Mike had better stay out of the way.

I called Jenny.

"Jenny, this is Tatum, come in."

"Go, Sheriff."

"Well, we got a situation up here in Rat Creek. Ritter is down. Lenny shot him. He's holed up in his cabin with a rifle. Mike Stanford is with him."

A long pause. "Are you okay?" she asked.

"Roger. I evaded him, but my options are . . . limited."

"You gonna take him out?" Jenny caught on fast.

"We'll see. Maybe he'll give himself up before it comes to that."

"Yeah, right. What do you need me to do?" Jenny was amazingly calm, considering we had a federal agent dead in the road, and I was on my own.

"You'd better call the Denver office, tell them one agent is down and the other is missing. That'll get 'em riled up. Then just stay on the horn. I'll keep you posted."

"You got it, Sheriff. Good luck. Shoot straight." She knew me.

"Roger, out."

My heart rate slowed and my breathing shortened; then I started getting cold. Without the churning heat of pumping adrenaline and desperate movement, my wet clothes betrayed me. I lay on the slagheap and shivered. When the autumn sun finally came, I knew it would provide little warmth in this desolate trench. Always prepared, I pulled my black skullcap out of my coat pocket and yanked it on, ignoring the cold shock of the wet wool against my tender scalp. Oh, yes, the stitches reminded me of their presence once again, and I had to put weight on my left side to ease the pressure off my broken ribs.

Separated, you pussy.

Regardless, it was an awkward shooting position.

THE LIFELESS VALLEY REFUSED TO AWAKEN. No birds flitted in the bare willows by the creek. No deer risked the fate of their comrade hanging from the railroad ties. No eagle soared in the gray band of sky above the trench. Yellow-white sunlight lit the top of the west ridge. Only the faint gurgle of Rat Creek and the quiet hum of the chinook broke the tense silence of the Rat Creek standoff.

Lenny's screen door popped open, and out came Mike Stanford, looking pale and confused through the scope of my rifle. Bet your ass, I still had the reticle centered on the door and my finger poised on the trigger, but my target did not emerge from the darkness of the cabin. Mike held his hands in the air and rotated his head frantically around the lot.

"Don't shoot, Sheriff Tatum, don't shoot! It's Mike Stanford. I am not a hostage. I am uninjured." He kept searching for a face to send his plea. I wasn't about to give away my location. I let him flounder around in the yard. He tripped through the frozen mud, unable to keep his balance with his hands above his shoulders. I kept my scope on the door and waited for movement. Mike was not my target. Still nothing from the interior. I heard the familiar honk of Mike's keyless entry. He was the only man in Mineral County who locked his doors.

Mike revved his Tahoe and tore out of the driveway. *There goes my ride.* I figured I could drive Lenny's truck back to the station. He wouldn't be needing it when I got done with him.

Good. It was just Lenny and me, now. No more federal agents or CPAs to interfere with the standoff. A little half-smile pulled at the side of my mouth, and I snuggled in behind my rifle. Gone were the cold, the ache in my ribs, the sting of my stitched scalp. I nestled my cheek against the warm wood of the Ruger's stock and waited. I could wait all day, and all night, and into the next day.

As it turns out, I didn't have to wait that long.

The screen door opened again and Lenny Leftwich emerged from his cabin. He wore the same blue flannel shirt, untucked and stained with food and grime. Black sweatpants hung down from his big ass and underneath his bulging gut. His untied work boots threatened to send him hurtling off the porch. It looked as if he had just rolled out of the rack and pulled them on. Could this pathetic form be a terrorist? Responsible for the death and destruction at Army posts across the West? Of course, it didn't take much gray matter to rig a truck bomb.

Just as I had expected, he looked straight out from his front porch, searching plaintively for death, or mercy. Just as I hadn't expected, Lenny was unarmed.

"Now, Sheriff, you know I ain't got no rifles, see?" He held up his beefy hands and pleaded to the rocks. "You took 'em when you was still a deputy. I don't got no quarrel with you. You're local. We recognize local law." He pointed a fat arm toward the dead agent. "That goddamn federal had no business here."

I released the pressure on the trigger and took a breath. I wasn't going to gun down an unarmed man, not yet. I kept Lenny in my crosshairs, which wasn't very hard. The stock pressed deep into my cheekbone.

Lenny stepped off the concrete stoop. He tripped in the gray silt in his untied boots, but caught himself before planting his face in the dirt. Told ya, Fat Boy. He kept his hands high, but kept moving.

"I aim to give myself up to you, Sheriff, but I ain't done nothin' to offend the laws of Mineral County." The narrow valley swallowed his pleas. I lifted my head from the rifle, ready to call out to him.

I hesitated. Were there more in the cabin? Was Lenny trying to roust me out of my position, so a fellow Minuteman could put a bullet in me? I put my face back down behind the scope to reacquire him.

Lenny used my hesitation to his advantage and scrambled across the tiny lot, ducking around the side of his truck and out of sight. He was quick for a fat man. I had underestimated him.

You lost your target. There goes your goddamn decisive point.

The truck door slammed. Lenny was going to break away, and I would be left with a long walk home through Indian country. He could set up anywhere in the narrow canyon and ambush me. I would have to wait until dark to move again. Great.

I desperately angled my scope to find him, as if I could bend the optics around the corner of the shack. I heard the starter whine and catch.

A blinding yellow flash filled the scope and the rest of the dim valley, followed by an earsplitting double roar. Twin shock waves rattled my spine and jammed the rim of the scope into my eye. Charred debris landed all around me.

When I'd recovered, I looked down into the trench. Lenny's cabin had transformed into an orange-and-black pile of smoking, glowing rubble.

Eighteen

As I stared at what was left of Lenny's pitiful shack, my first thought was to see if his truck was still intact. I wanted to know if I would have to walk down the mountain. Only four smoking tires and the black undercarriage remained. A fitting end to a domestic terrorist—blown up by his own demolition.

No point in freezing my dick against the cold ground any longer. I got up, slung my rifle behind my back, and plodded down the hill. Lenny's neighbors would be here soon. The rifle barrage didn't draw them out, but I assumed the explosions would.

I stopped halfway down the slope, feeling stupid and exposed. What if Lenny just wanted me to think he was dead? What if he had scurried out the back of the truck and found a nice spot of his own up the west ridge? Lenny might be dead, but what if there were another Minuteman up there, eager to avenge his comrade's incompetent demise?

Nice one, you squirrel.

Lucky for me, Lenny wasn't that smart. From the road, I could see his fat, black body still in the truck, sort of. The force of the explosion had blown him out of the driver's seat and over the front bumper. An acrid mixture of burning cordite, burning flesh, and burning wood assaulted my nostrils. The hanging mule deer burned silently from its crossbeam, then fell to the ground when the flames ate through the rope. I didn't get any closer, not knowing what unexploded ordnance remained inside the smoking ruin. This was the FBI's mess, now.

I wondered what had happened to Ritter's partner, Agent Vilicek.

From the corner of my eye I caught a glare. At first, I thought it was one of the other residents of Rat Creek, but then Jenny's Bronco topped the last rise below Lenny's lot. She zoomed up the slope and braked hard right next to me. Odd, I didn't hear the normal pop and grind of the off-road tires tearing up the gravel, but I tasted the dust she kicked up. It was better than dead Lenny fumes.

Jenny Lange stepped out of the Bronco, and, for once, had nothing to say. Her mouth was open, but no sound came out. She wore the same ski hat and yellow jacket. She left the door open and walked slowly to where I stood, her eyes locked on the charred pile of cabin and truck. When she saw Lenny's body, she covered her mouth with her hand, but didn't turn away.

"What are you doing here, Jenny?" I asked. My voice sounded strange and muffled, as if I had plugs in my ears.

She was talking, now, too, but I couldn't hear her. Her lips moved, but still no sound came out.

"What?" I yelled. Well, I guess it was a yell. The explosion had given me temporary hearing loss. It would clear. Frag grenades did that, too.

Jenny gave me a look, but understood when I pointed at my ears and shook my head. Her look changed from confusion to concern. She came over to me and touched the skin above my right eye where the rifle scope had cut me during the explosion. I jerked back in new pain. She showed me the drops of blood on her fingers. She wiped the blood on her jeans and put a hand on my shoulder, drawing my ear to her face.

"I heard the explosion downtown!" she shouted into my shocked eardrum. "We all did! Felt it, too! Then you didn't respond to my transmission! I was afraid something else had gone wrong! Is that Lenny?"

I nodded. "You call the FBI?"

"Just like you said, they have a chopper coming, but I don't think they're gonna make it! There's a huge storm coming that'll probably beat them to Wolf Creek Pass! Probably close down the whole valley!"

We were on our own. I looked north and felt the wind change—cold and full of snow. Gray, angry clouds had already gathered near the continental divide. They would come, banish the warm chinook, and claim the Belmont Valley for winter once again.

"Get in the Bronco. Stay near the radio. Keep people away," I said. A tall order for a girl wearing a yellow ski jacket and wool cap, but she would just have to handle it. I was out of help.

"Where are you going?"

"To find Agent Vilicek."

* * *

I HAD SEEN A FAINT SWITCHBACK TRAIL ON THE WEST
ridge above Lenny's cabin. I had a hunch I would find the
missing partner somewhere along it.

I gave Lenny's lot a wide berth, as if the space were toxic.
Walking up the road, past the dead bodies of my Bronco and
Agent Ritter, I cut back along the middle of the ridge. The
steep terrain forced me to plant my downhill foot decisively
to keep from tumbling down into the trench.

Scrub juniper and bare cottonwood covered the hillside
like moss, but I found the trail. It had been traveled recently, multiple times. I assumed it was Lenny's access
trail to his local poaching area, but part of me knew there
was another reason for the increased traffic.

As I climbed, the blood pounding through my ears re-
stored my hearing, and, for the first time, I heard the cold
wind out of the north. At least it blew the stink down the
valley. I stopped to catch my breath, to take in fresh air, relieved of the carnage below. I looked down at the tragic
scene in Rat Creek and nearly lost my balance. I guessed
the semicircular canals in my ears were not completely
back to normal. Jenny ignored my orders and stood next to
the Bronco with the door open, watching me through her
binoculars.

The trees grew tall and thick closer to the summit of the
ridge and the steep terrain eased slightly. A good place for
an observation post, I thought. Vilicek thought the same,
because I found his body tied to a tree fifty feet from the
top. At least, I thought it was Vilicek. I'd never met the man.

UNLIKE THE BODY OF THOMAS PITCHER, AGENT
Vilicek was naked. Lenny had made no attempt to dress the
body in a token gesture of staging a suicide. As with the

body of Thomas Pitcher, his hands were tied behind him, wrapped around the trunk of an old spruce, and duct tape clung to his lips and cheeks. He looked like an obscene crucifix. Gravity pulled him away from the tree. Cold, rigor, or some strange quirk of physics kept him upright on bent knees. His long, thin arms extended at full length, as if he were straining to break the bonds on his hands. His head hung limply on his blood-splattered chest, and I could see both the entrance and massive exit wounds from the bullet that had torn through it. Once again, in the left mastoid process and out the right cheekbone.

Vilicek looked too fair and young to be an FBI agent, an innocent martyred in violent death. His light crew cut seemed to be the only hair on his body, and the blood corrupted his pale skin. The ligatures gnarled fine, delicate hands, and deep, red scratches marked the translucent skin where he'd dug his nails in a helpless attempt to free himself.

Vilicek had piled his clothes neatly a few feet uphill from the tree. Somehow, I knew he had done it himself, that Lenny had made him do it himself. Next to the folded clothing lay his binoculars and gun—a statement: the Minutemen were no scroungers.

But no radio.

Radio silence, Ranger. Who do you need to talk to when it's just you and your target?

Lenny had known we were coming. No one in the Belmont Valley used stupid call signs like Ritter and his partner. Even Lenny could figure that out. Ritter had called in his own death.

I found the bullet buried in the turf in front of Vilicek's knees. It was easy to find because I knew where to look. The common duct tape and cheap yellow nylon rope could have been purchased at Bernie's Hardware downtown. I walked slowly around the tree, but found nothing else re-markable, except the tracks that led away from the body, up the ridge.

I followed the faint trail of booted feet through the scrub forest. Did the agents use this back trail to enter and exit the area, or had Lenny come in behind the agent, not from the valley below? Probably both. How had they gotten so careless? Lenny was fat and stupid, but he had pulled off the most successful string of domestic terrorist attacks in U.S. history. They had underestimated him. I had not, which was why I was alive, but I took little solace from my survival.

Big snowflakes tumbled sideways across my vision. From my vantage point, I could see the dense green of Miner's Creek, choked with ponderosa and Engelmann, rich with life compared to her barren sister, Rat Creek. The snow already raced through Miner's Creek canyon and into the mother valley of the Rio Grande.

I have always loved snowstorms. We had our fair share of them in Iowa—gray behemoths rolling out of the plains of Nebraska and South Dakota. I used to watch them with excitement and fear as they crept across the cornfield out-side my living room window. We lived far enough to the north to get a real winter, but near enough to the south for the road crews to lack in both funding and training, so we had a lot of snow days.

This storm felt different. Alpine weather could turn on you in moments, sneak up behind a warm sunny day and slam you with a cold front, led by an ice storm of freezing rain and plummeting temperatures. The chinook winds had lulled our valley into a quiet peace for some, agitation for others, as if winter would never come. To remind us of its inevitability, winter drove the warm reprieve out of the valley and replaced it with the snowstorm of the year. At least we could use the moisture.

By the time I returned to Vilicek's body, a layer of snow had covered the scene. Time to make decisions.

"Jenny, we need to bring up Dr. Ed," I called over my radio.

"He's on the way, Sheriff."

"I hope he can get up here in time. Snow's getting pretty thick for the coroner-mobile."

"It's already here, Sheriff," said Jenny. "I meant, he's on the way up to your position."

I looked down the abrupt slope and saw the black rectangle of Dr. Ed's vehicle, smartly parked facing downhill, rear gate open, ready to accept the newly dead.

A charge of fear flipped my stomach. Ritter's body was gone.

"Did he load up Agent Ritter?" I asked. I knew the answer, but my subconscious needed to know, too.

"Roger. I helped him." Jenny was made of sterner stuff than I'd ever imagined.

"How did he get up here so quickly?" I asked.

"Are you going to keep yakking on that walkie-talkie, or do you want to preserve this crime scene before it's covered by three feet of snow that won't be gone until spring?" Dr. Ed emerged from behind a clump of juniper, breathing hard. He wore an old black ski coat like the one my father used to wear on our trips to Summit County, complete with the nylon belt across the waist. His black cap and Gore-Tex gloves matched my own. Even his Sorrel boots were black.

"Nice outfit," I said. "Is that what all the coroners wear in the winter?"

"Be quiet. Youth is wasted on the young."

"You brought a toboggan." I nodded to the red plastic

sled he pulled by a white nylon cord. "Aren't you a little old, and this ridge a little steep?"

"Very funny," said Dr. Ed. "This is a secret technique employed by all Rocky Mountain coroners tasked to bring dead bodies out of the unspeakably precarious places they choose to die. I assume that is Agent Ritter's partner."

"Yup. I don't think he chose to die here, though."

"No, no. Lenny did that for him."

"Speaking of Lenny, did you bag him up, too?" I asked.

"No, I saved that for the two of us. Jenny is a brave girl, but not that brave."

I scowled at the thought. Maybe there would be a little less of him.

"Well, he ain't gettin' any deader," I said.

We strapped the stiff, pale Agent Vilicek to the red sled and covered his naked body with his FBI windbreaker, as if to keep the snow off his bare skin. I rigged a rear line to the toboggan, handed it to Dr. Ed, and we descended, a macabre parody of the Belmont Ski Patrol.

Vilicek was a walk in the park compared to recovering Lenny's charred corpse. We might have left some of him stuck to the front grill of his truck.

Finished with that unpleasantness, I surveyed the dismal scene of Lenny's lot. It didn't seem as tragic now, buried in the first layer of white. Snow erased the blemishes of man's folly.

"What else can I do?" I asked. "We just can't leave it like this."

"Best we can do is pick up the bodies and wait until the experts get here. This is over your head, Sheriff," said Dr. Ed. He turned his wrinkled face to the blizzard. "But they might have to wait until spring, or come out with a regiment of hair driers."

I crossed the pallet bridge and stepped over the ruined threshold of Lenny's front door.

"What are you doing?" Dr. Ed called out. "There could be more explosives in there."

"You'd better get down the mountain before we have to use your sled to get out, Dr. Ed," I answered. Snow fell relentlessly down the valley from the north. Dr. Ed didn't wait for me. I heard his vehicle start and pull away, the crunch of gravel muffled by the snow drifting on the road.

I gently toed the remains of Lenny's cabin, sifting through the white snow and black rubble. The storm responded by adding more of the white stuff, as if to deny my search. I moved to the north side of the ruin, where Lenny would have fired on Agent Ritter. A portion of the wall remained intact, including the bottom sill of the single window. Jenny prompted me to hurry by starting her Bronco. I didn't need the prompting. The driving snow and impending secondary explosion were enough to encourage alacrity.

My boot bumped a hard object on the floor next to the window. The dusting of white powder fell away from Lenny's rifle. That was easy. I picked up the weapon in my gloved hands and brushed the feather-light snow from its bent barrel and blackened stock. It was a sport-model saddle gun, short barrel, plain, untooled woodwork, matte finish on the firing mechanism. No scope, just a peep sight and iron pin at the end of the barrel. We used to call them "brush guns" back in Iowa. An excellent weapon for shooting deer at close range in thick cover, or careless federal agents outside your living room window.

What the hell do you hunt with a brush gun, brush?

I shot back the bolt, or tried to. Heat and impact had warped the chamber, and the bolt jammed halfway down.

A bright brass shell casing shone inside the charred magazine. I set the butt of the rifle on the floor and stomped on the bolt with my right foot. The unspent round flew in a graceful arc across the room and buried itself in the thickening snow. Nice one, chucklehead. I leaned the ruined rifle against the half-wall and delicately flicked the snow away from the spot where the round had disappeared. Once again, fortune prevailed, and I withdrew the cold brass from the drift in Lenny's front room.

The bullet rang a familiar bell inside my head. I had loaded countless rounds like this one into aluminum M16 magazines in my other life. This was a 5.56mm NATO cartridge.

And it said so on the bottom. Instead of the American name, ".223 Winchester," the simple digits "5 5 6" were stamped neatly around the center-fire primer.

It made sense for a former Army soldier to have his familiar 5.56mm rounds handy, especially one who acquired much more dangerous material from his former employer, like C4, det cord, and blasting caps. Unlike the custom-made precision rifle bullets that Marty Three Stones used in her killing spree, the mass-produced 5.56mm bullet was not a signature round, but you just couldn't pick them up in the hunting section at the Trout House. This ammunition came from the black market, like the demolitions. Lenny might have a fellow Minuteman still in uniform, one with access to some very dangerous stuff.

But that's not why the bell went off in my head. Mike Stanford's rifle fired the same bullet, the expensive rifle with the thick barrel and fancy scope that he couldn't hit jack shit with. Odd for two men to fire the same varmint caliber in a county filled with big guns and big game.

I felt for the warm brass shell from Mike Stanford's gun in my coat pocket and pulled it out. Stamped on the bottom were the numbers "5 5 6." The shells were a perfect match.

Retrieving the rifle, I stepped lightly through the living room and out the door. I was relieved when I crossed the pallet bridge for the last time.

"Time to go, Sheriff?" Jenny asked. She stamped her feet next to the open passenger door and eyed the white wall of snow to the north.

"I hate to leave, but I'd also hate to get stuck out here." I took another look at the cabin, which was almost covered with snow. "I'll never hear the end of it from the FBI, leaving a crime scene this way. We'll have to hope the snow will preserve the scene for us."

"Screw them. They're not here," said Jenny. "Well, not anymore."

I popped the hatch on the Bronco.

"Whose rifle is that?" she asked.

"Whose do you think it is?" I asked. "It's Lenny's. It's why I went into the cabin."

She pushed her dark hair out of her face. "That's not Lenny's rifle, Sheriff."

I held it out and looked at it, then looked at her. She blinked at the snowflakes gathering on her long eyelashes, but her stare was unflinching.

"I don't see anyone else's name on it," I said.

"That's not Lenny's rifle," she repeated.

"How do you know?"

She pointed to the bolt. "Lenny's left-handed. Why do you think we call him 'Leftwich'?"

Jenny was right, of course. The bolt was on the right side—a right-hander's weapon, impossible for a lefty to shoot. I tossed the rifle in the back and slammed the hatch closed.

"Son of a bitch," I said quietly.

"What's the matter, Sheriff? Whose rifle is that?" asked Jenny. She didn't let up.

"Mike Stanford's."

Nineteen

S ON OF A BITCH IS RIGHT," SAID JENNY. "STANFORD damn near ran me down on my way up here."

"That's nice," I said. "Get in. We need to move."

I jumped in the Bronco and instinctively reached for the radio to report in, but whom would I call? My deputy sat in a cell and my dispatcher sat right next to me. I put the truck in gear and gunned the engine. The Bronco fishtailed and slid sideways down the gravel road, unable to gain purchase in the thick powder.

"Didn't you lock down the hubs?" I said.

She paused, then spoke. "You don't drive in snow, much, do you Sheriff?" She was amazingly calm, considering her window seat on our unabated slide. "Just ease off on the brakes and wait until we hit that drift, then take her out slowly." As she finished, we bumped into a deep pile of new snow. The Bronco rocked to a halt.

"I hope we can move again," I said.

"This is nothin'," she said. "Nice and easy."

I responded by spinning all four wheels. I pounded the steering wheel. Jenny stared patiently out the windshield. The storm blew a waterfall of thick snow over the top of the truck and down the front glass. I had the irrational fear that we would be buried in Rat Creek.

"You want me to drive, Sheriff?" she asked, deadpan. "I've lived here all my life. This isn't my first snowstorm."

I let out a sharp sigh, then opened the door. A gust of snowflakes churned inside. Jenny slid over and I walked through knee-deep snow to the passenger side. I wasn't about to have my pretty young dispatcher crawl over me and take over.

I didn't say a word when she freed us from the snow with two expert rocks of the Bronco.

"Buckle your seat belt," she said.

The sinking feeling I always get when I forgot something overcame my embarrassment.

"Shit," I said, then turned around in my seat. All I saw was a barrage of snow against the rear window.

"What's wrong?" asked Jenny. She kept her eyes on the road, or the flat gap in the white madness.

"I forgot everything in my truck," I said. "We need to go back."

"We can't go back, Sheriff," said Jenny, "and don't worry about your stuff. I unloaded your Bronco. It's in my backseat. Except your hat. I couldn't find it."

I craned my neck over the headrest and saw a pile of familiar gear laid neatly across the rear bench seat.

"What's up with the leather folder?" asked Jenny. "Someone get that for your birthday?"

"That must be Agent Ritter's," I said. Curiosity got the better of me and I reached over and picked up the portfolio. I needed something to take my mind off the treacherous scene in front of me, anyway. I opened the folder.

"There he is again," I said to myself.

I stared straight into Mike Stanford's blocky face.

The shot had been cropped from a promotion photo. His hair was shorter, a military-style flattop I'd worn for years in the Army. His baby-face cheeks were thinner, and he had hair, but beyond that, the man hadn't changed at all.

The two silver bars on each shoulder of his green class-A uniform revealed a part of Mike Stanford's history that I had never known. Mike was an Army captain, an officer, a leader of men. The edge of a yellow tab at the top of his left sleeve stood out against the green wool.

"Jesus. He's a ranger, too," I mumbled. I had more in common with Mike Stanford than I thought.

At the bottom of the photograph I recognized the top halves of two brass tanks on his lapels—an Armor officer. That fit Mike Stanford perfectly. He was a poster-boy for the Armor branch, but why did Ritter have his 201 file?

I scanned through the text of the document. It wasn't an Army personnel jacket, or 201 file, at all. It was an FBI psychological evaluation. A wave of bureaucratic guilt washed over me. I had no right to look at the man's psych profile.

Screw it. What Mike didn't know wouldn't hurt him, and Ritter was beyond caring at this point.

Words like *"unstable," "personal tragedy," "needs significant counseling," "anger,"* and *"bitterness"* jumped out from all over the file. *"Psychologically unfit for federal service"* concluded the report.

Mike had applied to the FBI upon resigning his commission from the Army. No wonder Ritter had recognized him during his initial visit. The agent's name was at the bottom of one of the reports. Ritter had interviewed him during the final phase of the screening process.

And Mike had killed him for it. That was pretty clear now. I had his rifle in the back of the truck and Dr. Ed had Ritter in the back of his hearse. I wondered what Ritter knew that made Mike want to kill him and his partner.

I leaned my head against the rest, closed my eyes, and transformed Mike Stanford into a domestic terrorist.

Lenny as the key terrorist had never sat well with me, regardless of what Agent Ritter had said. Lenny took orders from someone in town, someone he called "Sir" in the dark kitchen at the Halfmoon Ranch. Lenny had assaulted me to protect his superior. Lenny was the minion. Mike Stanford was his boss.

While Lenny was plodding and incompetent, Mike was meticulous and intelligent. Lenny reacted to stimuli. Mike planned, schemed, and projected outcomes. Mike was the leader, the former officer in the tank corps, trained to move men and machines in a synchronized effort of destruction. Lenny was just a nug who followed orders.

I had known captains like Mike Stanford in the Eighty-second Airborne—hard-charging men of will and grit, brilliant men who never slept. There were some duds, too, but few of them. The combat arms branches did not send many clowns to command their frontline soldiers. If Mike directed his vast mind and boundless energy toward a desired outcome, it would happen. He would make it happen.

Other elements snicked into place. The car phone in the back of Mike's truck wasn't for business calls while traveling in the mountains. All of Mike's clients lived in Belmont, and we didn't have any cell coverage in the valley at all. He used the long-range three-watt bag phone transmitter to trigger his explosives.

Now that I understood Mike's mental instability, even the Velcro in the back of the truck made sense. Velcro upholstery was a glaring indicator of his looniness. I should have picked up on that.

The vulgar display of Vilicek's frozen corpse flashed through my head—another example of Mike's psychosis. But there was more. The method of the agent's death and the positioning of the body were eerily reminiscent of Thomas Pitcher's demise. I had shoved that connection to the back of my mind, but now it thrust itself right out front, not to be denied.

I had no choice but to confront the similarities and admit the possibility that I had arrested the wrong man.

Mike Stanford had been a suspect from the beginning. He was part of the "Group of Five" that emerged from the mountains the morning I'd found Pitcher's body, but I'd had no reason to suspect him beyond proximity. Why would Mike Stanford kill Pitcher, his fellow Mason, his worshipful master? Another thing I knew about successful junior officers was their loyalty to command. I imagined that Mike held Thomas Pitcher in high regard, like a young captain to his brigade commander.

Then, I remembered the fax of Lenny's operations order, sent from Pitcher's office. Had Thomas Pitcher discovered the Minutemen using the Freemason's cloak of secrecy as a cover for their terrorist operation? Knowing Lenny, he'd probably left a copy of the operations order on the coffee table in the lodge. Pitcher must have picked it up and sent the fax in an attempt to alert the FBI to the militant cell working out of isolated Belmont, Colorado. When

Mike found out that Pitcher had turned him in, that must have thrown a big turd into his well-planned punch bowl.

Which is exactly why Mike Stanford had killed Thomas Pitcher.

I worked through the time line in my head. Someone had sent the fax to the FBI. Three days later, Pitcher had gone to the Halfmoon Ranch and disappeared. Three days after that, the hospital had blown up at Fort Leavenworth, and I had found Thomas Pitcher dead in the mountains.

Mike had discovered that Pitcher betrayed him. Mike had used his cover as a member of the Halfmoon Gun Club and followed Pitcher up to Wason Plateau. He'd ambushed the old man on the ridge and tied him up, freezing and naked, in his deer stand. Then, rather than killing him right there, Mike had let him live, and suffer, through two nights of sub-zero temperatures. He'd kept hypothermia at bay by forcing coffee down Pitcher's throat, the hot liquid burning an acid hole in the man's stomach.

But why risk discovery? Someone might miss Thomas Pitcher and start poking around the ridge, like his own son. The reasons for Pitcher's torture had eluded me, until now.

Mike had had to assess the risk to his terrorist bombing in Leavenworth. He'd had to find out his level of exposure. He'd kept Pitcher alive to extract what the old man knew about the operation, and to find out who else might know. I guess Mike was satisfied he'd gotten everything, because he'd blown up the hospital, driven back to Belmont, and put a hole in Pitcher's head.

There was one problem with my theory—Mike couldn't be in two places at once. He couldn't set off the bomb in Fort Leavenworth and keep Pitcher alive, staked to a tree in the middle of the Wason Plateau. He'd have to get local help.

"Holy shit," I said out loud. "Emmet."

"What's that?" asked Jenny. Her eyes were still glued to the windshield and her knuckles were white on the steering wheel.

"Nothing."

Emmet also had the perfect cover for being on the Halfmoon Ranch. He was such a common presence on Wason Plateau that no one would suspect that he was secretly torturing Councilman Pitcher. Why did he need to take pictures of elk for a sculpture that was nearly complete?

With Pitcher's imminent takeover of his studio, Emmet had plenty of reasons to participate in Pitcher's suffering. The sculptor could easily slip onto the plateau, force-feed Pitcher his coffee, and slap him back into consciousness. Mike probably coerced the artist into performing the unpleasant caretaking. Emmet had a secret to hide and a studio to preserve. His art was his life—he had nothing else but a mangled hand and bad memories.

I wondered what had sent Captain Mike Stanford over the edge, transforming him from uniformed patriot to domestic terrorist. I had a hunch, of course.

"How did you say Mike Stanford lost his family?" I asked Jenny. It was cowardly, wording it like that, as if they'd gotten separated at Disneyworld.

"His wife died having their baby," she said. I didn't press. I wanted her to concentrate on driving through the blizzard.

I flipped a page and there it was, a clinical report on the tragic end to Mike Stanford's life before Belmont. They'd summed up the most significant event in his former life in five sentences.

The candidate has significant emotional problems coping with the death of his family. The candidate's wife died in 1999 of inconclusive complications during childbirth at Evans Army Medical Center, Fort Carson, Colorado. The female child died as well. Although the candidate's skills in accounting would limit his federal service to desk work, this report recommends strongly against acceptance. The candidate should not be allowed into federal law enforcement, let alone permitted to carry firearms.

That explained Mike's target choices—military hospitals. It wasn't about hitting soft targets or inducing terror, it was about avenging the death of his family.

Mike blamed the entire Army medical infrastructure for losing them. Down deep, I couldn't blame him—he had been a victim of the only socialized medicine system in the country. The level of incompetence present at every hospital and clinic was unconscionable, even criminal. I had no reason to doubt that the ob-gyn staff at Fort Carson had made mistakes during his wife's labor, but that didn't give him a license to blow them up.

I tried to empathize with the man. His wife and child were dead, he had resigned his Army commission, then was rejected by the FBI. Did he come to Belmont to escape or to hide? Was Belmont part of his terrorist plan or did he hatch it afterward?

Two words, however, eluded me in the report. I flipped through the pages, but they were missing altogether.

Those words were "Mike Stanford."

The candidate's name in the report, the one below Mike's picture, was "Michael Petry," son of former Marine Sergeant Denver Petry.

Twenty

RITTER WAS RIGHT ALL ALONG. DENVER PETRY was our chief terrorist, the leader of the Minutemen. He directed the hospital bombings through his son, Michael.

Michael Petry had rejected his father's hatred for his country, choosing to serve it, willing to die for it. But when the Army medical system had killed his family, his patriotism had disappeared, and he'd turned to his father for an outlet to his grief. Denver had provided a release for his son's anger, harnessing Michael's boundless energy and broad intelligence to the most successful series of domestic bombings in U.S. history.

The word "successful" galled me, but they were. From an operational standpoint, they were perfect, airtight in their planning and execution. Stanford—Petry—had transferred his superior skills from combat arms to domestic terrorism.

But this plan had certainly turned to shit. Michael's lack of foresight surprised me. For someone who had eluded the FBI's counter-terrorist division for this long, he had really blown it. Michael should have known Ritter would remember his interview—especially Ritter, with his photographic memory. Once they had Lenny, Michael would be next, yet he remained in Belmont.

Contingency plans, Ranger, don't leave home without 'em.

"I can't see the road, Sheriff," said Jenny. "Can you?"

I looked up, disoriented by the transition from near-sight to far and the torrent of white flakes driving against the windshield. For all I knew, we could have been in Alaska.

Before I could answer Jenny's question, a white shape filled the glass in front of us and we slammed into something hard, heavy, and evidently invisible. A violent shudder rocked the Bronco.

My seat belt kept me from cracking my skull against the windshield, but the tightening strap crushed my chest, and I was thrown back in my seat. I sat there, dazed and winded, then turned my head to look at Jenny. She wasn't so lucky. Although her belt had restrained her, she had smacked her head against the steering wheel—no air bags in these old Broncos. A smudge of blood smeared the top of the wheel and a trickle ran down her forehead, her black hair matted and wet, but she was breathing.

My door opened. A blast of wind and snow stung my cheek. Standing in the swirling white, holding a gun in my face, was Mike Stanford . . . Michael Petry. I guess he had a plan after all.

"Get out," he said. I didn't move fast enough for him, because he unbuckled my belt and dragged me out. He did this with one arm, tossing me into the snowy gravel like a small child.

"I said get out," he repeated. "Do as I say and you might live a little longer."

"Fuck you, Michael," I said. "You don't have the balls to kill me." Nice comeback, Chief.

He drove the barrel of the gun against my head, pushing my face into the snow. Snow and gravel ground my cheek. The hard barrel burned my scalp.

" 'Don't have the balls,' " Michael said. "You want to reconsider that assessment, Sheriff?"

He waited for a response from me, but I was done with witty conversation.

"I thought not. Get up." The barrel's pressure eased off a touch, and I slowly rose out of the snow and dirt. Michael's gun tapped my head every second or so and reminded me who was in charge. I wobbled on my feet, then got steady.

"Gun," said Michael. He stood behind me. I hesitated. He thumped me with the barrel. The mountains started spinning and I dropped to my knees.

"When I tell you to do something, I expect you to do it immediately," said Michael. "Now slowly withdraw your .45 from its holster and place it in the snow behind you." I complied. "Very good. Now your backup gun."

"I don't have a backup gun," I said. I really didn't. Michael thumped me again. I managed to catch myself before kissing the snow.

Michael reached down and felt at my ankles and around my waist. Satisfied I wasn't lying, he grabbed me by the back of the collar and stood me up, one-handed. He spun me around and half-carried me to the passenger side of his Tahoe, my toes barely touching the ground. Jesus, the guy was strong.

"You're taillight's out," I said. "Maybe we wouldn't have hit you if it was working."

"Always maintain your sense of humor, Ranger," said Michael. "That's what they told us at Ranger School, wasn't it?"

"At the start of every phase," I said.

"Good for you, but I don't think it's going to help you, this time, Ranger. Get in."

"We going somewhere?" The next thing I knew, my face slammed against the tinted glass. I thought I heard a crack, but I was uncertain if it was my head or the window. At least he didn't hit me with his gun again. I got in.

"Slide over behind the wheel," he said. I did.

The interior of the vehicle was immaculate. Floor mats vacuumed, seats clean, vents free of dust. A fresh layer of protectant shone on the charcoal gray dashboard and leather steering wheel. It looked as though he'd just detailed it with cotton swabs and dental tools.

"Start the truck," said Michael. I looked stupidly down at the steering column. "The keys are in the ignition, Bill." I used to be "Sheriff." Now I was just "Bill." It kind of chapped my ass.

I turned the key, and all eight cylinders responded happily, eager for me to drive to my imminent demise. I put both hands on the steering wheel, right where Michael could see them.

"Turn the vehicle around," said Michael.

"Where are we going?"

Michael said nothing for a moment. I waited for the blow. It didn't come.

"Listen, Bill, I know you're trying to stall, to hold out until someone comes by," he said quietly. "Well, no one is going to come by. This is the biggest storm to hit the San Juans in fifty years. They just closed La Veta Pass, and the Blue Mesa Cutoff is shut down. I doubt you could get through Slumgullion without a snowmobile. There is no way in or out of this valley." He let that sink in, then continued.

"I've been planning this for a long time. It will not fail. The FBI won't be here for days, and by that time, you'll be long gone. Now drive."

"What about Jenny?" I asked. "She'll freeze to death out here."

"I left your Bronco running. She'll be fine."

"You left her there to die," I said.

"No, you did." Michael smiled. "And I will save her from your abandonment. Shall we turn around now?" He pressed the barrel against my temple and with his other hand spun his finger in the air.

My dying wouldn't help Jenny, so I reluctantly pressed down the gas pedal and worked my way around the Bronco. The new, dry snow squeaked under the tires, but held. Once I got the vehicle pointed in the right direction, we moved slowly back up Rat Creek Canyon.

"I have to tell you. I'm a terrible driver in the snow." I squinted through the blaze of white.

"Unlike yourself, I have installed chains on my tires. If you get us stuck, I will kill you, and not easy like Agents Ritter and Vilicek."

"Is that your plan, Michael, just kill all the cops?" I asked. "There's more of us, you know, especially the FBI. It might take them a while to get out there, but they'll come, and they'll come for you."

"That's where you're wrong, my friend. Keep your eyes

on the road and your self-righteousness in check. You think their file on me makes me an easy mark, and you're right, it does. But I have nothing to hide. The FBI doesn't like the easy mark, and I will help them to reach other conclusions."

"You're staying in Belmont?"

"Of course," said Michael. "Like I said, I have nothing to hide. If I leave town now, that will only confirm their suspicions. When you disappear, however, leaving a pile of bodies in your wake, they will naturally direct their focus from me to you. Did you ever wonder what your FBI file looks like?" He held up Ritter's portfolio. "It probably looks a lot like this one." He opened his file. "Young face, tight haircut, an American patriot. What's your story? A former Army sergeant, a sniper, leaves the service under extreme circumstances and ends up in Belmont, Colorado. Were you hiding or escaping?"

"I could ask you the same question," I said.

Michael told the story. "I imagine escaping was your first intent, then it turned to hiding when you and Lenny started bombing hospitals. Two ex-buck sergeants getting back at the Army. 'Fuck the Army'—isn't that the disgruntled soldier's motto?"

I didn't rise to the bait—I was thinking through Michael's scheme. I fit the militia profile as much as he did, maybe more. I, too, had a reason to hate the Army, a reason to strike back at the federal government. I had run away to isolated Mineral County, entered law enforcement, then systematically removed everyone on the sheriff's staff.

You have a reputation for applying deadly force in your former and current occupation.

Now that I was in charge of the department and the only

sheriff in town, I had the perfect cover. No one would suspect me. Like Dr. Ed had said, I was their savior, their Boy Scout. I cleaned up the scourge of drugs poisoning their children and killed the demon sniper terrorizing them from the ridges above town.

I could blow up military hospitals and disappear into the mountains.

I could kill Thomas Pitcher and his mistress with my own weapon and still pin the deed on his son.

I could lead the FBI toward other suspects, like Mike Stanford or Denver Petry.

I could rig an inert device to my vehicle to make me look like a target.

I could ambush two federal agents and leave their bodies in the dirt.

I could blow up my terrorist comrade, then disappear into the mountains, seeking another remote refuge to begin the cycle again.

But I would really just be dead, and Mike Stanford would be there to paint the picture for them. Or Michael Petry.

"They'll know," I said. "They'll know who you are."

"Who? Michael Petry? So what? So I changed my name when those incompetent fucks at Carson killed my wife and newborn daughter. Wouldn't you? I needed to put the past behind me, start a new life in Belmont."

"But your father lives here."

"So what? He respected my privacy. We spend time together. How do you think he got so big? I'm his weightlifting partner. You see, Bill, I had this all planned out. They taught me that in the Army, you know. Command and Staff Service School, Fort Leavenworth, Kansas. They just don't have a hospital anymore."

"You coward," I said. "You killed all those people."

"Those people kill every day: an overdose here, a forgotten procedure there, a missed drug allergy on a chart. They got what they deserved. There's your socialized medicine for you. And people like Hillary Clinton want that for everyone."

He was rambling. I saw the real Michael Petry for the first time.

"I knew they'd find us, eventually," said Michael. "It was only a matter of time before Lenny screwed up, or the FBI got lucky, so I brought them here myself. That way, I could control their investigation."

"You brought who here?" I asked.

The gun snapped out and smashed my fingers against the steering wheel. My eyes watered, but I didn't take them off the white road or my hand off the wheel. I had given Michael enough sadistic pleasure for one day.

"It's *'whom,'* you stupid enlisted fuck, and *whom* do you think? The Harlem Globetrotters? Anyway. The FBI was getting too close. I knew a team from Denver would start sniffing around Belmont eventually. It's too perfect, too ideal, a militia's dream hideaway, so I threw them a bone. I gave them Lenny."

"You gave up your comrade."

"My comrade. Don't start saying the Ranger Creed. Lenny was a tool. You saw his place. Ted Kaczynski was his decorator. He might as well have put out a sign over his front door: DOMESTIC TERRORIST, PLEASE RING THE BELL."

"Ritter had your file," I said. "He saw you at Lenny's."

"Yeah, so did his partner. That was fun. A perfect place for an observation post, which is why I found him so easily. I guess they never went to Ranger School, like us, huh? The FBI is as predictable as Henry Earl's bowel movements."

"You know a lot about this town," I said.

"I know more than you think. Situational awareness, Ranger. Gotta have it. It allows me to plan on the fly, come up with contingencies for contingencies. I guess you wouldn't know much about that, being a buck sergeant. Not much planning that far down."

I said nothing. His smugness was getting to me.

"That's your biggest weakness as a sheriff, you know that?" He continued to press me. "You have no idea what goes on under your nose, and you have no desire to find out. If you know your operational area, you can predict reactions, project outcomes, and stay one step ahead of everyone. Two steps, three. That's what being a planner is all about."

"You know our invasion into Iraq a few years ago? I planned it. Yup, that's right, little old Captain Petry in the Third Division Planning Section. They had me and another guy locked up in the secure vault for months, and he was an idiot."

"You're delusional, Michael," I said. "You were here in Belmont when we invaded Iraq."

"Yeah, right. You don't think *maybe* we had a few plans put together long before President Bush gave the word? They probably dusted off my operations order and put new dates on it. I watched the whole thing on Fox News Channel, followed the division on the Internet. Every objective, every time line, every refuel—all my plan. Why do you keep calling me 'Michael'?"

He was right. I'd been calling him Michael since he put a gun to my head. To me, he became Michael Petry when I'd seen the name under his promotion photograph. "That's your name, isn't it, Michael Petry?"

"Michael Petry died in the waiting room at Evans Army Hospital."

* * *

WE PASSED LENNY'S LOT, THE CHARRED RUIN COM-
pletely white and smooth under the snow. It didn't even
smolder. I inched around my shattered Bronco. This little
part of Rat Creek looked like a war zone, an old one, forgotten, like so many Sergeant Richter and I had found in
the mountains of Afghanistan.

We topped the rise where I'd turned around. The storm
had taken a breath, an operational pause, and I could see up
the canyon. More dark, low clouds lingered, waiting to
strike at our valley again.

"Turn around and park it," said Michael. "We walk from
here."

We walked up the east side of the canyon, Michael a few
feet behind me, gun pointed at my back. The pall of imminent death made this winter hike particularly unpleasant.

"Where are we going?" I asked. There was nothing out
here—no cabins, no trail, not even a deer track, just a barren
slanting field of rock and dormant alpine scrub. The rounded
top of Bulldog Mountain loomed overhead. The dark clouds
to the northwest, tired of their waiting, unleashed a new
round of white fury.

"Up, then down," he said. "Keep going, Ranger. It's not
far."

Our climb settled into a shallow draw. I slipped on the
rocks beneath the snow. I started feeling sorry for myself.

"Come on, Ranger, you can make it," said Michael.
"You can rest very soon."

The ridge flattened into a broad step that ran along the
entire length of the canyon. I gained the rocky lip and
paused to take a breath.

"Very good, Ranger, we made it," said Michael.

I looked around. Made it where?

Michael noticed my confusion. "See those rocks over there? That's your final destination."

A pile of boulders and smaller rocks topped a knoll to our left. Snow covered the rise and worked into the cracks between the rocks.

"Let's go check it out." He sounded like a twelve-year-old looking for buried treasure.

I climbed the knoll and stood there. Tiny crystals of snow stung my face. Michael stopped halfway up.

"Reach down and clear off some of the snow. You'll find it."

I dusted off a six-inch layer of snow from an old Army poncho staked down in the alpine turf.

"Very good. Remove the poncho."

I pulled, but the stakes had frozen in the cold dirt.

"Try harder, Ranger. You can do it."

I got down on my knees and grabbed the first stake. I felt the hard, cold steel through my leather gloves. I worked at the orange stake, just like the ones I'd been issued as a private in basic training. I jerked it back and forth, freeing it from unyielding earth. I was sweating by the time I pulled up all four.

I tore away the tough nylon fabric to reveal a deep crevice in the earth. A new jolt of panic gripped my pelvis, and my breath came short and fast.

"That's an old mine shaft, left here one hundred years ago," said Michael. "I guess it was a dry hole. They didn't expand it beyond the initial penetration."

He let me look into the shaft for a few moments, barely three feet across. I couldn't see the bottom. Snow blew into the hole and disappeared. My panic didn't get any better.

"Take off your clothes," he said from behind me.

"What?"

"You saw Agent Vilicek. You know the drill. Take off your clothes. Boots, long johns, everything. Fold them up neatly next to you. Let's go. I'm freezing my ass off out here."

I stood in the blowing snow and removed my clothes, even the Ace bandage holding my separated ribs together. I tried to bury the humiliation, as if it mattered now. The wind assaulted my bare skin. I felt like I'd jumped into a lake just after the winter ice had melted.

"Now, get down on your knees, put your cuffs on your right wrist, then show me your hands behind your back."

After digging through the pile of clothes, I found my handcuffs. I found the key, too, palming it in my right hand. Keeping my back to Michael, I pretended to fumble with the cuffs and brought my hands close to my face. I slipped the little silver key in my mouth. My hands shook as I cinched down the cold steel. I didn't have to fake that. The ratcheting cuffs sounded like a death rattle. I hoped the key would give me some kind of margin. I put my hands behind my back and waited. I felt the snow melting and freezing underneath my bare knees. My feet burned.

"Very good, Ranger. You follow directions very well, just like a good soldier." I heard him come up the knoll. He would need his other hand to close my left in the cuffs. Another margin, another very narrow margin. I steadied myself and waited. I closed my eyes and envisioned my moves, sending early commands to my joints and muscles, rehearsing the motion in my mind.

I never had the chance. Michael was very fast. He shoved me into the snowy rocks. The force of the impact knocked the wind out of me. He put one knee on my back and the other on my neck. He closed the cuffs on bare wrists, exquisitely tight. My hands would freeze in hours.

He lifted me up by the links between the cuffs. Both shoulders nearly dislocated, but I managed to get my knees under me and relieve some of the torque. He turned me around and put his face in mine. My lip had split against a sharp rock, and a welt rose beneath one eye.

"You look like hell, Ranger," he said.

"Why don't you just kill me now?" I rasped, sending blood and spittle onto his coat. He grimaced.

"You should know this by now. You are a liability. I need to know what you know. A few hours up here in the cold should soften you up, but I don't think it's the cold that'll break you. Lenny told me about your little episode in the stairwell."

He was going to bury me alive. Ice filled my lungs. He was going to put me in the hole and leave me there to die.

"I . . . I . . . Don't."

"Go ahead, Bill, take your time." He grabbed me by the hair and dragged me across the knoll. I kicked at the rocks with my numb feet, helpless to stop what was coming.

Michael hopped over the hole and dangled me over the lip. I pushed against the wall, struggling to stay out of the blackness.

"Stop squirming. I'll be back." Michael thumped my temple with his gun. The strike sent me into semiconsciousness. I fought the full blackout. Part of me wanted it, needed it, to cope with the hell that I was about to endure.

Michael held me effortlessly over the hole, then let go. I slid down the shaft, feet first. My body clattered against the rocks on the way down. My chin struck a granite shelf, and I crumpled in the black, letting it consume me.

Twenty-one

I WOKE UP IN A PANIC, BUT IT WAS ONLY THE beginning.

I struggled against consciousness, the fear in me not wanting to comprehend the squeezing darkness.

Squeezing. Hard, angular surfaces bit into my aching flesh. I pushed away the tangible and sought the void.

I slowly came around, as if each nerve fired on its neighbor, one at a time, until all senses returned. I held shut my eyes and denied the horrible reality of full wakefulness, but it was coming.

As I gained consciousness, my rate of breathing increased, measure by measure. Then I couldn't breathe at all. Something crushed my chest, dug into my broken ribs, pushed against my back.

I couldn't breathe. It felt as though I were running again with my gas mask on. Before Sergeant Richter had made me his shooter, I was in a line infantry squad in the Eighty-second Airborne. My platoon sergeant was Staff Sergeant Willie Jenkins, a white trash, rawboned hillbilly straight out of West Virginia. He had a bug in his ass for gas-mask training. We road marched in them, did push-ups, fought hand-to-hand, everything, but the worst was his five-mile run. I am a good runner, but I could never get a breath in the gas mask. Now I knew why—I panicked, taking shorter and shorter gasps until all I did was move my chest up and down. I usually collapsed from hypoxia by the second mile. Jenkins had always left somebody with me to make sure I didn't take off my mask. What a son of a bitch.

It felt like that now, only the weight of the earth sat on my chest this time. I thought about all the rock and dirt above me. That didn't help. I felt the familiar tingle of hypoxia creep into my face and toes. At least I could still feel them, but I wanted to give in to the panic, let my autonomic system take over and let me breathe free of my phobia.

Fuck that, Ranger. You sleep, you die. It's too damn cold out here for that shit.

I shook my head. My bruised cheek smacked against a nearby rock. The fresh pain brought me around completely and I opened my eyes. Not much had changed.

Dark as four foot up a bull's ass.

I smiled in the darkness, and my frayed nerves reknit, just a little. I held the fear at arm's length. I didn't know how long I could keep it out there.

I was wedged in the mountain.

Miners had drilled into the side of the mountain at an acute angle, but obviously hadn't found a new vein of silver. As they had drilled deeper, the hole had narrowed from a three-foot bore to an eighteen-inch crack; then they had stopped and taken their tools elsewhere.

The force of my fall had jammed me tight inside the narrowest termination of the drill hole. I couldn't feel the bottom. I flexed my ankles, pointing my toes down for a purchase to ease the pressure on my chest, but found nothing.

Thoughts about crucifixion filled my head—the slow suffocation caused by your own weight bearing down on your chest. I wondered if Michael had engineered this specifically for my phobia.

That didn't help. The fear gripped me again and I couldn't breathe at all. I squirmed and fought in my rocky straitjacket, which only allowed gravity to pull me farther into the earth, and the rock to squeeze tighter. I smelled old dirt, cold rocks, and gritty dust from the earth, blood, urine, and sweat from my own body. I passed out again.

It could be worse, Ranger. You could be tied up to a tree. Hypothermia and exposure'll kill you a lot quicker than this little squeeze, but you can't just sit down here and die. Get up.

My mentor's common sense revived me.

I wondered where my hands were, because I sure couldn't feel them, or my arms either. They had been locked behind my back on my rapid, rocky descent, and I pictured a horrible tangle of broken limbs behind me. Either way, they were dead to me. I could not rely on them to get out.

Get out. There it was. A sliver of hope had returned. My phobia backed off and hid somewhere in the darkness. Nothing like a little involuntary aversion therapy to work out your issues.

Looking up for the first time, I expected a circle of light, but saw nothing except more inky blackness. At least I

knew which way was up, the way out. Now I just had to figure out how I would get there. I couldn't move my dead
hands and arms or feel anything below my feet, but I could
bend my knees.

Bending my right leg, I placed my bare heel against the
rock and pushed. I didn't move. I was really jammed.
Maybe my dead arms were wedged into an adjoining
crack. I bent the other leg and pushed, exhaling at the same
time. I felt the pressure on my chest let up. I breathed easier. I held the position for only a few moments, then my
legs started quivering. I was afraid I'd lose the tiny victory
and jam deeper into the hole. I spun my head around and
caught my chin on a shelf of rock.

I strained my neck muscles, keeping my chin's purchase
on the rock. The bones bit through the skin against the
rough granite shelf, but combined with another surge from
my legs, I moved upward a few more millimeters. My butt
found a lip in the hole and I rested on it. The pressure on
my chest released me. I was free of the rocky grip.

I took deep breaths and laughed out loud. The black
swallowed my merriment, but I didn't care. Now I wouldn't
suffocate, at least.

My new position eased the pinch of blood vessels in my
arms, and I felt them tingle. At first, I was happy, eager to
know my arms again, but then the needles came. With each
heartbeat, the pain increased. At the apex of their return, I
pushed my forehead against the cold rock and screamed in
the darkness.

THE PAIN RESIDING IN EVERY PART OF MY BODY
decided to remind me of its presence. I probably had the
nastiest road rash on my ass and back from sliding down

the shaft. It felt like most of the skin had scraped off the length of my backside, and Dr. Ed had just dumped a full bottle of Bactine on it. I thought at least two toes were broken on my right foot. They would slow me down considerably when I got out.

Got out. There it was again. *Keep it up, Ranger.*

Of course, once I got out, I would be naked in a snowstorm in the San Juan Mountains. I didn't know when Michael would return, either. He could be sitting in his truck, drinking coffee and waiting for the cold, tight space to reduce me to Jell-O. Well, that just wasn't going to happen.

What else would I do, sit here and wait for him to come back and put a bullet in the back of my head? Not hardly. There were a few things Michael hadn't considered in his master plan. The first was my overcoming my claustrophobia. I could thank him for that. The second was the handcuff key I still had in my mouth.

How could I not have swallowed the little piece of metal? Hell, I would have put it in my ass, given the chance. Either way, it was stuck to the roof of my dry mouth, near the soft palate. I peeled it off with my tongue and held it there like a Jolly Rancher. Then I realized I had no idea how I was going to get the key from my mouth to my hand, then unlock the cuffs, in the dark behind my back, body contorted in a narrow chamber of granite. Houdini I was not.

If I dropped the key, I was fucked. I was pretty fucked anyway, but that would make things exponentially worse. My hope hung on a little silver key. Drop it, and I might just trip back over the edge of oblivion. Michael wouldn't have to kill me, just leave me raving in this hole until I died.

Enough of that shit.

The first few feet were the toughest. My muscles ached from the slide and hours of inactivity. I bumped my broken toes on the rocky wall a few times and almost blacked out with the pain. The raw skin on my back tore and bled. The pain kept me sharp, adding needed adrenaline to the effort. I got my legs out of the crack below me and pushed upward, inches at a time. I had no idea how far I had slid down the shaft, but it didn't matter. My life had purpose again. I held the key tightly in my teeth.

After what seemed to be hours of shimmying, ripping skin, and stubbing broken toes, my legs were almost straight out in front of me, knees bent at a forty-five-degree angle. Time to do the Houdini thing.

I pressed against the wall with my left foot, then dropped my right foot from the wall. I stretched my cuffed hands down and felt the cold metal against my heel. Almost there.

My left leg began to quiver, then shudder. I willed it to steady. It ignored me. My shoulders, slick from the blood, slipped an inch, then another. The rock wall jammed my chin to my chest, and my neck felt ready to snap. Terrors of falling back down the hole, headfirst, flashed through my head. I lunged my hands around my heel and thrust my right foot back against the wall just as my left leg gave way. Broken toes wracked my nervous system with waves of pain, punishing me for the violent move. My left leg dangled, worthless, but I was halfway there.

I didn't have much time before the lactic acid in my right leg would sell me out. I slipped the cuffs around my left foot and returned it, gently, to the opposite wall. I scooted up the shaft to a more comfortable position. Comfortable was a relative term.

My hands felt cold and dead against the hot skin of my chest. Michael had vised them much too tightly. I would never play the piano again.

I brought my hands to my mouth and gripped the key, but I couldn't feel the hard metal with my fingers. I wasn't even sure that I held the key at all. My brain told my right hand to close, but I would have to put it on faith that it obeyed. I had come too far to hesitate.

Screw that. How the hell could I put the key in the little hole if I couldn't feel my fingers? I kept the key in my teeth and guided it to the hole. I worked the key inside the lock, found the sweet spot, then twisted my wrists. The metal gate fell away with a blessed ping of releasing metal.

I flexed my hand in the darkness, waiting for the undeniable pain of blood forcing open thousands of dormant capillaries. When it came, I squeezed my right hand into a fist and hoped the pressure would make the reincarnation of my hand go more quickly. I didn't scream this time.

When I could trust my tingling fingers to grip the key, I freed myself from the left cuff.

Having hands and arms to climb up the shaft was a luxury, but fatigue threatened to send me back down the shaft. I had to keep going, all the way to the top and out into the snow, or stay here forever. I ignored the nagging fact that I had no plan for escape and evasion once I hit the top and emerged from my rocky prison. One life-or-death challenge at a time.

Snow dusted the rocks higher up and melted against my warm skin. I scraped handfuls into my parched mouth. I had to be near the top now. It was much colder here, but still no light came from above. I kept climbing.

My head bumped something solid, not rock, but not yielding, either. I reached up and felt the cold nylon of Michael's Army poncho. It bulged, filled with heavy snow. No wonder it was dark in the mine shaft. I really had been buried alive. I ignored the twinge of panic in my gut and listened for movement outside.

I didn't hear anything, but whether that was because no one was out there or the thick layer of snow muted all sound, I didn't know. I had to get out of the hole.

That wasn't going to be easy. Michael had staked the poncho back down in the frozen earth. If I had a difficult time getting the poncho up when I was on the other side, how the hell was I going to do it from below? I reached into my trick bag and came up empty, but I tried anyway.

I steadied myself over the shaft and beat on the poncho with both hands. It didn't budge. Kicking it only dislodged me from my already unstable position. I caught myself before slipping back into the hole. I tried to bite a tear into the fabric. Nope. I thrust my head between the nylon and the rocks. That failed, but I snaked my arm through the tight gap and grabbed the edge of the poncho. I pulled on it, hard, putting most of my weight on the grip. Sharp rocks dug gouges in my forearm, and the stakes held the poncho fast.

I was getting very tired. I'd made it all the way out of my own little hell, only to be blocked by a plug of snow and nylon.

Then I heard something coming from the other side— just a vibration in the earth, transmitted by snow, dirt, and rock. It was the drone of something man-made, but I didn't know if I should feel relief or fear.

I chose fear. Better safe than sorry. Michael had returned to find out what I knew, to find out who else he needed to kill before he killed me. I decided right there that I wasn't going to let him do that. I didn't just climb out of the depths of the earth, naked, bleeding, and broken, to be shot in the snow like a wounded coyote by that crazy fuck

Michael Petry. When he poked his head over the edge, I would rip it off.

The engine noise increased. Michael could not have driven his truck up here—he had returned by snowmobile.

Michael cut the engine right outside the shaft. I heard him shuffling above me, clearing the snow from the poncho, then I heard the back-and-forth grind of each stake as he pried them from the rocky soil. I got ready. My only advantage was surprise. I had only seconds to take him down.

The poncho disappeared and a cold gust of snow-filled wind shocked my naked skin. I shook it off and let my adrenaline build up. A circle of gray dusk had opened above me. I'd been down in the hole for hours. It seemed like days.

A flashlight shone on the far edge of the hole a few inches above my feet. Almost there. I waited.

A blocky head and broad shoulders broke the circle of sky. I reached up, grabbed his collar with both hands, and pulled down with all of my weight. I didn't care about falling. I could catch myself on the way down. I could wedge his body in the hole and use him like a platform. Whatever came next didn't matter.

Only he didn't come down. I struggled fruitlessly against him. He grunted with the effort, but didn't budge from the edge of the hole. Instead, he put a vice-like grip on my forearms and pulled me out of the hole the way an ice fisherman withdraws a fish from a frozen lake. I flopped in the snow like a walleye.

"Don't worry, Sheriff. I got you. Easy there, son. You're out now."

That was Michael's voice, but an older version, hoarse and weathered. Did he just call me "Sheriff?" I didn't trust my ears anymore.

I scrambled to my hands and knees, then pounced on his back. He lay on his stomach next to the mineshaft, but didn't try to get up. I locked my right forearm around his neck, ready to choke the life out of my tormentor. Michael didn't resist at all.

"Sheriff, goddamnit, what are you doing?" he wheezed through a shrinking larynx. "It's not Michael, it's me! I just let you out! Get the hell off!"

The man didn't get up because he couldn't use his legs. It was Denver Petry.

Twenty-two

DENVER . . . WHAT ARE YOU . . . WHERE'S MICHAEL?"
I hopped off him and huddled in the snow.

After hours in total darkness, the half-dusk seemed like full day. Snow continued to fall unchecked. Multiple layers covered our tracks from the climb. How had Denver found me in this field of white?

"I don't know where he is, but he ain't here right now. That'll help us to clear out," said Denver. "I got a blanket on the Ski-Doo." He turned on his stomach and crawled over to the decrepit snowmobile parked a few feet away. His dead legs dragged behind him like forgotten laundry.

"How did you find me?" In my bewilderment, I blocked out my nakedness to the snow and wind, but I couldn't stop the violent shudders ripping through my exposed body. Hypothermia threatened.

Denver hoisted himself onto the torn padded seat and tossed me a greasy wool blanket. I wrapped it around me. I noticed an old M14 rifle lashed lengthwise to the seat where the blanket had been.

"I watched Michael leave town early this morning," said Denver. "Then I saw you and that federal go out in your truck. After the explosion, Jenny tore through town like her skirt was on fire. Only she didn't come back, and neither did you. Only Michael. I figured no good come of that, so I got the Ski-Doo started and followed his tracks."

"Did you find Jenny?" I asked. "In her Bronco?"

"No, Sir. I followed Michael's tire tracks to Lenny's place, but that's where they stopped. I saw your Bronco all shot up and found your Resistol down the hill, mostly buried in the snow, so I knew you were close. I been up and down the valley for hours, lookin' for you. This here knoll kind of bumps up in the middle of the ridge, so I checked it out and saw what was left of the tracks in the snow from you and Michael. They're almost gone."

I couldn't believe what I was hearing or seeing. I had never seen Denver outside, let alone riding around on a snowmobile in the middle of a snowstorm.

"Your legs," I said.

"Don't need 'em to drive the Ski-Doo." He patted the fuel tank. "She don't look like much, but she still starts on the first pull. I get out more in the winter, no tourists ridin' around, makin' fools of themselves." He tugged his dead legs across the seat and started the engine. "You comin'? You don't look so good, Sheriff. Bet you can't even feel your ass anymore."

I couldn't feel my feet, either. I stood up and shuffled through the deep powder as if I were walking on air. This vaguely bothered me, but I was out of the hole. The worst part of my day was over. I could suck up a cold ride on a snowmobile. I sat down on the bench seat behind Denver.

"Now, don't you be ashamed to put your arms around me," he said. "We don't need no heroes today. I know you're cold as them rocks over there. Wrap up and get yourself some body heat. I gotta drive slow to keep the wind chill down."

I complied and didn't think twice about it. I'd spooned with my share of grown men at Ranger School.

Like a good soldier, Denver had parked his snowmobile facing downhill, just like the other Minutemen.

Oh, yes, I had no doubt of Denver's involvement in our local militia, but he gave me freedom, a blanket, and a ride. Survival had to take priority.

When the bullet burst through his chest, I felt the spatter on my bare skin against his back. I was lucky Michael had used a .223 Winchester. A larger caliber would have killed us both.

I tumbled backward into the snow, instinctively pulling Denver on top of me. He was graveyard dead, but still useful. No time for eulogies. I crawled back toward the hole, dragging the dead marine like a shield. Puffs of snow exploded around me and pinged off the boulders near the mine shaft. I didn't feel their scrape on my raw skin, either from numbness or adrenaline.

The cluster of rocks around the hole formed a natural parapet and provided cover from Michael's rifle down in the valley. I had the angle, for now. My temporary protection didn't stop Michael from blasting away at me—his futile attempts ricocheted ineffectively into the snow. His helpless volleys gave me time to strip off Denver's clothing and put it on—boots, hat, bloody shirt, and all. No time to be squeamish, either. I reveled in Denver's body heat still lingering in the fabric.

The snow muffled the reports of the rifle and prevented me from pinpointing Michael's location, but I knew it was Michael. No one else could shoot so poorly so rapidly. I was surprised he'd connected with his father's chest on the first round.

I let that shock roll off me. I'd have to deal with the issue of patricide later.

The shooting stopped. I launched over the low wall of rocks. I hit the deep powder and rolled to the snowmobile, keeping it between Michael and me, just like they'd taught me in Basic Training.

I'd never driven a snowmobile before. I usually got around in the winter on Pancho, skis, or snowshoes. I guess I could learn.

I lay behind the sled, reached over the vehicle, and gripped the right handlebar. I found the throttle and squeezed it all the way to the handgrip. The snowmobile lurched down the slope and dragged me along with it.

Down was bad. Down got me closer to Michael and made it easier for the incompetent rifleman to put a bullet in me. I groped for the left handlebar and yanked it. The sled swerved and cut into the snow, but started traversing the side of the hill. My legs nearly caught under the churning treads. I flew across the side of the ridge with a death grip on the handlebars.

I couldn't keep up this blind flight for long. I'd have to see where I was going before I ran into a boulder or fell off a cliff and made Michael's job easy. I pulled myself onto the bench seat. The throaty whine of the old Ski-Doo rang in my ears and kept out the report of Michael's rifle.

The lower reaches of Bulldog Mountain pushed a wide knuckle of terrain into the valley. I had to get around it and put the hefty terrain feature between me and my shooter.

I sped toward sanctuary. With every meter and every second, I put distance and darkness between myself and Michael. If he wanted to kill me, he would have to get into his truck and come after me in the mountains. I opened the topographical map of the valley I carried in my head and projected his course of action. A jeep trail wound up the spur of Bulldog Mountain on the northwest side of Monon Hill, but he would have to race out of Rat Creek and back-track to Highway 149 to access the narrow road. He would never make it before I disappeared up the Willow Creek Valley and made it back to town.

But did I want Michael back in town? A murdering ter-rorist, capable of killing his own father in cold blood? Nope. I would have to end this now, here in the mountains. I found the headlight switch and snapped it on. The light did nothing but illuminate the falling snow in front of me, but it gave Michael a beacon to follow.

I looked down the slope to my right. The ghostly white Tahoe bounced down Rat Creek Road. His line of flight ran parallel to mine.

The spur flattened at its apex and I sped across the field of pristine white. Tall Engelmann spruce lined the far side and continued upward to the top of Bulldog Mountain. The improved gravel trail, two lanes wide, ran beyond the trees and into Windy Gulch. A good place for an ambush.

At least it looked pristine, like a frozen lake or a soft-ball field, unbroken in its smooth perfection. I felt com-fortable, even cocky, on Denver's old sled. That's when I hit the hole.

One moment, I was flying across the open spur, a self-taught snowmobile driver. The next moment, I was flying through the air, an idiot who should have known better.

I guess the map in my head lacked a few man-made features, like old mine strikes, and I had just hit one. I tumbled headlong into the snow, like a skier wiping out in deep powder on his first black diamond run. Only a few rocks lay hidden beneath the white duff. Trying to sort old pain from new pain, I gave up and rolled to my knees. The sled sat upended in the snow, its front buried to the windshield. I hustled over and pulled down on the back end, righting the machine. Its headlight and front skis were smashed. I yanked furiously on the cord, to no avail. The old Ski-Doo had made her last run.

Not her last run. She had one more job to do. The edge of the trees lay less than a hundred meters away, and the road just beyond that. I could haul it.

I detached the rifle from the side of the snowmobile and quickly checked the weapon—full magazine, round in the chamber. Can't have that nasty metallic click of the firing pin on an empty chamber when you're trying to ambush somebody. Denver's rifle was an immaculate Marine Corps M14 with iron sights, no scope, but plenty of range. It fired a .308 caliber bullet—the Marines were the last branch of service to switch from the .30 caliber rifle to the 5.56mm M16. A thirty-round clip extended from the magazine and matched the one in Denver's coat. Good for me.

Turning the rope and straps that held the rifle into a sling, I looped it around my chest. Inertia and deep snow kept the snowmobile locked in place, and my feet slipped in the sugary powder. This sled didn't have the light, sporty construction of the new century—Ski-Doos of this vintage were made to last. I felt as if I were dragging an elk down the mountain and getting nowhere. I dug trenches in the snow with Denver's boots, pumping my legs, but only kicking up puffs of fine white. My ribs screamed against the strap across my chest.

When I hit the frozen turf, I gained traction and the sled budged. That was all the momentum I needed. The snowmobile loosened from the drift and slid across the field. Blood flow from the effort warmed my muscles and dulled the pain.

The sunset had given up on Belmont, but the snow and overcast sky reflected the remaining light against the other, bathing the valley in silvery twilight. The surge of blood and muffled footfalls in my ears could not drown out the constant wind. It blew at my back and assaulted my exposed neck. I even heard the whisper of fine crystals sweeping across the snowy field.

The downhill slope increased on the back side of the spur. I simply guided the machine through the snow. The line of stately Engelmanns stood a couple dozen meters away. I closed the gap quickly, more quickly than I expected. The slope dropped off rapidly on its way to the roadbed, and the sled picked up speed. I did my best to aim for a break in the trees, but the snowmobile ignored me and went its own way. I tugged at the sling in a desperate attempt to guide the machine. I gave up, threw off the sling, and let gravity take over. The snowmobile bounced off three trunks, sending bark and snow flying, but maintained its downward course.

Miners had cut the road into the side of the ridge, and the sled fell the last few feet and hit the gravel head-on. This was good. The abrupt cut kept my future obstacle from tumbling the rest of the way down the mountain and into Main Street. The sled settled crossways in the middle of the gravel road. I wasn't done. I hopped down to the snowy surface of the road and frantically threw snow on the machine. I had to make it look like a drift, but my efforts didn't stand up to close inspection.

I stood back from the sled and surveyed the ambush site. I could not have planned it better—the road and terrain formed a classic L-shaped kill zone. To the south, the road made a short straightaway, then dropped off into the valley. To the north, twenty meters beyond the sled, the trail entered a spruce grove and turned sharply to the left. I would set up in the short side of the L, just up the hill to give me a little height advantage. The terrain would keep Michael in the kill zone—he could neither plunge into Windy Gulch nor climb the steep cut. He'd be trapped in my line of sight.

Michael would feel confident in his pursuit—I was driving an unfamiliar vehicle in the dark over uncertain terrain. He would assume that these conditions forced me to seek this trail for my own safety, which it did, but I don't think he knew I had his father's gun.

I looped through the spruce grove and found a nice deadfall to get behind—just ten feet above the road and only thirty meters from my trigger point. Thirty meters made me a little uncomfortable. I was used to at least ten times that distance in my old line of work, but this was not a sniper engagement—it was an ambush. Iron sights and darkness forced me to employ close quarters combat. Fine with me. I'd done this before. I settled into position just as the glow of his headlights appeared at the far end of my kill zone.

Headlights. Shit.

The headlights lit the snow flying through the air and reflected off the intense white cover all around. His high beams struck me square in my wide-open pupils, and I had to look away. In all of my training and combat experience, I'd never encountered a target with high beams. Soldiers and terrorists lived in darkness. Light compromised your position. Even if the obstacle froze him in the road, his lights would continue to blind me. How could I engage?

I would have to move, but not yet. I had to bring him down to my level, remove his advantage. If I couldn't kill him right away, I could kill his truck. I had to let my obstacle do its job.

It did. Michael drove as if ghosts were chasing him. He had lost the meticulous deliberation of his former self and completely embraced the psycho within. That worked for me.

The truck roared as it gained the straightaway, unleashed after miles of uphill grind. The chains bit through the twelve-inch powder and grabbed the frozen gravel underneath. The tires churned white devils into the swirling wind.

Michael hit the buried snowmobile as if it were just another drift. The snow surrounding the sled provided a short ramp for the truck, so rather than stopping in its tracks, the Tahoe rode up on its right wheels. The truck hovered at the tipping point for what seemed to be minutes.

Then, to my horror, the Tahoe plopped back down and Michael regained control, but not for long. He missed the sharp left-hand turn and drove off the far side of the road. He disappeared over the edge. The snow muffled his descent into Windy Gulch; then the howling wind regained its dominance over the valley.

I lay shivering in the snow behind the ancient fallen spruce and tried to comprehend the quick violence that had flashed before my eyes.

Well, get up, Ranger. Go see if he's dead.

I obeyed my inner team leader and stumbled into the road. I looked down the slope. Taillights glowed like red eyes through the driving snow. The vehicle lay at the bottom of a deep wash, two hundred feet down the steep angle of the mountain. It looked as if Michael had just driven down the hill and parked it. The interior lights came on.

I vaulted over the edge and sidestepped down the slope, taking long leaps through the deep powder. Haste bred stupidity. My broken body didn't respond to my eagerness, and I tumbled down the wash, but I managed to hold on to the rifle. I regained my feet and took my time.

Although the truck looked like it had driven straight down the hill, its tracks told a different story. One-third of the way down, he hit something under the snow. This obstruction turned the truck to the right and the vehicle rolled for at least fifty feet. Then it somehow flipped end over end and slammed headfirst into the bottom of the wash. The fall must have scrambled Michael inside.

I approached the vehicle cautiously, swinging out to the driver's side, rifle at the ready. The door lay wide open, but the cab was empty, except for a couple of pints of blood spattered shiny on the dark gray interior and the shattered window glass. Even the globe on the ceiling had fresh blood on it.

A bloody rut led away from the truck. I wouldn't need Michael's Coleman lantern to follow this trail.

I found him forty meters from the truck, near a little juniper grove. He hadn't quite made it into the branches. I was impressed with his stamina, but like a fatally wounded animal, blood loss had abruptly ended his flight. He lay on his back in a snowdrift, his ruined legs askew at broken angles in front of him. His right hand was buried in the snow up to his shoulder. The fingers of his left had were deep inside a gash in his neck. Dark blood oozed down his wrist as he desperately pinched the jugular vein.

"Forgot to wear your seat belt?" I asked.

"Fuck you," he gurgled.

"Where's Jenny?" I enjoyed his pain. "What did you do with her?"

He coughed up a gout of black blood onto the snow. "I can't tell you."

"Yes you can. Just spit it out." I almost laughed. I wanted to put the barrel into his mouth to convince him, but that would keep him from talking.

Michael just lay his head back into the snowbank. I wasn't going to let him die before finding out what I needed to know.

"Just sit tight, Michael. Hold on. I'll get you down to Dr. Ed."

"No you're not." His right arm came up from the powder with a 9mm Beretta at the end of it.

I fired from the hip. The M14 bucked in my hands. The first two rounds hit him in the chest and throat. I put the third bullet in his eye. I took a little more time with that one.

Twenty-three

I HAD TO KEEP MOVING. FULL DARK HAD SETTLED ON the Belmont Valley and with it a frigid blanket of bone-dry cold. Our protective layer of snow clouds slipped over the edge of Wagon Wheel Gap, and whatever heat remained escaped into the starry sky. The cold reality of spending twelve hours in an alpine snowstorm returned to my abused body. I hopped, rolled, and fell through the knee-deep powder. Windy Gulch had never seemed so steep or so cruel.

Fighting the snowy mountain, I lost track of time. I figured I had a mile or so of cross-country travel, but nothing looked familiar in the dark, covered in fresh powder. I knew gravity would get me back home eventually. It could have been hours. I finally slid down the scree field above Amethyst Trail and tripped into town.

The wind sent snow devils down Main Street and small drifts crept up the dark storefronts. Everything was dark, except for the blue-black glimmer of new snow. Where were the streetlights? Only the narrow wedge of stars lit the Belmont box canyon.

A series of clanks broke the snowy silence and answered my question. They came from behind the municipal building. I limped around the corner. An ancient Coleman lantern hung from the open door of the Cat generator. Joe Bender's lanky form disappeared inside the yellow box.

"Hey, Joe."

"Evenin', Sheriff." He didn't turn from his work on the old Cat. "Helluva storm, ain't it? Got up to take a leak and noticed the lights was out all over town. Didn't hear the generator runnin', so I came over to get 'er started. We'll have you up and goin' in a jiff. Sometimes you just gotta bang on 'er a few times."

He whacked the old diesel with a ball-peen hammer, and the Cat sputtered to life like an Army cargo truck. The backdoor lamp snapped on over our heads, lighting the evil green door of the coroner's locker. I wondered how many bodies Dr. Ed managed to fit inside.

"See, now? There she goes! Just like I know what I'm doin'!" he yelled over the diesel engine, then looked me up and down for the first time, "What're you doin' out in this weather, Sheriff, and what's up with them clothes?"

"Let's go inside!" I yelled back.

Joe retrieved his lantern and slammed the engine door. "You go ahead, Sheriff! I'm goin' back to bed! Jody'll wonder where I am!"

He pulled his blue-and-orange Broncos cap over his ears, threw his cigarette butt into the nearest bank, and left me standing in the snow.

Smoke dampened the dim light of the back hall.

Smoke? Great. The place was burning down. Could anything else happen tonight?

I sniffed again—Captain Black.

I found Dr. Ed smoking in the circle of green light from my desk lamp.

"What are you doing, sitting in the dark?" I flipped on the bright overhead.

"Waiting for Joe to get the generator running, and someone has to stay with your prisoner." He pulled the pipe out of his teeth and pointed it at me. "Why are you wearing Denver Petry's clothes?"

"He doesn't need them anymore," I said. I didn't want to ask my next question. "You haven't seen Jenny?"

"No, just your prisoner."

"He's not my prisoner anymore. He's innocent. We need to find Jenny."

I gave him the highlights while I put on my last clean uniform. I smiled inwardly when I felt the icy floor against my bare feet.

"Mike Stanford . . . Michael Petry . . . was our resident terrorist," said Dr. Ed, "and he tortured and murdered Thomas Pitcher for finding out."

"That's about it. You were right all along. I arrested the wrong man. I need to let him out."

"Denver Petry was Mike Stanford's father," said Dr. Ed. "I should have known. The resemblance is uncanny, now that I think about it. I even saw them lifting weights together."

"They were probably planning out the next hospital bombing."

"I doubt it," said Dr. Ed. "Denver hated the government,

but he was honorable. He saved your life. Then his own son killed him for it. That is inconsistent."

"Yeah, whatever. They're both dead now, and Jenny's out there in the cold."

"We will have to retrieve the bodies," said Dr. Ed.

"We got bodies all over this valley," I said. "They'll keep for a while. We need to find Jenny." I jammed my extra hat on my head, then opened the lockbox and pulled out Jerry's gun belt. My Beretta lay beneath it. I picked it up and cleared it. Still clean. I nestled it in the small of my back. Michael had my .45 and my rifle, too. I would have to hold on to Denver's M14 with the iron sights for now. That was fine. It had served me well.

I closed the lid of the lockbox, grabbed the key ring from my desk, and walked down the hall to Jerry's cell.

Jerry sat in the same patch of cold concrete I'd left him in the night before. I found the right key after three tries and opened the cell door. "You're free to go, bud. I guess I was wrong about you." I smiled, having nothing else to offer in the way of apology.

Jerry just stared at the same midpoint. I walked inside and stood over him.

"No time for drama, Jerry," I said. "I fucked up, but you really can't blame me, after you took off and tried to drown me and all. Let's just call it even and forget the whole thing. My false arrest for your assault."

He looked up at me with red eyes that had aged ten years since his father's murder. At least he was alive. I reached out my hand. He took it. Jerry stood and tossed the blanket onto the cot.

"Is that my badge and gun?" His voice was dry and brittle.

"Yup. Strap it on and come with me. Lots of shit has gone down, but we only need to do one thing."

"What's that?"

"Find Jenny. Your Bronco still at the house?"

THE LITTLE TOWN LOOKED LIKE THE NEXT ICE AGE had swept through it. I heard the scrape and grate of snow blade two blocks away. Joe Bender had again forsaken his warm bed with Jody and attached the yellow plow to his old Ford pickup. By the time the rest of town woke up, he'd have the roads clear.

Jerry's Bronco looked snowed in. Snow had reached the bumper and drifted across the wheelchair ramp in front of the Pitcher house. No column of wood smoke crept out of the chimney. A plume of guilt spouted in my gut—I hoped the baby lay with her mother, staying warm.

The diesel rumble of the municipal generator and the scrape of Joe's plow carried through the frigid snap of air in the valley, but another mechanical hum permeated the dense cold. I couldn't place it.

"I need to go inside and get my keys," said Jerry.

"Aren't they on your belt?" I asked.

"Oh, yeah." He put a hand on his keys and thought of something else. "Maybe I'll get some coffee made while the truck's warming up."

"Jenny's out there somewhere. Let's get this thing fired up."

"I need to get my coat," said Jerry. He had left the night before in the warm chinook with only his shirt.

"It's not in the truck?"

"I don't know, maybe." He stood there and thought some more. "We should put the chains on," said Jerry.

"Bet your ass we do," I said.

"They're inside."

I gave up and followed Jerry up the snow-covered ramp. Jerry opened the door without a key, breaking the seal protecting the Pitcher women from the bitter cold of an early Belmont winter. A puff of warm, humid air escaped onto the front step. I waited in the cozy foyer while Jerry looked for the tire chains. I wondered why he'd keep his chains in the house, instead of the garage, but we didn't have many garages in Belmont.

Warm? Cozy? How the hell is it warm in here? The power's been out for hours.

The ancient wood stove in the corner looked like it hadn't been used for a decade and the brass firewood holder lay shiny and empty. The living room smelled of new baby and potpourri—a mixture of infant and grandmother, but no wood smoke.

Lack of movement made me sleepy and I rocked in the dark, half-lidded, like some new private in his first formation.

I jerked my head and opened my eyes. The shadowy box shape of Mrs. Pitcher's wheelchair had appeared in front of me.

"Good evening, Sheriff, or good morning." Her well-bred voice came out of the spot where her head would be. "I am glad to see you have found it appropriate to set my son free from your jailhouse."

"Yes, Ma'am," I said. I scraped through my tired brain to think of something nice to say about falsely imprisoning her son. I came up short.

"Can I offer you something warm to drink?" she asked, her hospitality unchecked by the hour or my blunder. "I know it's late, but I'll be up for the rest of the night."

"How do you have power, Ma'am?" I asked.

Mrs. Pitcher awkwardly pivoted her chair in the deep white pile and led me to the kitchen. "Years ago, my late husband installed a quiet generator on an automatic transfer switch. Can't you hear it? The hum actually provides white noise to sleep by. It's very comforting. It will not, however, help me get back to sleep."

Now I knew where the heat came from. My desire for coffee overcame my embarrassment.

"At least let me help you make coffee," I said.

A single light burned above the sink, recessed and unobtrusive, the kind of light left on for old people who can't sleep and new parents who aren't allowed.

"You forget, Sheriff Tatum, that we do not have coffee in this house," said Mrs. Pitcher. "I know it seems like a very long time since you were here last, but it was just one night ago."

"That's right," I said,

"Tea, then? Your choices are the same, Earl or green."

Jenny was out there freezing somewhere and I was having tea with Mrs. Pitcher.

"We really don't have time, Mrs. Pitcher."

She was already filling the teapot. "I could put it in a thermos. You can take it with you."

"A thermos . . ." I stopped at the threshold between the front and back rooms of the house, caught on something that had lain dormant in my withered consciousness.

Wendy had made green tea for Thomas Pitcher every morning for his hunt. I had found it in the thermos that had disappeared on Farmer's Creek Trail.

Wendy had prepared a thermos of coffee for Jerry every morning, too.

But Jerry didn't drink coffee. Neither did his father. Mrs. Pitcher didn't even have it in her kitchen.

Come to think of it, I'd never seen Jerry drink coffee at the station, either.

I heard the rattle of linked metal behind me. Jerry shouldered past and into the kitchen, tire chains in one hand, rifle case in the other. He wore his red hunting coat instead of the department sheepskin. I didn't care what the hell he wore.

"Found 'em," he said. "Ma, what are you doing up?"

"You walk like an elephant, young man," said Mrs. Pitcher. "I was going to make a pot of tea for you to take into the snow."

"We don't have time for tea, Ma," Jerry said quietly. "Why don't you go back to bed?"

Twenty-four

W E STRUGGLED WITH THE CHAINS FOR A GOOD half hour before we finally got them on right.

"You want to drive, Sheriff?"

"No."

We sat in the truck with the dome light on, looking over my topographical map of the valley. I shook my head and tried to think clearly.

"We should start where I left her, just north of the Miner's Creek intersection," I said. "Maybe we'll see some sign."

Jerry drove slowly down Joe's freshly plowed lanes. The cold snow squeaked under the tires. He had the heat on full blast and I let him. I was still cold from putting on the chains and my ordeal on Bulldog Mountain.

"Wake up, Sheriff Tatum."

My head jerked back against the seat. I had fallen asleep. I peered out into the snowy black and recognized nothing.

"Where are we?" I asked.

"We just made the turn by Airport Road." Jerry drove like an old woman, leaning forward with his chin almost resting on the steering wheel. That was fine with me.

"Man, I could use some of Wendy's coffee right now," I said, rubbing my eyes.

"That fuckin' bitch. That goddamn home wrecker. I can't believe Orville let her get away with the shit she pulled up there."

Jerry's bile woke me right up. "Hey, bud, don't hold back. Tell me how you really feel."

"I'm sorry, Sheriff. I shouldn't speak ill of the dead, but that woman was the devil incarnate. She ran a brothel up there in our lodge, poisoning every man who walked through the front doors."

"It couldn't have been everyone," I said.

"Just about. Why do you think the place is so popular? Orville's been through some rough times, especially with the drought. The herd numbers have been down for three years in a row and the big bucks are getting taken without any to replace them. How do you think he stays afloat, keeps bringin' 'em in?"

"He depended on Wendy to keep the place running," I said. "You know how it is—Orville knows hunting and shooting. Women run the rest of it. Mandy does the books and Wendy runs the lodge."

"That's why he turned a blind eye to her whoring. He doesn't want to upset his operation, even if it's a nest of sin. If my mama found out—"

"If she found out what?" I asked.

His breath plumed on the windshield.

"It would kill her."

"What do you care, Jerry?" I asked. "You're faithful, right? You never took the candy."

"I would never cheat on Julie, especially pay for it," he said.

"What about your father?"

The leather steering wheel creaked beneath Jerry's choking, twisting grip.

"My father did what he wanted up at the Halfmoon and he stayed away from me. He wanted to be alone. Whether it was in the field or at the lodge, he was always off by himself."

"You sure about that?" I asked. I was goading him. It made me feel like a shithead, but it kept me awake.

"I told you. I hardly ever saw him once we got up there."

"You think he indulged in Wendy's services?" I asked.

"How the fuck should I know?" He took his eyes off the white road and glared at me. In the dim light from the instruments, I saw tears pooling on his bottom lids.

We made the turn onto the road to Rat Creek, and it just got darker and snowier. The canyon wall loomed on our right. Jerry crawled down the lane, guided only by the reflector poles every hundred meters or so. It took us another half hour to go half a mile. Jerry kept driving like his grandmother, but we didn't get stuck. The west wall of the valley appeared next to the truck.

"Hold up here," I said. "I think this is it."

"How can you tell?"

"I can't."

I opened the door and got out. Jerry stayed in the truck. That pissed me off, but I was too tired to reprimand him.

I'd locked him up for a day and a half, so I owed him a little slack.

I did five circuits around the truck. Each one grew out from the last, but I found nothing. I walked two hundred meters north and south, kicking through the powder down to dirt and gravel. Nothing. The storm had covered up any evidence of the collision and whatever happened after.

The cold crept into my vulnerable fingers and threatened to bite them again. They would always feel that way now. I ignored the numbness and kept looking. I knew my search was fruitless, but I had to keep looking. Jenny was out there somewhere, but not here. I fought back horrible thoughts of Jenny in her own hole in the earth, naked and frozen, lost to the world. The same fear squeezed my chest again. I had to find her.

I got back in the truck and made Jerry drive a quarter mile up the road. I repeated my search, then again, and again. We drove into the lower reaches of the Rat Creek Canyon, far beyond where we'd run into Michael's Tahoe, then back down the watershed, close to Dana Pratt's Shallow Creek Ranch. Each time, my search was futile in the dark.

The truck door slammed. "What the hell are we doing out here, Sheriff?" Jerry stood in the headlights and voiced my frustration. "How the hell are we supposed to find Jenny in the middle of the night with all this snow? When did she run into Mike's truck, yesterday afternoon? There's about two feet of snow covering everything."

I sighed and got very tired. I shuffled over to the Bronco.

"What else are we supposed to do?" I tapped out a Marlboro and lit up. The cold skin on my face soaked up the spot of heat from the butt, melting the ice crystals on my lids and whiskers.

"I'm freezin' my ass off out here. What you gonna do now?" asked Jerry.

The nicotine snapped my tired and wasted body into an artificial state of awareness, and I got to thinking out loud.

"I wonder how Michael got rid of the Bronco by himself," I said. "He couldn't just drive it away, then walk back to his own truck. It would have been easier to throw Jenny in his Tahoe and drive away, but then the Bronco would still be here, right?"

"Maybe he had help," said Jerry.

"No, I don't think so. He blew up his help in Rat Creek," I said. "Wait."

"Wait? Wait for what?"

"For fuck's sake—Emmet." I whipped the cigarette into the snow. "Get in the truck. Back to town, and don't drive like your fucking grandmother this time."

"WHY ARE WE GOIN' AFTER EMMET?" ASKED JERRY.

We passed the gate to the Shallow Creek Ranch and turned east onto Highway 149. A silver line of twilight lingered above the mountains.

"He owed your father lots of money," I said. "Your dad was going to take the studio, so Emmet helped Michael kill him, and he must have helped him with Jenny. He might even be one of the Minutemen."

Jerry looked at me like I was a crazy person. "Emmet didn't owe my father any money. Dad wanted the studio, sure. Emmet's art sells like crazy, and my dad could smell money two valleys over, but Emmet is solvent."

"I heard different," I said.

"From who?"

"Michael."

"Right. Why do you keep calling him 'Michael?' No one called him that."

"Long story," I said. "How do you know all this? About your father's business? I thought he kept you out of it."

"Dad left me everything, except a little for my mom to live on," said Jerry. "Isn't that one of the reasons you arrested me?"

That shut me up. I sat in the passenger seat and let my mind swirl around. I was just flailing about and Jenny was still missing.

"Emmet rides up Farmer's Creek every day during the season," I said. "He told me he always saw you on that ridge near your father's stand. He must have been trying to lead me."

Jerry didn't say anything for a couple dozen rotations of the snow tires.

"That's pretty convenient for him," he said quietly.

JOE BENDER HAD CLEARED THE CENTRAL BLOCKS OF Belmont and worked his way outward on the side streets. Fresh piles of plowed snow were heaped on the corners and narrow sidewalks, even blocking a few front doors. Joe would come back with his silver coal shovel and dig out those folks, too.

Charcoal gray and night shadow enveloped the town, still dark from lack of power. Only the municipal building glowed resolutely at the top of Main, thanks to our fickle generator. Many of the cabins sent silent columns of wood smoke into the early twilight. The residents of Belmont were veterans of power loss and bitter cold.

Jerry drove straight down Main Street and stopped at the pale front of Emmet's gallery. He came around the front of the Bronco and was opening the unlocked door before I put both feet on the snowy curb. He had his hand on the butt of the .45 on his belt and moved with a purpose.

"Hold on, Jerry," I said to his back as he went inside. I hustled out of my trance and into the building.

Jerry's flashlight beam jerked from corner to corner, as if Emmet were hiding behind the grizzly bear display. He moved quietly and efficiently, light on his feet for a former fat boy. I guess losing weight freed his inner grace. He didn't bump one statue.

I stood on the bare wood of the entryway and watched Jerry bustle around. The air inside the studio felt as cold as the valley.

A low snarl came out of a dark corner of the room. Jerry's light whirled.

"Get it off me!" Jerry shrieked.

"Simmer down, Chief. It's just Roger."

I did my best to remove the attack cat from my deputy's neck, but it took a little longer with all my laughing.

"I think we could have knocked, first," I said. "But I don't think he's here."

"Where's your gun?" Jerry shined his light where my duty belt would be.

"I'm not certain," I said, "but I don't think I need it in here. Snap yours back up."

I turned toward the narrow plank staircase. Jerry grunted and followed, but I didn't hear the snap click on his holster.

"I thought you said he was a terrorist," said Jerry. He crowded me on the stair. I felt his eagerness too near. Again, I didn't want him behind me, like the day I found his father dead on the mountain.

"My speculation doesn't give us a license to bust in here like the gestapo," I said.

We reached the top of the stair and stepped into the dark room. Dozens of stars cast pale light through the skylights above us, but Jerry shined his light into the darkness anyway. The place still looked like a machinist's shop—mechanical implements waited in dim corners. Winter crept through the windows in the old roof and saturated the upper floor of the gallery. No cheery heat from the wood stove in the center of the room, just a cold lump of black iron next to a colder mound of clay.

"What the hell did he do?" I asked myself under my breath. "Shine your light in the center."

Jerry turned his light onto the pedestal where Emmet had been working on his next creation—the wounded bull elk beset by wolves—but instead of the bunched haunches and thick neck of the old bull, a pounded hill of clay lay in its place, smashed into an undefined mass of base material. The wolves had lost their form as well.

"Jesus." I walked across the gap to the center of the Emmet's world. "He ruined it. Six months of work, just a lump of shit now."

"Something he was working on?" asked Jerry.

He was behind me again. I turned to face him and he shined his light in my eyes.

"Yes. I think Emmet's lost it." I blocked the glare with my hand. "He's not here. The place is cold. Get downstairs." I wanted him in front of me. Jerry kept his light on me for a few moments too long, then disappeared down the stairwell.

Joe Bender's red pickup with the yellow snow blade idled outside. Clouds of white exhaust billowed into the cold air. The charcoal gray morning had turned a few shades lighter. Joe had a wrench going on the scarred plow and a cigarette going in his chapped lips.

"You lookin' for Emmet?" he asked. The wrench and the cigarette kept going.

"You seen him?" asked Jerry.

"Yup." He made one last crank on the wrench, then leaned against the blade. He sucked a long drag from the cigarette and I noticed Joe's bare hands. I stopped feeling sorry for myself about my cold fingers.

"Him and Henry trotted out of here when I was hookin' up the plow." He adjusted the Bronco's cap over his forehead. "Soon as I got in, Jody reminded me about clearing the streets, so I turned right around. Snow's real light, like pushing air. Half of it'll blow away in the next day or so."

"Did you see where he went?" I tried to get Joe back on track.

"Where he always goes, every mornin'," said Joe. "Snow won't keep him home, an' Henry's a good horse. Named after Henry Earl Callahan, I think, but don't think he knows that. I sure ain't gonna tell him."

"Where, Joe?" I asked.

"Up Farmer's Creek Trail, like always."

Twenty-five

Y OU THINK HE'S GOT HER UP THERE?" ASKED
Jerry. He put the truck in gear and pulled away from
the curb.

"We have to find out," I said, "I don't know what else
to do."

"How should we get up there?"

"The trail up from the valley is too narrow and rocky for
the truck, especially with the snow," I said. "We'll have to
go up and over, across Wason Plateau. Maybe we can intercept him."

"He can't be in a hurry," said Jerry. "He doesn't know
we're coming."

"We need to hurry if we want to find her in time," I said.
"Don't get stuck."

* * *

JOE HAD PLOWED A WALL ACROSS THE ENTRANCE TO the pack trail that led up the east side of the Belmont box canyon. Jerry plowed right through it. I never knew our Broncos could do anything like that.

"Gotta keep moving when you're going uphill," he said. "The switchbacks are the hardest part. Can't really take 'em too quick. Wouldn't want to fishtail and go ass over teakettle back down the mountain."

I said nothing. When we crested the ridge above town, I breathed a little easier. The white shoulders of Mammoth Mountain rose to our left.

The wind on the plateau helped our crossing. This wasn't the pleasant, unseasonable anomaly of the chinook, either. This wind tore across the top of the mountain, carrying the new, dry snow with it, as if the wind were angry that something so impermanent would try to cling to the frozen turf. On the jeep trail, patches of bumpy gravel peeked through the thin layer of snow that managed to remain. Slanted drifts angled into the road.

"It's all about momentum," said Jerry. "You can't be afraid and let off the gas. You slow down and you're done."

I gripped the oh-shit handle above the door as he plowed through drifts as high as the front grill.

"Hard part's over, now. We're on top," said Jerry.

"You don't have to go so fast," I said. "Emmet's got a long ride up Farmer's Creek."

"I just want to get there. Get settled in."

"Settled in for what?" I asked. "We're looking for Jenny."

"You think he's got her tied in the same place?"

"The same place . . . you mean, as your father?"

"Uh-huh."

"Guess we'll find out," I said. "The turn's up on your right."

"I been here before, Sheriff," said Jerry. "I could ride a horse in the dark on this mountain and know my way around."

We cut across the lateral sidetrack that led to Farmer's Creek Trail, then down the mountain to the spur that had held Thomas Pitcher captive for three days.

"That's close enough," I said. "We'll walk from here."

Jerry quietly snicked his door closed. "Let's get the rifles," he whispered. It was like we were hunting.

"You think we'll need them? I don't think Emmet owns a gun."

"Do you want to be out here without a weapon?" asked Jerry. I hadn't told him about the 9mm under my coat.

"Pop the back," I said.

Jerry drew his left-handed .270, checked that it was loaded, and slung it over his shoulder. He handed me the spare radio and I put it in my coat pocket. I grabbed Denver's M14 with the banana clip and patted the extra magazine still nestled in my other pocket.

"Where'd you get that old relic?" Jerry stared at the M14. He closed the tailgate with barely a click.

"Denver lent it to me."

"No scope? How are you going to hit anything?"

"Don't worry. I can hit a man center-of-mass at six hundred meters with the iron sights on this rifle," I said. "Nothing like a seven-point-six-two round to reach out and touch someone, but I don't plan on killing anyone else today."

"Anyone else?"

"Michael," I said. "I left him in the snow on Bulldog Mountain. We can pick him up later."

We walked up the last rise to the top of the spur. The first stages of dawn glimmered faintly in the east, and the snow-covered valley responded to the early light. We stepped into the narrow line of evergreens that hid Pitcher's stand. I led the way. My eyes adjusted to the morning twilight. The rifle, heavy on my shoulder, comforted me. The wind had died in preparation for the day, a quiet hiss across the crystal field and a whisper in the spruce trees.

Would we find Jenny, tied to the same tree as Thomas Pitcher? Naked and frozen like Agent Vilicek?

I pushed through the silent pines and emerged in the small clearing where I'd found Pitcher's body, but Jenny wasn't there. The new snow had settled fresh and unblemished on the evergreen boughs and alpine turf.

I stood in the center of the clearing and rubbed my eyes. The Belmont Valley and its surrounding mountains seemed to get bigger each minute we didn't find Jenny. Colder, too.

Jerry made some noise behind me. "What do we do now?" he asked. I remembered I didn't like him behind me. I turned toward him.

"Now we wait." I said.

"Wait? For Emmet?"

"That's right."

"Maybe we should go after him."

"No," I said, "he's coming."

"How do you know? He could be anywhere. We could backtrack . . ."

"Shut up, Jerry. We're staying right here."

"We shoulda followed him up Farmer's Creek," Jerry muttered.

"I said shut up, Jerry. Find a spot to watch the trail and stay out of sight."

"We gonna ambush him?" Jerry slipped his rifle from his shoulder and checked it again.

"No," I said, "we wait for him to show, then we question him."

"This is kind of like hunting," said Jerry.

THE MOUNTAIN SCENE CHANGED FROM WHITE AND shades of gray to white and shades of green. The wind remained dormant.

I didn't trust myself to sit or lie on my belly, so I stood in the spruce grove and watched down the slope for Emmet to come out of the draw. Jerry cleared a spot in the turf behind a rock ledge and fidgeted.

I looked at him as he lay there squirming and I noticed a shiny piece of brass working out of his coat pocket. I bent down and picked up the object. It was a 9mm shell.

"You're leavin' shit in the hide site," I said. I sounded a lot like my old team leader.

"Huh?" Jerry turned around and saw the brass in my fingers.

"You're leavin' shit all over the place," I said. I pocketed the shell.

"I must have put it there the last time we fired our Berettas."

"Whatever," I said. "Just hold still."

"He's not coming," said Jerry. "We should go after him."

"Be quiet," I said. "There's no need to talk. He's coming."

Jerry grunted, but obeyed.

The cold air stung my face, then numbed it. My feet were lumps of wood. I wiggled my toes in a vain attempt to send blood to them. The skin on my ears was lost to blood flow and nerves. Good. It helped me focus on the spot where Emmet would emerge from the draw. I ignored Jerry's annoying movement and centered myself.

Orange light nicked the tops of the mountains, and the sky turned red in the east, indigo in the west. Jerry clicked the safety on and off on his rifle. I toed him in the leg to stop. Steam rose out of Farmer's Creek.

Steam?

White puffs of condensation drifted upward from the wooded draw below. I could see the contrast against the snowless green boughs of the tall Engelmann spruce reaching out of the low ground. The white field in front of us had a rounded slope, then dropped down to Farmer's Creek Trail. Emmet was down there, but I couldn't see him. The trail lay in a perfect defile from my position in the spruce grove. All I saw were Henry's billowing exhalations rising out of the defilade.

"He's not coming," said Jerry.

"He's here," I said.

"Where?"

"He's down there," I said.

"How can you tell?"

"Look through your scope, just above the drop—see the vapor?"

"Yes."

"That's Henry."

"Henry? Henry Earl? Is he smoking up here?"

"No, Jerry, Henry is Emmet's horse. He's breathing."

Jerry peered through his scope. "Oh, yeah. Now I see." I didn't believe him. "What's he doing?"

"Waiting for us," I said.

"How do you know that?"

"Because he isn't moving."

Jerry thought about this for ten whole seconds. "What do we do now?"

"You sit tight." I stepped around him and out of the spruce grove.

"Where are you going?" he hissed.

"I'm going to talk to him. Keep your eye in the scope, but your finger off the trigger."

"But, Sheriff—"

"*Off* the trigger, Jerry. And don't use the radio unless I call you."

Farmer's Creek Trail swung to the west of the spur, then down into the draw. I silently toed through the powder. I followed the first switchback into the draw and turned on a short straightaway. There stood Emmet's horse, Henry, thirty meters down the trail. Henry's white patches disappeared in the snowy background, making him a ghostly entity in the gray light of the draw.

Emmet leaned on the pommel and looked at me. I was right—he was waiting for me. He wore his winter cowboy uniform—long, dark riding coat, denims, leather gloves, red scarf around his neck. Frost covered his walrus mustache. A single, snotty icicle clung to it. His dark brown Resistol looked black. His gray-green eyes gathered light and fixed me through his wire-rims. I didn't see a gun or a scabbard on the saddle, but his coat could have hidden two Colt Peacemakers and a shotgun, for all I knew.

I approached him, hands in my pockets, M14 slung barrel-down. I could whip the rifle and shoot from the hip in one quick motion, if I needed to, and the 9mm rested comfortingly against the small of my back. I stopped fifteen meters from Henry's nose. The horse didn't snicker and Emmet didn't move.

"Emmet."

"Sheriff."

"Ever seen this much snow up here?" I asked.

"It'll blow off the mountain in a few days, but the cold is here to stay."

Henry's nostrils bristled with frost and the horse blew clouds of vapor into the slack wind.

"Jerry needs to learn a little ambush discipline," said Emmet. "I heard him snapping his safety a hundred meters down the trail."

"How did you know it was Jerry?"

"I know you wouldn't do that, Sheriff."

I studied his posture, his face, his eyes. Same old Emmet. "You know why we're here," I said.

"Can't say that I do. Hunting, maybe?"

"Where's Jenny?"

He raised frosty eyebrows. "Jenny Lange? I hope she's sittin' back snug and warm in your radio room. Seems your building's the only one with emergency power."

"She's not, and she's not here, either," I said. "What've you done with her?"

"What have I done with her? What would I want with Jenny? Orville would kill me if I looked cross-eyed at his granddaughter."

"Don't fuck with me, Emmet," I said. "This is over. The Minutemen are all dead. There's no point keeping Jenny tied up in the cold. Just tell me where she is."

Emmet stared at me like I had a dick growing out of my forehead.

"Sheriff, what in *thee hell* are you talking about?"

I took a few steps back. I didn't liked the angle. "We don't have time for this bullshit. I know about your little militia. I know that you kept Councilman Pitcher up here while they were blowing up that hospital in Fort

Leavenworth. I know about your bad conduct discharge and your hatred of the government. I know you took care of Jenny so Michael could finish me in that dark hole. I know you ruined your own sculpture. I saw it sitting in your studio this morning. There's nothing left for you, now. Denver, Michael, and Lenny are dead."

Emmet's mouth shifted under his thick mustache. Then he shook his head and chuckled.

"You ain't thinkin' straight, Sheriff," he said. "You look tired and beat up, like ten miles of bad road. Now, I don't understand much of what you just said, so let's start with what I do know." He slowly wiped the frost from his mustache with a gloved hand, then settled it back on the pommel.

"First of all, my bad conduct discharge is public record. I told you myself, didn't I? I ain't keepin' that a secret from nobody. Not somethin' I want to talk about much, though. Now, that lump of clay in my studio ain't my elk and wolf sculpture. I took that piece to the foundry in Pueblo yesterday. I got stuck in Walsenburg last night when they closed La Veta Pass. Can't say that bothered me too much, because I stayed with a lady friend of mine, a kindred spirit, you might say. You can check with her. I woulda stayed longer, and she woulda let me, but that new lump a clay is rollin' around in my head, and I was itchin' to get back to the mountains, see the snow before it all blows away. So I followed the plow out here this morning. Joe Bender saw me come in."

"Joe saw you go out, too," I said. "He didn't mention your late arrival."

"You probably didn't ask him," said Emmet.

We stared at each other for a few moments. Henry snorted.

Emmet shifted his skinny butt in the saddle, then reached into his coat. I eased my hand over to the rifle sling.

"Easy there, Sheriff. I'm just gettin' me a smoke." He pulled out a pack of Marlboro Reds and lit one up.

"Want one?" He held out the pack. I did.

Before I walked down into the draw, I thought I knew all the answers. After five minutes with Emmet, my suspicion of him had all but disappeared, and only questions remained.

"I thought you quit," I said.

"So did I," said Emmet.

We smoked in silence. Henry stamped his front feet.

"Where's Jerry at?" asked Emmet.

I just stared at him and smoked. My gut told me I was wrong about Emmet.

"He's probably up in his father's old stand," Emmet answered his own question. Thomas Pitcher had been dead for only three days, and people already referred to the murder scene as his "old stand."

"He's gonna have a hard time hittin' me from up there," Emmet continued. "We're in a nice bit of defilade. I know all the covered spots in this valley, keeps me alive from all the hunters slingin' bullets around. Why do you think I stopped here when I heard Jerry clickin' his safety?"

Emmet's question triggered a flood of answers. Time to listen to my gut.

I had assumed Thomas Pitcher had found Lenny's operations order and faxed it to the FBI. I had assumed Michael had found out and killed him for it. I had assumed Emmet was a Minuteman and assisted in Pitcher's captivity.

But Emmet wasn't a Minuteman at all. He had no reason to participate in Pitcher's torture. Without Emmet's help, Michael could not have kept Pitcher alive while bombing the hospital in Fort Leavenworth.

I shook my head, trying to recall something from Michael's rant at Rat Creek. He said he had alerted the FBI himself, not Thomas Pitcher. He knew it was only a matter of time before they found him, so he gave up Lenny, made him the patsy. If Pitcher didn't send the fax to the FBI, Michael had no reason to kill him.

I had arrested the right man all along.

The fragments of truth in my head began to form a clear picture.

Emmet had seen Jerry on this ridge every day, wearing the red wool hunting coat that matched his father's.

The drunken hunters from Denver had nearly run him over on the mountain road to the Halfmoon Lodge. Jerry had just left his father freezing in the cold. His recent comment in the truck echoed in my head: "I could ride a horse in the dark on this mountain and know my way around."

Jerry had run like a wounded animal when I came to arrest him. It wasn't the chinook messing with his psyche—it was guilt.

Wendy had made a thermos of coffee for Jerry every morning before his hunt, but Jerry didn't drink coffee. He forced it down his father's throat to keep him alive, punishing him. Punishing him for what?

For betraying his invalid mother.

Jerry had killed Wendy to punish her as well. She hadn't wandered into the mountains naked on a meth high and died of exposure, not with the bullet hole in the back of her head. Jerry had forced her to walk barefoot through five miles of alpine snow. Then he'd killed her in the same spot he'd killed his father and dumped her body into the dry wash of Farmer's Creek Canyon.

Now Jerry waited for Emmet, the last remaining witness who had identified him at the murder scene. I had set up the ambush for him, and I stood right in the trigger point.

Jerry would get away with it, too. He had a legitimate reason to kill Emmet, one that no one would question— Emmet was a Minuteman. Jerry would be the hero for eliminating the last member of a vicious domestic terrorist cell that had eluded the FBI for months.

Then an icy chill ran from my frozen head to my numb feet—Jerry had a good reason to kill me, too. I was his patsy.

My weapon had fired the bullet into Thomas Pitcher's head. The Beretta burned against my back. The FBI could easily match the ballistics from my Beretta with the slug I pulled out of the dirt. The bullet still had Pitcher's blood on it. Jerry could easily kill us both and make up any story he wanted.

One last thought snagged in my head—not only did I have the murder weapon in my belt, I had the shell casing in my pocket, the 9mm shell that fell out of Jerry's coat, the one that was missing from the murder scene. I was a walking evidence locker.

While I was standing there, thinking instead of moving, a bullet tore through Emmet's neck. The gunshot boomed through the valley like tank fire.

Twenty-six

BLOOD POURED OVER BOTH SIDES OF EMMET'S collar. He looked at me with surprise and confusion, then tipped off his horse like a drunken cowboy and disappeared into the wash.

I dove over the edge where Emmet had fallen. I rolled once and put my heels in the dirt and snow. Instead of tumbling, this time I kept my feet moving and half-stepped, half-slid down the steep slope.

I landed heavily in the bottom of the draw and started scrambling away, then hesitated. Emmet lay in a bloody heap ten feet away. I could not leave him, not an old soldier like that, to bleed to death in the cold dirt. I still believed in the Ranger Creed.

I will never leave a fallen comrade to fall into the hands of the enemy.

I had seen a wound like that before—I had inflicted a few myself just like it, but I couldn't stay in the open and provide first aid, both fingers jammed into the holes in Emmet's neck.

Goddamnit, Ranger. Drag his ass out of the line of fire.

I grabbed Emmet by his coat and pulled him under a rocky cut protected from Jerry's fire. I ripped open his coat and stripped off the red scarf, now damp and redder. The bullet had passed cleanly through the thin muscles of his neck. The entrance and exit wounds were small and perfect, and both seeped blood. I yanked off my right glove and felt for his carotid. My numb fingers slipped in the blood and felt nothing. I was wasting time. I cut two pieces of cloth from the scarf and stuffed them in the holes, then wrapped the scarf around his neck, not too tight. That was all I could do for him.

"Hold on, Emmet," I said. I didn't know if he could hear me, but maybe he did. "I'll come back for you."

I had done the honorable thing. I could hide here and die, hovering over Emmet, or I could eliminate the threat. It was time to shoot back.

I scrambled in quick bursts from rock to tree to cut. I made the end of the wash and started climbing out. The terrain here was gentler than the steep sides, and not as high. Juniper clustered at the water source and provided me with spots of cover and concealment.

No shots followed me. Jerry was moving. I could feel his confusion and pursuit. Every nerve screamed when I exposed my back to the canyon. I climbed faster, grasping for any purchase, rock, or tree, scrambling up the terminal notch of the draw before Jerry put a bullet through my spine.

It never came. I had evaded him, for the moment. He

had not seen me climb out. The terrain eased and softened. The tide had turned slightly in my favor.

I stopped inside a thin grove of juniper and unslung the M14. The rifle had taken a beating on my trip down the slope, but you could throw a military-issue M14 in the mud, kick it around, pick it up, and fire three rounds into your nearest enemy. I silently thanked the ghost of Denver Petry for not mounting a scope on the rail. The optics would have smashed with my first tumble, the zero horribly marred, but the cold iron sights didn't budge, ready to center their next target. I pulled the bolt back an inch and saw the brassy cylinder of a .308 Winchester round in the chamber.

Keep your enemies closer.

I would have to keep Jerry near and fight him at the belt buckle. If I strayed into open terrain, his greater stand-off range would give him the advantage and I would be done. Now I just had to find him.

"Sheriff, this is Jerry," came his tinny voice out of the radio in my pocket. I instinctively pulled it out and listened again.

Radio silence, Ranger. Who do you need to talk to when it's just you and your target?

Sergeant Richter's words came a second too late. Jerry depressed the signal key on his handset and sent a warping tone into the silent morning air. I flung the radio and rolled away just as a bullet smacked into the thin juniper to my left.

I kept moving and Jerry kept firing. I imagined him smoothly working the bolt action on his Ruger M77, just like Marty Three Stones had trained him. It was as if she were shooting at me again. Snow, rock, and dirt blasted behind me with each impact, following me across the ridge. I had to get out of his scope.

I rolled behind a rock ledge and brought up the M14. I had revealed my location, but so had Jerry. I pumped out five rounds of suppressing fire in his general direction, then moved again.

I found another fold in the terrain and fired. Bullets came as fast as I could pull the trigger. I squeezed quickly, fast and slow, five more rounds onto the opposite ridge. Maybe it wasn't so bad having the M14 after all. I'd be finished with my single-shot Ruger.

It don't fucking matter if you hit anything, just keep up your volume of fire. You can kill 'em later.

Sixty rounds to play with. I could use fifty-nine to get away.

Across the slope, I found another bit of dead space and sent Jerry another burst of withering fire. He'd stopped shooting. Maybe my barrage had kept his head down.

The next one would. I needed to get across a small open area and I didn't want any shit from my deputy. I fired two quick three-round bursts across the ridge, the muzzle blast making that beautiful St. George's cross through the fire suppressor. I then sprinted uphill and to the west, quartering away from his line of fire. Jerry didn't follow me with his .270—he was reloading or pissing his pants. Either way, I made a bold move through the open space without harassment. I found a sturdier grove of spruce with a big rock in the center. I crashed into the cover and leaned into the cold granite.

"That was fun," I said out loud. I crawled around to the opposite side of the rock and peered through a tiny gap in the spruce boughs. I saw nothing but quiet Farmer's Creek Canyon to my front, but my front wasn't the problem. I looked back at the long, high ridge behind me. The feature would provide Jerry with covered lateral movement, and

nothing but bare, white turf would protect me from his precision fire. I was up too high. I had to get down into the
shit, into the rough terrain and evergreen concealment. He
would have no choice but to follow.

The main branch of Farmer's Creek lay on the other
side of a little spur, below me and to my right. A line of
pine trees marked the end of the alpine meadows and the
beginning of the wooded canyons on the lower reaches of
the foothills. There the terrain would drop and contours
would become erratic. That was my sanctuary, and my kill
zone, but I would have to cross an open field of fire to gain
the spur.

I loved my big chunk of granite, but I had to leave it. I
gripped the M14 in my left hand and exploded out of the
grove.

You got to move like bears are chasin' you.

I crashed through the lateral line of evergreens, then the
slope fell away under my feet. My momentum carried me
over the lip like a downhill skier and I was airborne. Lucky
for me, deep powder had gathered on the spur. I hit the snow
in a white cloud, rolled forward once, regained my feet, and
kept going. The spur lay a little too exposed for me to slow
down. A crescent moon of juniper lined the lower rim, and I
lunged for the cover.

The junipers hid another step in the terrain. I dropped
over the lip and tucked myself under it. The move had
taken me over two hundred meters of terrain and through
two layers of forest cover. I gave myself a few moments to
breathe, then took off again.

This time, I rounded the spur to the west, ninety degrees
from my original direction of movement. I wanted to get to
the far side of the open area and watch for Jerry. If he saw
my frenzied tracks across the field, he would project my

flight into the trees and look for me farther down the slope, but I would be to his right and slightly behind him.

Jerry had let me escape his reticle. He didn't know it yet, but it was the biggest mistake he would ever make. He would have to come after me. If he ran, I would find him. His escape lay in a snowy hollow with an old M14 and no radio.

I fought sleep. If I fell asleep, I would die, and Jerry knew that. He knew how tired I was—I hadn't slept in thirty-six hours, unless you call passing out from claustrophobia sleep, and I didn't. Shit, I'd fallen asleep on the way out to Rat Creek, sitting right next to him in the Bronco.

I will never leave a fallen comrade to fall into the hands of the enemy.

I'm not sleepin'!

I shook myself awake. Emmet and Jenny. Had I forgotten? The sun broke over the La Garita Mountains to the east. How long had I been out? My numb right hand told me a long time. I'd left my glove in the wash with Emmet. I would need that hand. I flexed it and let the glass-shard pain jolt me into consciousness.

Jerry must have been freezing his ass off, too.

"You dumb fuck," I said to myself. "He's got the Bronco. He's up on the ridge, waiting for you to come out or freeze to death." I looked around for a covered path out of my hiding place.

My backtrack on the spur had led me to another line of trees that overlooked the main branch of Farmer's Creek. I eased out of my position and found another in the protective layer of evergreen. Beyond it lay the open slope to the top of the ridge where I knew Jerry sat in the warm Bronco, waiting for me.

I'd left my binoculars with Michael Petry, but I didn't

need them to find the white truck on the ridge. The sun behind me glinted off the driver's window. I smiled at that bit of advantage. I would take all I could get.

My smile faded quickly when I saw Jerry's hostage.

Twenty-seven

I NEVER FIGURED JERRY TO TAKE A HOSTAGE, BUT I never figured he'd torture and kill his father, either. There he was, big as shit, flaunting his new tactic.

Orville James sat on his old gray horse in front of the Bronco and chatted with my last deputy. I could recognize the old man's squat form and quick movements from two mountains away.

I looked for Jerry so I could put a bullet in his head.

It was a long poke with the iron sights, maybe four hundred meters. The wind had picked up, too, out of the east, stiff and sure. A rooster tail of snow whipped off a sharp contour in the ridge. I would have to account for the crosswind and the difficult uphill angle. I could probably do it, if I could see my target. Jerry stood on the far side of the truck.

That's when I realized Jerry's second mistake. He'd parked his Bronco close enough to the edge for me to shoot out both driver's side tires. I could remove his vehicular advantage and bring him to me with two well-placed shots.

I found a comfortable depression in the turf and twisted my elbows into the thin layer of snow and dirt. I kept the muzzle deep within the low-lying boughs. I cradled the rifle in my hands, seated the butt into the pocket of my right shoulder, and welded my cheek to the stock. I found the back tire in my sights, adjusted for crosswind, distance, and angle. I took a deep breath, then exhaled. My finger grazed the trigger.

The grunting crack of the M14 split the morning air. The shot surprised me when it launched out of the barrel. I hadn't noticed the hair-trigger on the M14—Denver must have made that modification himself. The Bronco settled back on its haunches. I pulled the rifle to the left, located the front tire, and squeezed off the second round. Again, the Bronco listed to the left with the loss of air pressure. Now Jerry and I were equals in transportation.

Change mags, Ranger.

I dropped the banana clip and checked the load—two rounds left, one still in the chamber. That would be my reserve. I stuffed the clip in my coat pocket and brought out the fresh one. Its weight in my hand comforted me. I pressed my thumb down on the first round. It barely moved—a full load. I blew away some lint and jammed it home. The solid, metallic click of the magazine seating into the rifle made my heart sing.

I checked the ridge above me. Orville's gray horse was already kicking up snow on the way down the slope. True to form, the old man wanted to choke the living shit out of the jackass who'd fired in his direction, on his own ranch, for Chrissake. The wind carried his cursing a blue flame to my ears. Jerry walked right behind Orville's horse, using it as cover from me.

"No problem, bud," I said to myself. "I can fix that real quick." I got up and backed out of my position. I sprinted laterally behind the line of evergreens, away from Jerry and Orville. One hundred meters to the left, the trees arced gently uphill and gave me the angle to put a bullet into Jerry's head. I flopped down and waited for the pair to get in range.

They came off the slope and onto the flatter terrain of the spur. Jerry still walked in the fresh horse tracks, but now he was in the open. They had split the distance from the top of the ridge, and I could pretty much guarantee a kill shot from my new position, even with the iron sights.

There was only one problem—Jerry held his .45 low next to his right leg, so I could see it. I would have to kill him with the first round, otherwise he'd take Orville with him. I could probably make the four-hundred-meter shot, but was I going to risk Orville's life on "probably?" Not a chance. Jerry knew it, too.

They approached the line of trees where they would find my last position, then follow my tracks around the spur. I had precious little time to move before I lost my advantage.

I could descend into the low ground and try to lead them into another ambush. Once they picked up my trail in the snow, however, I would lose the element of surprise. My only other option was to cross the open area and get behind them before they realized I'd backtracked. I might have a chance—the center of the field lay at least four hundred meters from the tree line. Jerry was a good shot, but not that good, especially if I was moving.

Jerry and Orville disappeared into the trees on the opposite side of the spur. I would be exposed for at least two minutes. A long sprint—I hated long sprints in high school.

I tore across the open field, knees high in the ankle-deep snow. It seemed to take an hour; the snow got deeper and heavier and dragged on my tired legs.

That's it, Ranger, run across a wide open danger area in broad daylight.

I ignored Sergeant Richter and asked for one more surge of adrenaline from my depleted reserves.

It didn't come. My long-abused body failed me. My feet couldn't keep up with my ambition, and I stumbled. I fell into the snow just as Jerry's bullet snapped over my head.

The crack of his rifle got my adrenaline going, finally.

You're in the shit, now, Ranger. Better get small.

I low-crawled to a minuscule fold in the terrain and hoped the dwindling layer of snow would obscure my movement. I pointed the M14 toward the sound of the gunfire and pulled the trigger in a desperate attempt at suppression. A single round exploded out of the barrel, then a cold, deadly click snapped the air. The firing pin had fallen on an empty chamber.

I frantically yanked the bolt back and forth, trying to coax in a round. The chamber refused to accept another bullet. I dropped the magazine and looked at it—the metal leaves at the top had bent over the first bullet and kept it from feeding into the rifle.

Jerry fired again. He took his time—the quarter-mile shot lay at the very edge of his skill, but the bullet broke the sound barrier right next to my ear. I dropped the full, worthless clip, rolled to my left. I dug the two-round clip out of my pocket, jammed it in the magazine well, and jacked in a bullet. No more suppressive fire for me. I'd have to make my last two shots count.

A low cairn of snowy rocks lay ten feet in front of me. I made a bold move for sanctuary.

You're up, you're seen, you're down.

Jerry fired behind me as I lunged for my last position. I crashed into the white turf, but kept my head up. I shouldered the M14 and sought anything human in the green, gray, and white, four hundred meters away. I could almost feel Jerry's scope centering my stupid head in the reticle.

The red wool coat was his third mistake. I found a tiny patch of red at the base of a giant spruce. That was all I needed.

Another round cracked over my head. I ignored it.

I laid the bead over the red spot, held myself back, held it, breathed out, felt the wind, let my heart beat once more, visualized the bullet arcing across the snowy field.

The M14 bucked against my shoulder before I knew the round was away. The hair trigger almost dropped the firing pin on its own. The red patch disappeared and Jerry stopped firing.

I got up and sprinted for the trees. The downhill slope aided my flight and I kept my feet this time. Another eternity of running. Still no return fire.

I burst through the trees and the terrain fell away. I hit the ground, rolled a few feet, and came up with the rifle in my shoulder. The forest lay empty and quiet. I crouched against the lip in the terrain and slid around the spur. The snow muffled my footfalls and the wind masked my breathing. I moved quickly. I had already lost one friend. I was not going to lose another.

Bloody snow and crushed evergreen marked the spot where Jerry had fired at me. I followed the spots of his blood into a trio of juvenile pine. Their low branches nearly touched the new snow. I kicked something hard—Jerry's rifle.

I paused before I emerged into the clearing on the other side. Jerry would be there, pointing his department-issue .45. Could he still point his weapon?

"Come on out, Sheriff," came Orville's craggy voice from the clearing. "I think we got us a situation here."

Jerry stood between us, the .45 in his left hand aimed at Orville. Jerry's right arm hung limp and worthless at his side. An ugly .30 caliber entrance wound and an uglier exit wound marked the spot where my bullet had torn through his flesh. Blood soaked into the sleeve and dripped off his fingers. A pool of red melting snow lay at his feet. He whipped his head back and forth, eyes white around pale blue irises. He blew short puffs of white vapor into the still air.

Orville turned his horse. Jerry let out a whining groan and lunged a step in his direction, but he planted his feet too close together and listed to the side. Jerry shook his head and righted himself. Blood loss. His racing heart pumped the blood right out of him.

"Easy, there, big fella," said Orville. "I'm just turnin' a little so I don't have to crane my neck around to look at you." The old man winked, one hand on the reins, one hand on his hip. "I'm gonna get a cigarette, now, son, so don't shoot me." He reached into his coat and pulled out a hard plastic cigarette case, the kind with the slot for a Zippo lighter. I had always wanted one of those. He tapped one out and lit it with the oldest Zippo lighter I'd ever seen. The chrome had rubbed off at the corners and revealed the brass underneath.

"Sheriff?" Orville held the pack out to me like Jerry wasn't even there.

"No!" Jerry grunted.

"I'll have to take a rain check, Orville." I kept my rifle trained on Jerry's head.

Orville returned the pack to his shirt pocket and rebuttoned his sheepskin coat. He took a few deep drags on the cigarette. The smoke hissed out his chapped lips. He looked over the top of Jerry's head at me, then stared down at my young deputy.

"Now, son, I don't know what the hell's goin' on, but I don't like starin' down the big black hole of your forty-five. Can you lower it a touch?"

"No!" Jerry thrust his .45 at Orville. His head swiveled between us.

"I guess you'd call this a San Juan standoff, then," said Orville.

Orville sat in the saddle and smoked his Marlboro. I breathed deeply and rested an elbow against my side. The M14 was not a light weapon. Jerry kept his gun trained on the old man, but I noticed a slight quiver at the end of the barrel. His arm was getting tired, too. I heard the drops of blood spatter the snow at his feet. The quiver increased. Jerry tried to bring his right arm up to steady his left, but gasped with the pain of the effort. When he spun his head at me again, I slowly lowered the M14 from my shoulder to my hip. Maybe I could de-escalate the situation, just a little.

Nope, just the opposite. Jerry took one more blink at me, hedged his bets, and pivoted on Orville. He took a combat shooter's stance, just like I'd taught him. His wider feet stabilized the ever-increasing list.

"I already killed one old man. I'm not afraid to kill another," he said.

"But it's just Orville," I said.

Orville flicked his butt into the snow. I heard it sizzle out. "So, that's what this is about?" he asked. "You're the one who blew away your old man, huh? Damn shame."

"Not really," said Jerry.

"No, I mean it's a damn shame I didn't get to do it, first," said Orville. "Your father was a genuine horse's ass."

"D-don't talk that way about him," said Jerry. "You let it happen."

"Let what happen?" asked Orville.

"You let him and Wendy . . ."

Orville scowled, then let out a coughing laugh. "Your father was a grown man, son. He did what he wanted, and it wasn't none of my business." He squinted at Jerry with comprehension. "Did you kill Wendy, too, walk her out here in the cold, dark, night 'til she froze to death?"

"No, I shot her in the head," said Jerry. "Sh-she deserved what she got. Fuckin' whore."

"Where did you hide her, you son of a bitch?" said Orville. "You can't leave her out here, gettin' torn apart by animals."

Jerry had turned his back to me, and I stepped toward him.

"Don't move, Sheriff, or I swear to God, I'll kill him! Knock him right off his horse!" Jerry thumbed the hammer on the .45. "Put your gun down. Throw it down in front of you. I want to hear it."

The M14 clattered through the snow against the rocky turf.

"You don't want to do that," I said quietly. "We've both

done enough killing. Why don't you put your gun down, so we can go find Jenny?"

Orville jerked his head toward me. "What's wrong with Jenny? Where is she?"

"We think Michael's got her stashed somewhere in the mountains," I said. "She's been missing since yesterday afternoon."

"Who the fuck is Michael?"

"Mike Stanford," I said. "His real name is Michael Petry. He was a terrorist."

"Denver's boy. Shoulda figured that out," said Orville. "She's been gone how long?"

"Eighteen hours," I said. "We were up here looking for her."

Orville pinched his mouth and frowned. The creases in his face deepened.

"Listen here, son," he said to Jerry. "Right now, I don't care who you killed. You just put that gun down and let the sheriff and me go find Jenny."

Jerry's shaking increased down the length of his left arm. Orville and I had stalled him since my arrival, waiting for the blood to drip the strength and will out of his body.

The 9mm Beretta burned against my back. I had almost forgotten it. Jerry thought I was unarmed. I reached inside my coat and felt for the butt of the pistol.

Orville saw me move and made a move of his own. He got down off the horse. He spoke while he did it. "Now, pay attention, you little prick. I'm gonna take that piece away from you, so if you're gonna shoot me, you better kill me dead, 'cause no little fuck like you is keepin' me from savin' my granddaughter." Orville settled in the turf and walked toward the deputy. Jerry backed away, right into the barrel of my 9mm.

I pushed the warm, hard steel against the back of his head. Orville kept coming. A panicked wheeze escaped Jerry's lips, and he jammed the gun in Orville's face. I pressed the trigger on my Beretta.

Twenty-eight

Two METALLIC CLICKS SNAPPED IN SUCCESSION. The hammer of Jerry's .45 clicked forward on hollow metal—he'd forgotten to jack a bullet into the chamber. So had I.

Orville's right hand shot out like a rattlesnake and snatched the .45 from Jerry's fingers. The old man whipped him on the temple with the handgrip. Jerry crumpled in the snow.

I eased back on the trigger of my 9mm, then worked the slide, putting a shell into the chamber.

"It's a good thing you boys weren't with me during the breakout of the hedgerows," said Orville. "I'd a shot you both myself."

I handed the Beretta to Orville. He held both guns on

my slumped deputy while I pulled off Jerry's belt. Jerry let me do it, groggy from loss of blood. I cinched the leather belt as high and tight as I could. He yelped, and the pain revived him, but the double caverns of Orville's pistols kept him from struggling.

When I'd finished, Orville handed the pistols back to me, then lifted Jerry by the collar. He pulled the young man's pale face to his own. Jerry tried to turn his head away from the old man's wrath.

"You put a gun on me, you little fuck, you better kill me," he said. "I'm gonna find my granddaughter. That'll give you some time to think. Then you better come out with where you stashed Wendy, or that little pinch on your shoulder will feel like a horsefly bite."

Jerry went slack. Orville released his grip on the boy.

"He ain't in no shape to walk," said Orville. "And you don't look much better."

"Well, I'm fresh out of vehicles," I said.

Just then, down the quiet valley, I heard an ATV engine laboring. I plucked the radio of Jerry's belt.

"Dr. Ed, that you down there?" I called.

"Yes, Sheriff."

I would never convince Dr. Ed to use the word "roger" on the radio. At least he conceded to carrying one.

"Meet us at Pitcher's old stand."

"Yes, Sheriff."

We hauled Jerry's limp form onto the front of the saddle and Orville rode behind him. The short old man had trouble seeing around him, but every so often Orville shoved Jerry against the neck of his gray horse to keep him out of the way.

We plodded through the snowy upper field and met Dr. Ed. He pulled his red plastic sled behind the four-wheeler.

Strapped to the toboggan and looking very dead was Emmet. Dr. Ed had wrapped him in a wool blanket with only his face exposed.

"Doc, you are a very lucky man this morning, otherwise I'd tear up your membership card right now," said Orville. He looked up the mountain, "No sense goin' back up. I'll have a truck meet us down below at the trailhead, then we can go find Jenny. I can have them call Pueblo for the medevac, too. The bird can land in the parking lot and we'll put both these bleeders inside." Orville worked the radio while Dr. Ed and I talked.

"Is he dead?" I asked.

"Just about," said Dr. Ed, "but I closed and sutured the wounds as best I could in these conditions. He's lost a lot of blood, but if we can get the medevac out here in time, he will survive. You gave him that chance, you know, with that field dressing."

"Never leave a fallen comrade," I said.

Dr. Ed stared at my listing deputy in Orville's saddle.

"So, you arrested the right man, after all," he said.

"Yup, that's the last time I listen to you."

"Hardly."

"How did you know to come up here?" I asked.

"Well, I saw Emmet leave first, like he does every morning, then I saw you two speeding up the mountain like the devil was chasing you."

"And that made you drive up here with your little ATV medevac setup?"

Dr. Ed smiled. "I puttered out to the trailhead and heard the gunfire from up the canyon. It sounded like a war up here. When the shooting stopped, I figured someone was dead."

I saw the truth in this, but not the humor.

We roped the toboggan between the horse and the ATV to keep Emmet from sliding down the canyon. Orville led the way. I rode behind Dr. Ed and tried to stay awake.

I didn't. I woke up on the lower stretch of Farmer's Creek Trail, my face smashed against Dr. Ed's back. Frozen drool dripped down his parka.

A keening roar overhead had roused me. I looked up and watched the twin-tailed Kawasaki BK117 LifeFlight helicopter zoom past our caravan and bank 180 degrees along the mountain. The pilot flared the red bird over the parking lot and settled in the swirling snow and dust.

I squinted against the brilliant white of the Rio Grande Valley. I knew this view would not last. Snow rarely came and never stayed in Belmont. The powdered dome of Bristol Head met blue sky to the west. Snowshoe Mountain actually had snow and towered over my little A-frame cabin on the other side of the river. I hoped Pancho would speak to me when I returned.

Nick the paramedic ducked his head as he passed under the circling blades. The rotors whipped the dry snow around our legs and heads. He brought a real stretcher, and the four of us transferred Emmet to it and carried him to the rear doors. Nick checked Dr. Ed's work on the wounds in the artist's neck and gave the town doctor a pat on the shoulder. I didn't get any credit.

I grabbed Dr. Ed before he stepped into the bird. I cleared and safed my 9mm and handed it to him. He pushed it back. I unpinned the sheriff's star on my hat and attached it to his black parka. I mouthed the word "deputy," pointed at his chest, and pointed at Jerry. I didn't care how much blood he lost, the boy was still unstable. Dr. Ed scowled, but took the weapon and got in the aircraft.

Nick shot me a look, too, but I gave him a thumbs-up

and walked away. He shrugged and closed the rear doors. As soon as the latches caught, the twin turbines on the BK117 whined with a surge of power and the chopper dusted off the ground. The aircraft sped nose-down across the valley. The pilot barely lifted the bird in time to clear Wagon Wheel Gap.

I CRAWLED INTO THE PASSENGER SEAT OF THE MONster Ford F350 Orville's men had brought down and the old man pounded the accelerator to the floor. All six wheels spun in the snow and gravel.

Orville had the driver's seat jacked up to its highest setting, and he still could have used the Denver phone book to sit on. He yanked the shifter through the gears. His windburned cheeks were glossy red, and he burned a whole Marlboro before we hit the pavement. He left the pack on the dash. I pulled one out and pushed in the cigarette lighter.

"Pour yourself some coffee, too," said Orville. "You look like shit."

His boys had left coffee in the largest thermos I'd ever seen. It looked like an eight-inch artillery shell.

"Where we goin'?" he finally asked.

"Turn up by Dana Pratt's place," I said. "We'll start there."

"But you said you already checked up Rat Creek," he said.

"I know, but it was dark. I might have missed something."

Orville lit another Red and tossed the old butt through the crack in the window. "You have no idea where he took her, do you?" he asked.

"No."

"Then how the fuck are we goin' to find her?"

"We have to start somewhere," I said. "At first, I thought Michael had Emmet pick her up, take her somewhere, and ditch the truck. Turns out I was wrong. Emmet knew nothing."

"Why didn't you squeeze it out of the lawyer?"

"He was an accountant and I killed him before he had a chance to tell me."

"Now, why'n hell did you do that?"

"He pulled a gun. Gave me no choice."

Orville grunted.

A lump of futility joined the guilt in my stomach. I didn't want to find another dead body in the snow. I didn't want to find Jenny naked in some hole or tied to a tree, stiff from cold and rigor, eyes wide and terrified. I didn't have the heart, or the guts, to tell Orville how we'd find his granddaughter.

Orville glanced at me. "She ain't dead, Sheriff," he said quietly. "I would know. You just keep it together, and we'll find her."

I looked at the little old man, sitting high in the driver's seat of a big-man's truck. Most folks who didn't know him would laugh at his statement. I didn't laugh. If anyone could will his granddaughter alive, it was Orville James. I felt a little better.

THE WIND HAD RETURNED WITH THE SUN, AND IT blew the new, dry snow down the mountain and out of Rat Creek Canyon. Snow devils danced across the sloping watershed, stirred to life by the alpine gusts racing out of the north. Packed snow on gravel muffled the tires. The truck was so warm.

"Say when," said Orville.

"What?" I was drifting again.

"Tell me when to stop, where you left her."

"It's up a ways, just inside the canyon." I tried to keep the hopelessness out of my voice.

We turned up the sad little canyon of Rat Creek, the ugly sister of the three who shared the watershed.

"Stop here," I said.

We got out and started the same search I had done the night before, finding the same nothing I had found twelve hours ago. I tried not to think that we were just going through the motions. I tried not to think about my failure.

Orville stood in the road and stared across the open field. Dana Pratt's cattle fence ran straight and true all the way to the highway. I walked over to the old soldier.

"Somethin's wrong with Dana's fence. It's new damage, too," he said. "He'd never leave it torn up like that. Have his boys out here in a hailstorm if he knew his fence was down."

Two fence posts and a triple-strand of barbed wire lay ragged across the snow. The rest of the boundary stood firm.

A burst of hope jump-started my spirits. We left the gravel road and kicked over to the fence. The tattered strands pointed in the direction of the Pratt homestead.

"Someone broke through here last night," I said, "and kept going."

Orville almost beat me back to the truck.

WE PASSED UNDER THE ARCHED GATE OF THE SHALlow Creek Ranch. Dana Pratt's complex sprawled at the bottom of an easy slope in a grove of spruce and cottonwoods.

"That your Bronco over there?" asked Orville.

In all the white, I'd missed it. Jenny's truck was parked against the big white barn. Not parked—crunched. The damaged front end pushed a dent into the side of the building. Hope blossomed in my shrunken gut.

Orville skidded his pickup next to the line of black trucks in the parking area. We jumped out and crossed the footbridge over Shallow Creek.

Dana Pratt stood on the wide front deck of his timber and stone ranch house, steaming mug of coffee in one hand, burning cigarette in the other. I never liked the short, abrasive developer, but today I could have hugged him.

"'Bout time you men showed up," he said. "I'd have to charge your granddaughter rent if she stayed any longer, but my boys are takin' good care of her."

JENNY LANGE SAT AT DANA'S LONG KITCHEN TABLE. Four burly ranch hands hovered around her like minions. She looked a little pale, and an awkward gauze pad clung over her right eye, no doubt applied by the meaty hands of one of the doting boys around her. Mountains of breakfast spread across the battered mess-hall table. They had placed her at the end of the table, nearest the stone fireplace. I could feel the heat from across the room. The boys ignored their feast, bent on filling Jenny's coffee mug or finding a muffin somewhere in the kitchen.

When she saw us, her eyes lit, and she leapt up from the table. She wore a red-and-black checked wool shirt that hung to her knees over gray long johns. She wavered a bit, caught the table's edge to gain her balance, then lunged toward us, but instead of falling into Orville's arms, she collapsed into mine. I looked at him. Her grandfather stood there, happy but surprised. Then he eyeballed me.

"You're alive. I'm so glad," she said into my coat. "I thought you were dead."

"You've . . . been here the whole time?" I asked.

She lifted her head and noticed all the men staring at her. She released me, patted her dark hair, and sat back down. Orville and I joined her at the table, as did the entire staff of the Shallow Creek Ranch. They weren't going to let her out of their sight.

"I woke up and the truck was still running. It was dark and you weren't there," she said. "I tried to drive back to the station, but I was still a little groggy. I guess I drove across Dana's field and ran into the barn."

"No harm done, my dear," said Dana. "One of these goons'll tow the sheriff's truck back to town. The others can fix the barn and the fence. It'll be good for them to quit playing video games and do some work."

"Why didn't you call someone?" I asked Dana. "We didn't know where she was."

"You know I have no telephones on my ranch, and we've been snowed in since yesterday," said Dana. "We knew someone would come looking for her sooner or later. She was in good hands."

"I didn't wake up until this morning," said Jenny, "on Dana's leather couch in front of the fire. By the way, you left your rifle in my truck." She looked me over and lay a hand on my arm. "You look awful. What happened?"

WE ALL HAD A NICE BREAKFAST AT THE LONG TABLE, except for the frequent glares from Dana's ranch hands. The color returned to Jenny's cheeks and she became more animated with each bite of blueberry pancakes. When she looked well enough to move, Orville was ready to leave.

We thanked Dana and his boys for the hospitality and drove away in the Halfmoon Ranch pickup. They all crossed the footbridge and waved as we drove out the gate.

We turned east on Highway 149. The sun sat high over the valley, giving the snow on the road a metallic sheen—the "silver thread." Orville craned his head around to look at his granddaughter. Jenny had stretched out in the extended cab and drifted to sleep. Satisfied that it was just the two of us, he started talking.

"You know, Sheriff, now that all the excitement's over, there's somethin' I been wanting to tell you for a while."

I didn't say anything. Orville didn't need my prompting.

"You coming to Belmont was probably the best thing that happened to this town since the Mother Lode."

"Thanks, Orville," I said.

He thumped the steering wheel with an open palm. The tops of his ears were beet red. "Now, don't you go brushin' me off. This town's been wrapped up in shit for a long time. We all knew about it, knew somethin' was wrong, but we're all so busy with our lives that we just let it go. 'Til something bad happened. Then it was too late."

"I'm not a savior."

"No, you ain't, but you are a lawman. A sheriff. We ain't had a real, honest, hard-working sheriff in a long time."

Hearing Orville call me a sheriff with such conviction felt like a coronation. I had more respect for this man than any decorated Army general or crusty sergeant major. He reminded me of Sergeant Richter, only fifty years older.

"I don't know jack about law enforcement," I said.

"We know that, but it don't matter," said Orville. He lit up another Red. "You are an honest man who don't take shit off nobody. When folks talk to you, they know what they're gettin'—the truth comes right out of your face. And you get shit done."

"I don't know about that," I said.

"Yes you do," said Orville. "You've had enough experience in the last year for a lifetime of law enforcement. This town don't need a supercop, anyway. You do just fine."

"I tend to kill a lot of people," I said. "Doesn't that bother you?"

"What are you s'posed to do when they shoot at you, use harsh language?" Orville let out a raspy laugh. "This is a big county, lots of range. You keep your rifle zeroed, Sheriff. You'll need it again soon enough."

Evan H. McNamara is a former Army officer and 82nd Airborne paratrooper. He now works for a wireless communications company in Kansas City, Missouri, where he lives with his wife and daughter. *Fair Game* is his second novel.

www.evanmcnamara.com

EVAN MCNAMARA

SUPERIOR POSITION

The author who's "C.J. Box [with] a pinch of Tom Clancy."
—VICTOR GISCHLER

When a reporter investigating "mountain sprawl" is shot dead, small-town Colorado sheriff and former Army sniper Bill Tatum must catch a ruthless sharpshooter who is locked, loaded, and ready to kill again.

Evan McNamara is the perfect author for fans of Nevada Barr and C.J. Box.

0-425-20390-5

"An action-packed outdoor thriller."
—JOEL GOLDMAN, AUTHOR OF
THE LAST WITNESS

**Available wherever books are sold or at
penguin.com**